# Pepper River Inn

## K.T. DADY

Pepper River Inn
Published by K.T. Dady

Copyright © 2022 K.T. Dady

Cover design by K.T. Dady.
Cover photography: Canva.

Serendipity: The nicest thing the universe can do for you.

# 1

'Look at the size of that fence. It's ridiculously high. What would you say it was, nine foot? It has to be. It started off with a three-footer, you know. I've seen it in a picture. They did that. Stupid Renshaws. Think they can do what they want, as usual. Well, they've bullied our family for far too long, Rosie.'

Rosie stared over at the dark wooden fence and the top half of the pristine white hotel on the other side. 'I think it's quite sad, Belle.'

Belle scrunched her nose. 'The only sad part is what their grandfather did to ours.'

'I'm not sure I know the exact story.'

'Nor me, but it was their fault. I know that much. Pops only wanted to open a hotel with his best friend, and look. Who the hell goes around cutting hotels in half anyway? I bet our grandad had little choice in the matter.'

The sisters gazed over at the six-foot-wide gap between their hotel and the one on the other side of the fence.

Rosie widened her hazel eyes in surprise. 'It really has been sawn straight down the middle, hasn't it?'

'Yep.'

'It must have been a terrible row they had back then, and Uncle Frank's been dealing with the fallout all these years. No wonder Dad left home straight from uni. He really did hate this place, and he wasn't about to stick around any longer than he had to.'

'Dad shouldn't have left his brother to it. I would never do that to you, Rosie. That Clive Renshaw made poor Uncle Frank's life a misery. Put him in an early grave, I know.'

Rosie turned to face her little sister. 'I think Clive Renshaw died first, Belle.'

'Well, he still made him ill, taking all his business, causing him stress in every way, shape, and form.'

The sisters stared over at their own hotel. The old rundown building looked ready to feature in a Stephen King book. Its paint was peeling, wooden shutters hanging off their hinges, and cracked steps led to a dark arched doorway that by no means looked welcoming.

Their eyes wandered over to the hotel sign by their side that told passers-by that the derelict holiday home was called the Inn on the Right. One of the n letters was missing and half of the R had faded on the dirt-covered white sign.

'We could turn it into one of those haunted hotels,' suggested Rosie.

'Not a bad idea. At least we wouldn't have to spend all our money doing it up. I could check out the local history. See what was here before. We could introduce a couple of ghosts.' Belle glanced at the old sign again. 'Perhaps we should change the name. It seems silly calling it the Inn on the Right, and over there is called the Inn on the Left.'

'The whole place used to be called Pepper River Inn.'

'See, now that makes sense, being next to Pepper River. Maybe we could have an uplifting name, like, Sunshine Inn.'

Rosie's brow furrowed as her nose scrunched. 'There's nothing about this place that screams sunshine.'

Belle combed her fingers through her long blonde hair and sighed. 'We really have got our work cut out for us with this place, but we have to get stuck in, Rosie. We're all that's left of the Trents now. It's our legacy.'

The sisters rolled their eyes glumly over the small hotel once more. Neither had anything to say for a moment.

'Let's be positive,' said Belle. 'How about we strip it back to its original name.' She raised her hands and pulled her arms apart as she added, 'Pepper River Inn.'

A deep, snorting laugh filled with sarcasm and meaning made the sisters jump and spin their heads around fast enough to make them dizzy.

Belle slapped her hands on her hips and glared her hazel eyes over at the man resting on top of the dividing fence, who was obviously standing on a stepladder.

'You can't have the original name,' he happily told them. 'It's against the rules.'

Belle felt her blood boil just looking at him.

*Who does he think he is? Just look at his stupid smug face, and what's with that hair? How is it flopping on his forehead like that? He looks like a Disney character, and he has one of those sexy, charming smiles. Well, he's not charming. I know exactly what and who he is, and I'm going to wipe the floor with him.*

'What rules?' asked Rosie.

He gave some sort of jazz hands wave over the fence. 'The contract.'

Rosie was clearly none the wiser as she turned to her sister.

Belle tugged her arm, pulling her around so that they had their backs to the smarmy face staring their way. 'He's winding us up. I don't know anything about a contract.'

His voice carried over their heads. 'Each family has a copy.'

Belle tightened her fists. 'Ooh, I really bloody hate him.'

'Have you met him before?'

'No. First time, but still. You know who he is, right?'

Rosie shook her head slightly. 'No.'

'Clive Renshaw had two sons, Elliot and Edward. They both own the Inn on the Left now, and that ugly dude leaning over the fence is the younger one, Edward.'

Rosie twisted her lips to one side. 'I'd hardly call him ugly, Belle.'

'He's ugly on the inside, just like all Renshaws. Did you see his stupid floppy Disney hair?'

Rosie muffled her giggle. 'He does look a bit like a Disney love interest.'

Belle huffed. 'More like the baddie. Well, old Gaston over there won't get away with picking on us. Their days of ruling the roost around here are well and truly over.'

'Gaston?'

Belle shrugged. 'Seems fitting. To be fair, he does have strong arms... that are currently hanging over our side.' She quickly spun around to face the grinning idiot. 'You're trespassing.'

His dark eyebrows furrowed as his aquamarine eyes glared her way. 'No, I'm not. I'm on my side.'

Belle took a step forward and pointed her index finger out at him. 'Your arms are on our side.'

He lifted his arms from the fence and made a show of raising them in the air and then lowering them to his side.

'Make sure you stay over there too,' she snapped.

'Oh, I plan to. Why would I want to come over to the Trent side anyway? Hardly draws you in. In fact, we'd be happy to buy the place from you. It needs tearing down. The land would make a nice garden.'

Belle felt her sister's hand rest upon her shoulder, attempting to silently calm her rattled adrenaline.

'It's not for sale,' Rosie told him, without raising her voice or showing any signs of the agitation Belle was feeling.

'Well, the offer's there, should you need it. We are willing to pay market value. You have to admit, it is an eyesore. It really does lower the tone around here.'

'You're the only one lowering the tone, Renshaw,' spat out Belle.

He raised his hands in the air and grinned at her. 'Hey, I'm just putting in an offer.' His bright eyes rolled over to their hotel. 'It's going to take a lot of work to get that place up and running again after your uncle ran the place into the ground.'

'What do you know about our family? Nothing, that's what,' said Belle. 'You don't know anything about us. Me and my sister are going to get this place back up to scratch, and your poxy little inn won't know what's hit it.'

He raised his brow in amusement. 'Oh, you reckon, do you, Trent?'

Every single part of Belle's body was clenched and ready for war with the cocky man. 'I do.'

'Well, good luck. You're gonna need it, little girl.'

Rosie pulled her sister away as Belle was about to vault the fence and punch Disney-boy in the face. 'Ignore him, Belle. He's just trying to wind you up. Don't let him win.'

The sisters climbed the five steps that led to the main entrance, both of them checking the floor below for any signs of a trapdoor, as the vibe was very much there that the inn would swallow them whole. Belle unlocked the large padlock attached to the doorframe and then pulled a different key from her handbag to show Rosie.

'Goodness, we've got Gaston behind us and a Disney key in front of us. That thing looks like it would open any enchanted castle.' Rosie giggled to herself as Belle placed the large, ornate, black key in the lock. 'I just had a thought. He's Gaston and you're Belle.'

Belle rolled her eyes. 'That's not funny, Rosie.' She struggled with the lock. 'Flipping thing won't open.'

'It's probably just rusty. Jiggle it a bit.'

Belle clenched her teeth. 'Is he still watching us?'

'I'm not going to give him the satisfaction by turning around to see.'

'Good idea.'

'Now, jiggle the key at the same time I wiggle the handle.'

Belle did as she was told and thumped her foot on the bottom of the door as she used all of her might to turn the key.

The door wedged open, reluctantly, and the sisters stepped inside to the distant sound of clapping hands.

'Blooming heck,' said Rosie, looking around. 'I feel like we should be doing the "Time Warp".'

Belle giggled. 'Shame it's November, because this place is definitely ready for Halloween.'

Across the way from them was a dark-wood, dust-covered reception desk that had a large chunk missing from the top righthand corner, revealing splinters and even more dust. A stairway to the left had a navy carpet embedded with so much dandruff-looking dust that even the biggest bottle of shampoo wouldn't have been able to clean it. And two spindles had no doubt got a better job offer somewhere else, as there was a large gap in the banister. Arched wooden doors that matched the main door were darted about. Double doors to their left and right, a single behind the desk, one to its side, and another behind the stairs. The parquet flooring looked as though it would come up a treat after about two weeks' worth of elbow grease, and the lone light bulb hanging from the middle of the ceiling just needed a decent lamp.

Belle shivered. 'It's freezing in here.'

'Yes, let's find the boiler and switch it on. You did call all the companies and tell them our moving-in date, didn't you?'

'Yes, Rosie. I'm not a complete idiot, and please may I remind you that I recently turned the grand old age of thirty, so you need to stop talking to me like I'm a child.'

'Sorry, Belle. So, where do you reckon the boiler is?'

She shrugged. 'Kitchen, maybe?'

Rosie flicked her blonde ponytail over her shoulder. 'And where might that be?'

Belle made her way across the foyer. 'Let's open some doors. See what we have here. You know, you would have thought that Dad might have brought us on holiday here at least once growing up.'

'In his defence, I can see why he didn't.'

Belle opened double doors to a dust-filled dining room that had long dark drapes hiding floor-to-ceiling windows. 'This room has potential.'

Rosie opened the door at the back of the stairway to see a set of concrete stairs heading down. 'Kitchen could be down here, Belle. We seem to have a basement.'

'Ooh, just what every haunted house needs.'

A large dull-white kitchen, with stainless steel features and a stone floor was at the bottom, looking every bit as untouched and unloved as the rest of the place.

'What on earth was Frank doing here?' Rosie said, flapping her arms. 'Did he even open this place to the public?'

'Maybe he gave up a long time ago. Probably put out of business by the Renshaws. Their hotel looks like it's made of money. Ours looks like it's owned by the first little pig out of the three. One gust of wind and this place is definitely coming down.'

'I wonder why they did so well and our family didn't? We're right next door to each other, and the hotels were probably exactly the same at one point.'

Belle flicked the light switch to see if it worked. 'I know the answer to that, Rosie. I did as much research on this place as Google would allow. That's how I knew what the Disney idiot looked like. Their hotel has a flashy website. I've seen all their rooms. Their dad won some money on the lottery a few years back. He spent loads doing up the place. Uncle Frank didn't stand a chance after that.'

'Lucky sods.'

'It must have been so hard for Frank. Dad should have stepped up.' She glanced up at the spotlights. 'At least we have electricity. Now we just need some heating.'

Rosie approached the boiler and switched it on at the wall. When nothing happened, she opened the flap on the front to reveal the control panel and turned the dial to ignite the old thing. 'Oh, no. It's not coming on, Belle. Great! That's all we need.'

Belle was busy looking in drawers. 'What did Frank do with all the cutlery? There's nothing here. Do you think he sold everything? Oh goodness, I hope there are beds in the rooms upstairs. This place is going to drink all of our money. Ooh, look, I've found something.' She waved a sheet of paper in the air. 'Boiler manual.'

Rosie took it from her hand, scanned the page, and then continued to faff about with the boiler whilst Belle searched the cupboards for any signs that someone once lived there not too long ago.

A rat scurried across the floor opposite Belle. 'Oh, hello. Looks like we've got our first guest.'

Rosie gazed over her shoulder. 'Rats. That's all we need.'

'Do you think we should feed him?'

'With what? There's no food here. We'll have to go shopping in a bit. Go and switch the fridge on. Let's hope that works.'

Belle squatted down to the floor to get a better look at the rat. 'I miss having hamsters. We always had them. I definitely think we should name the rat.'

'It's not our pet, Belle. Don't make it feel at home.'

Belle got up and switched on the fridge. 'It's working.'

Rosie shook her head. 'It's no good. We're going to have to call someone about the boiler.'

Belle whipped out her phone. 'No signal down here.'

'Let's go upstairs anyway. Check out the state of the bedrooms.'

The first-floor landing held five bedrooms all with their own small bathrooms and looked a bit cleaner than downstairs, which was a small blessing for the sisters.

'I'm pleased they still have beds, though we're probably going to have to buy new mattresses,' said Belle, assessing the quality under the dustsheets.

Rosie pulled back a thick dark curtain to allow the unaired room some daylight. 'Oh my goodness, the garden is so overgrown.' She peered through the dirty window. 'There's an outbuilding at the back. Hopefully, it's full of gardening equipment.'

'That can wait till spring.'

Rosie turned back to the room. 'It can't. Not if we want to try and get some rooms filled for Christmas.'

'Yeah, I think that idea died and went to hell the moment we arrived.'

'We could still try. We've got some friends back home who said they would come for Christmas if we were up and running by then.'

Belle admired her sister's optimism. 'They won't be our friends for very long if we inflict this place upon them. We're going to need a fairy godmother to get this all spick and span in time for Santa. We might as well face it, Rosie. We'll be lucky if we can get this place ready for action by Easter.'

'All the time we're closed, we're losing money, and next door is gaining from our closure.'

'Oh, I know that, but let's be realistic here. This might not be the dream we were hoping for. I actually feel like we've been conned.'

Rosie sighed deeply and turned back to the window to gaze outside at the small forest their grounds had become.

Belle looked her way.

*Don't worry, Rosie. It'll all work out in the end. I promise. I'm going to make this place work, and I'm going to make you smile again like you used to before that evil ex of yours destroyed you. We came here on a mission, and we will complete it. The Inn on the Right is going back on the map, somehow, and soon the whole of the Isle of Wight will know about it. We have to at least try. I really need to find that contract, if it does exist. Bloody Gaston!*

# 2

*Ned*

'Ned, what were you doing up a ladder in the front garden? Were you spying on our new neighbours?'

'Calm down, Elliot. I was just making sure they knew they had a way out once they saw the state of the place.'

Elliot raised his dark eyebrows. 'A way out?'

Ned slumped into the office chair and spun to his left. He struggled to hold back the smile itching to light up his face. 'You've seen the place, but have you seen those sisters who have taken over?'

Elliot ran his hands through his mop of dark hair. His aquamarine eyes gleamed. 'No, why?'

Ned shrugged nonchalantly. The smirk still sitting on his face.

Elliot's broad shoulders drooped. 'Please don't tell me they are two little old ladies who we now have to hate on. I really don't want any part of this family feud. It's gone on too long, and we don't even know how it started in the first place. No one seems to know. All I know is that our grandfather and Conway Trent were best friends once. They built this place together.'

Ned sat up straight. Anger filled his eyes. 'Not our hotel, they didn't. Dad made this place what it is, and with Frank Trent constantly on his back. That man caused Dad all sorts of stress. His heart attack was all down to that family. And, no, they're not two little old ladies who have inherited the place. They're his nieces. They look in their thirties, both blonde, hazel eyes, nice legs. The older one is slightly taller

15

and thinner, and the younger one has a gob the size of the island.'

Elliot grinned a matching smile. 'So, basically, she told you off then.'

*There's no way she got the better of me.*

Ned waved away the comment. 'She did not. I think she fancies me.'

Elliot breathed out a huff of a laugh. 'Of course. Why wouldn't she?'

Ned held his hand over his heart, faking being wounded. 'Hey, women like me.'

'That's why you're single, is it, Ned?'

'I'm single because I choose to be, thank you very much. I'm too busy helping you run this place. Plus, Kasey takes up all my time. Being a single dad runs me ragged.'

'Speaking of Kasey. Everything is ready for her Little Mermaid birthday party tomorrow, finally. I'll be glad when she turns eighteen and we can just take her down the pub. Turning six has stressed me right out. Her birthday parties are getting more extravagant every year.'

Ned rested his chin on his linked hands. 'We were always spoiled on our birthdays. Kasey should have the same level of fuss we had. Besides, she hasn't got a mum, and I just feel like we should do everything we can to make her feel happy and loved.'

'She is definitely happy and loved, Ned. You're doing a great job.'

'We are.'

'So, back to the neighbours. Did you make them a decent offer?'

Ned bit his lip to stop himself from laughing. His thoughts were right back there in the moment, watching the younger Trent sister getting annoyed with every word that he spoke.

*Too easy. I reckon I could just say good morning to her and she'd want to punch me. Perhaps that's what I'll start doing. See how far my politeness can go before she snaps. Those Trents have always been the weaker family. If she thinks for one moment that I'm going to go easy on her just because... I'm not even going to go there. She's a Trent, and that's all there is to it. My job is to torment the hell out of her before she gets a chance to do it to me, and I know she will. She'll try, anyway. She won't win. Not with me. She'll see.*

Elliot clicked his fingers, snapping Ned out of his thoughts. 'Are you going to tell me?'

'I said we'd give them market value. I played fair.'

'Good. You never know. They might take us up on the offer once they see how much work that place needs. We've always wanted to reunite the two hotels. This might be our chance, which is another reason I don't want you over there winding them up. The last thing we need is for them to decide to sell to someone else. Who knows what we'll get next door then. I wish we knew more about them. That might be helpful. Did you do any research on them at all?'

Ned leaned back in the black leather chair and scrunched his nose. 'Wasn't much to find out. I put someone on the case, but all I discovered was they're the last of their Trent line, and they've got stupid names like Begonia and Thistle or something.'

'Thistle?'

Ned shrugged. 'Don't know. Don't care.'

'For someone who doesn't care, you sure put a lot of effort into getting involved with them.'

'Yeah, only because of our offer. Besides, you need to get to know your enemy, Elliot.'

'Can't we just ignore them if they do stick around? Let's not think about enemies. We have our own lives to live.'

'And what if they don't leave us alone, eh, Elliot? Have you thought about that? What if they start lobbing eggs and rotten tomatoes at our windows like Frank used to. What then?'

Elliot peered out of the window to stare at the swimming pool in the back garden. 'We'll cross that bridge as and when we come to it, but I don't see why they would need to do stuff like that. Frank was a bit crazy. It doesn't mean his nieces are too.'

'We'll see. They are Trents, after all. We can't forget that.'

Elliot turned back to him. 'Maybe we should send them a gift basket, or we could invite them for dinner. Offer an olive branch.'

Ned's eyes lit up. 'Yes, you're right. Dad always said you catch more bees with honey.'

'That's not what I meant. I mean, let's try being friendly.'

'Why?'

'This can't go on forever, Ned. One day, Kasey might own this place. Do you want hostility in her future? Do you want her to constantly worry about what's happening next door?'

Ned groaned. 'God, Elliot, you sound like an old man sometimes. You're only thirty-seven. I remember when you were over there trashing the place when no one was looking.'

'I was a teenager. That's not something I would do now nor would I want that level of hatred to be drip-fed into

Kasey like it was into us. We can break the cycle, Ned. We can offer peace with the Trents. And it wouldn't hurt you to act your age. You're not that far behind me.'

'Erm, excuse me, but Frank was a lot older than us, and he behaved like a teenage rebel. Half the time, I couldn't let Kasey outside to play because I was worried he might throw something over our way.'

'Well, they're not Frank. They will be different, just like we're different from our dad. We can't judge people on their family members, Ned.'

'You can when they're Trents. Remember everything we've been taught about them. So far, we haven't had any reason to believe otherwise.'

'I just think we should be nice to them. Start off on the right foot.'

'Is this because I said they were cute?'

'You never said they were cute, but if you like one of them already…'

'Whoa! I never said I liked anyone. I'm just merely pointing out the fact that they were cute, that's all. Just a description. Nothing more.'

'Yes, well, if you were your usual charming self when you introduced yourself, then I guess neither of them would like you back anyway.'

'Cheers!'

'Should I be worried? What exactly did you say to them, Ned?'

*Not enough. I wish I'd said a hell of lot more now, especially to the mouthy one. I've got such an urge to rattle her chains. Why did Frank have to have nieces? Just another way to annoy us. I bet he thinks he got the last laugh. Ha! Think again, Frankie mate.*

19

He laughed out loud, mostly to himself, and it came out like some sort of disturbed cackle. 'I wasn't rude. I told them that they can't have the original name for their hotel. I overheard them talking about it. I mentioned the contract, but they didn't seem to know what I was talking about, and if that is the case, that will work in our favour. We can do all sorts to this place if they don't have their copy. Wish I never mentioned it now.'

'I can't blame them wanting to rebrand. That's what I would do in their shoes. I wonder how bad that place actually is. They'll need a good repairs team. Probably needs new pipes, and maybe rewiring too.' Elliot stopped talking when he saw the twinkle in his little brother's eye. 'What's that look for? What have you done, Ned? Please tell me you haven't messed about in there with their wiring or anything. That could be bloody dangerous.'

*Really! Does he actually think I'm that insane?*

'Calm down. I haven't.'

'You've done something. Your face is filled with world domination.'

'I just made a few calls to friends, that's all.'

Elliot folded his strong arms across his solid chest. 'And?'

'Told them not to be too helpful if they get any calls from next door.'

'Really, Ned! Why?'

He jolted forward in his chair, slamming his arms down hard on the desk. 'Because, Elliot, whether you like it or not, they are our competition, and I'm not about to make it easy for them. There is only room for one hotel along Pepper River, and it's not going to be theirs. Ever. They don't even deserve to be here. They're not even from Pepper Bay. Surrey, I think. Anyway, they're not coming here and doing us out of business. Like you said, Kasey might take this place on one day. Let's leave her something worthwhile, shall we?'

'I just don't think that going to war with the Trents is the best way forward, Ned.'

'We've always been at war with the Trents, and our family didn't start it, but we sure as hell aren't going to be the ones to wave the white flag and let them in the door. Think of our poor grandfather. He went through so much because of that family, and so did our dad. We owe it to them, Elliot. We can't let the side down.'

Elliot turned back to the window and sighed. 'Hopefully, they'll sell to us, and we can put this whole mess behind us once and for all.'

'So, no gift baskets or dinner invites, agreed?'

'Agreed, but only if you agree not to interfere with them anymore.' He looked over his shoulder. 'I mean it, Ned. No more silly games. Let them fail on their own. We both know they're likely to, what with the state of that place, so they don't need your input, okay?'

'Fine.'

*I don't want to go near that mouthy woman again anyway. Just thinking about her face is annoying me already. I don't know who she thinks she is. Well, good luck to her and her sister. They don't stand a chance. Ha! She really was pleased to see me.*

The thought of her made him smile, which led his face to fall flat. There was no way he was going to think about a Trent and smile. That was way off limits. And his mind, body, and soul needed to know that. No, he was just feeling warm inside because he had made himself laugh by winding her up. That was all it was. Simple.

# 3

*Rosie*

The long, dry, thick stems of overgrown grass and weeds were bugging Rosie with a passion. She had a small garden in her old house, and she enjoyed pottering around out there during nice weather. It was therapeutic and always left her feeling peaceful. The jungle she could see outside the office window couldn't be too hard to conquer, surely.

She glanced at the unorganised paperwork she had just piled onto the old, cracked, wooden desk. It could wait. Paperwork could always wait. There was so much of it, and the first few pages she had flicked through hardly made sense at all. She wasn't business-minded, but still, at least something about the way her uncle ran the hotel should make sense. Her eyeballs ached after ten minutes and a part of her soul died and drifted off somewhere far, far away. There had to be more to life than shoddy accounts and doodles of dying men.

*Seriously? What on earth was going through your mind, Frank?*

She glanced out the window again. The November sun was shining nicely and was warming her through the dirty glass, inviting her to step outside and enjoy it while it lasted.

She'd had a rough night, freezing in her dusty four-poster bed up on the top level of her hotel. The boiler man said he couldn't come out for two weeks, but at least the electric shower worked, so she had enjoyed a nice hot wash that morning.

*Oh, how have we ended up here? Maybe we should have just sold the place straight away. Looking at the state of it, I'm thinking that's the best option. We're crazy if we think we can make this place work. Neither of us know what we're doing, for a start. Some ideas always seem better the night before. Oh well. Frank lived here. He seemed to survive. Somehow. To think Dad grew up here. I bet it looked nice back then. It must have done. It couldn't have always looked like this. Perhaps we could rename the hotel... The Graveyard. Yes, that will draw in the punters. Blimming heck, so much for a new easy start.*

'Sod it. I'm going to see what's in that outbuilding while Belle's at the shops. It won't hurt to look.'

She peered down at her skinny jeans and white Converse pumps, feeling the need for overalls and wellies.

'This is good enough. Besides, it's a nice day.'

She slipped a black gilet over the top of her navy jumper and headed outside. Somehow, she managed to make her way across the back garden without getting trapped in amongst the brambles, weeds, and stinging nettles. Keeping to the side of the fence, which looked as though it had seen better days and smelled like decay, seemed to be the easiest path to take, or rather, the only path.

*I bet this end of the fencing is down to us. It's definitely older and doesn't have a nice concrete bottom like out the front. Well, if the neighbours think we're forking out for that, they can think again. Replacing fence panels is the least of our worries.*

The lock to the outbuilding covered her hands in rust and took a while to get into, but when she did finally open the door, she managed a smile. The place was filled with everything a garden needed, from deckchairs to secateurs. It held a musty, damp, earthy smell, and there were a few cobwebs high up in corners. Sitting to one side of the big shed was a large, red, ride-on lawnmower that looked brand new and for some strange reason hadn't been attacked by dust.

*Maybe it was the last impulse buy Uncle made before he passed away. Oh, Frank, it doesn't look as though you got to have a go.*

She sniffed away the dusty air and ignored the smell of wet earth as she made her way over to the contraption that had caused the biggest grin to appear on her rosy face.

'Hello, you beaut. I've always wanted to have a go on one of these.'

She stroked her hand lovingly over the shiny Christmas-red surface of the beast and peered inside.

'Looks simple enough. Yep, I can do this, and this will make light work of that forest out there. I don't think I'll need to use the strimmer at all.'

She looked around for any keys and saw a dirty wooden box nailed to the wall over by a workbench. Inside were a few keys hanging on a collection of different types of hooks. It would appear the whole box was handmade by someone with little to no carpentry skills and not an ounce of creativity. Still, it did the job, and the keys to the Beast of Pepper Bay, as newly named by Rosie, were now in her hand.

She went over to the doors of the building and fought hard to open them both fully, allowing the sunshine to warm the chilly area. A shiver filled her body, as the approaching-winter sun wasn't as friendly as it first appeared. She caught her breath and went into farmer mode.

The engine started straight away, and Rosie let out a little squeal of excitement. Even though she was the older sister, at thirty-three, she knew full well that Belle would not approve of her November gardening antics and would no doubt give a lecture about health and safety, all because she had a certificate in the subject.

The thrill of riding a tiny tractor, of sorts, was far too exciting for Rosie. Clapping her hands with glee, she jumped on and manoeuvred the machine into the jungle and got to work, wishing she had brought her earphones, because some booming rock music was something she felt would accompany her chore quite nicely. She could tidy the garden and play air guitar, she was sure.

The ground was hard and bumpy beneath her and even the Beast was struggling. Rosie guessed she should have used some muscle and taken down a lot of the growth herself first. It couldn't be that difficult. She'd seen Poldark do it numerous times. Her mind drifted off to Cornwall and was only interrupted by the sunlight making her left eye water.

'Goodness, sunglasses would have been a good idea.'

She went to remove her foot from the pedal, but it seemed to be stuck. She glanced down to see her shoelace had somehow tangled itself around it. There was an attempt to tug her foot to release it, but it didn't budge. The Beast plunged forward whilst Rosie re-enacted Kevin Bacon's tractor scene in Footloose. Wiping her watering eyes from the glare, she momentarily blinded herself by looking directly up at the sun. Her twinkling vision tried to home in on her footwear as she bent down to untie her lace from the pedal.

The Beast continued to move forward, and a sudden thump brought Rosie's squinting eyes level with the steering wheel.

'What the hell was that?'

She glanced down to her side as the wheels of her mower glided over what appeared to be a broken garden fence panel, uncannily like the one dividing her property to the one next door. A loud voice cried something, but it was muffled over the engine noise, the cracking of wood beneath her, and a new crashing sound that had just joined the mix.

Rosie jolted forward as the mower tipped down, and it was at that moment she realised her face was nearing water.

The chlorine hit her nostrils as the weight of the Beast pulled her under the swimming pool before she had a chance to hold her breath. Her hand immediately reached for her shoe, but her lace was still entangled with the pedal and panic had already ripped through her, rendering any logical action useless.

The memory of coming off her inflatable lilo in the ocean when she was a child filled her mind. She had almost drowned that day when a huge wave had caught her off guard. The swirl of stones and water had tortured her for years afterwards, causing many nightmares and eventually therapy. She was drowning again, but this time not in her dreams. This time, it was real. She was awake, and her foot was trapped, and there wasn't anything she could do to free herself, no matter how frantically she tried.

Suddenly, large hands were on her leg, tugging at her. A hand reached down to her foot and pulled it out of the shoe, and Rosie felt her body shooting through the water. She gasped in the cold air as her face hit the sunlight. Her head felt bruised and dizzy, and her body was shaky and weak. There was a burning deep at the back of her throat, and she was sure she would throw up. She couldn't tell if she could smell a swimming pool or the ocean. A large silvery-greenish-blue fishtail was flapping on top of the water alongside her moving body. She came to a stop and found herself resting against something hard. A rock, maybe? Large hands flopped to her sides, and a muffled voice was saying something in amongst the roar of the waves. Dark hair was stuck to the side of her cheek as a face was so close to hers. She rolled her eyes in an attempt to see the other end of the fishtail.

He had a man's face, and a blue tee-shirt clinging to a firm chest, and there were ink marks on his bare arms. His eyes were bright, like rock pools, and his wet hair was as dark as night. There was a faint outline around his cheekbones, or maybe it was in her eyes. She couldn't be sure if he was really there or somewhere deep in the ocean.

'Merman?'

His dark eyebrows tightened.

Rosie didn't feel very well. She couldn't figure out where she was, and why her parents weren't there to help her. Was she lost? Did they leave her on the beach alone? Why was she so lightheaded? Who was holding her? She shot up quickly, trying to free herself from the giant fishman. Her head swirled, her heart flipped, and everything went black.

# 4

*Elliot*

Elliot was dripping wet, could hardly walk, thanks to his merman costume, and was carrying the slumped weight of some blonde woman who had driven her ride-on lawnmower into his swimming pool. He was trying hard not to swear when his brother, who was also dressed as a merman, came running towards him as he approached the back doors of their hotel.

'What the hell happened?' shouted Ned, whilst in full sprint.

'Call the doctor, Ned. This maniac just drove into the pool, and now she's passed out.'

'Oh my God, is there a car in our pool?'

'No, a bloody lawnmower.'

Ned was already calling the local doctor. 'What?'

'Where's Joy? Find her and bring her to my room. Someone needs to get this woman changed before she freezes. I'm bloody freezing myself.'

Ned ran off whilst talking to the doctor and flapping his arms at a member of staff.

Elliot made it to his bedroom at the top of the hotel and slumped *Sleeping Beauty* down onto his bed. He tentatively tapped her face. 'Hey.'

Rosie stirred, opened her eyes slightly, sat up quickly, threw up on the floor, and jumped up. 'Merman! Ooh, I don't feel well.'

Elliot caught her as she passed out again. 'Great!'

A woman in her fifties entered the bedroom. 'What's happened?' She combed back her short dark hair and grimaced at the splodge of vomit by his feet. 'Ned said someone fell in the pool.'

Elliot gestured to the woman on his bed. 'Joy, can you get her out of those wet things. Put my dressing gown on her or something. Just get her warm. I'm going to jump in the shower quickly, and call Suzie to clean this mess up, please.'

Joy waved him away. 'Leave it with me.'

Elliot grabbed a navy tracksuit from his wardrobe and headed outside to use his brother's shower to give the soaked woman some privacy.

Ned met him at the top of the stairs. 'Doctor Tully will be here in a sec. He was on his way anyway to pick up his granddaughter from the party. Good thing they're all in the front of the hotel. So far, no one's noticed any of the commotion. How's she doing?'

'So far, she's passed out twice. Oh, and she thinks I'm a merman.'

Ned laughed.

'Oh, Ned, this so isn't funny.'

Ned stopped smiling. 'I'll tell you what's not funny. How are we going to get that lump of a machine out of the pool?'

'Call a tow company or something. Figure it out.'

'I've got twenty mermaids gathered in the front room singing "Under the Sea", and you want me to keep ringing people. Sod it, Elliot. When she wakes up, she can pay for it to be removed. It's her problem.'

'It's ours when it's in our pool.'

A young woman with blue hair jogged up the stairs. 'The doc's here. Shall I send him up?'

Elliot really wanted a hot shower. His hair was flat against his head, and he was pretty sure his costume had shrunk in the pool, because it suddenly felt so tight on him. He could see Suzie staring at his muscles poking through, and he wasn't in the mood to be gawped at, especially by a nineteen-year-old with a crush. 'Suzie, go and check that Joy has made the woman decent, and can you clean up the vomit in my room, please, and then send the doc up, ta.'

'Where you going?' asked Ned.

Elliot raised his clenched fists in annoyance. 'I just want a bloody hot shower and to get out of these clothes. Can you please supervise for five minutes? That's all I need. The mermaids are fine. They've got four mums down there looking after them, not to mention two entertainers, and a member of our staff. They will cope without you for five minutes, Ned.'

Ned raised his hands, showing his palms. 'Hey, calm down, Elliot. Go and have your shower. I'll meet you in your room in five, okay?'

Elliot took a calming breath. 'Okay. Thanks.'

It was the fastest shower he had taken in his life, feeling the need to get back to his room as quickly as possible. Doctor Tully was the first person who Elliot saw as he approached his bedroom. He turned his walk into a sprint. 'Hey, Doc. Is she all right in there?'

Before the doctor could reply, a blonde woman, who looked very much like the lady on his bed, ran up the stairs to pant in his face. 'Where's my sister? What have you done to her? The lady downstairs said she fell in the pool.'

Elliot went to speak, but the doctor interrupted any form of argument that was about to take place on the landing.

'Please lower your voice. The woman in question has had a nasty shock.'

Ned came out of Elliot's room and stared over at Belle and the doctor.

Doctor Tully turned to Belle. 'Your sister will be fine. She was a little disorientated when she woke and somewhat panicky. She asked for something to help her sleep. She told Suzie where her medication was, so Suzie brought it here and I have given your sister a couple of her light sedatives. She is resting now. May I ask you about your sister's mental health?'

Belle looked straight at the doctor. 'She's not a delusional person, if that's what you're thinking. She was probably disorientated because she almost drowned when she was a child. And then she had to have therapy for the nightmares that the incident caused her to have for three years afterwards. As soon as I heard she had fallen in the pool, I knew it would confuse her. When she panics, she gets confused, but she hasn't been like that for years.' She turned to face Elliot. 'My sister suffered a trauma, that's all. She's terrified of water. This has no doubt freaked her out.' She looked back at the doctor. 'She has that medication because a while ago her anxiety levels were high due to a personal matter. She has been doing great lately.' Her eyes flittered to Elliot.

Elliot felt a punch to the gut. There he was silently cursing the stupid woman, even wondering if she tried to destroy their swimming pool on purpose, and all the time she genuinely was so afraid, and now so traumatised the doctor had to sedate her.

Belle turned back to the doctor. 'Can I take her home?'

Doctor Tully shook his head. 'I'm afraid you'll have to wait till she wakes. I'd rather she slept. It will do her the world of good.'

'Plus, she's nice and warm here,' said Ned. 'I hear you've got no heating.'

Doctor Tully looked clearly alarmed. 'No heating. That won't do.'

'We're getting the boiler fixed,' said Belle. 'The man said he can't come out for two weeks. I'm going to ring around, see if I can find someone else.'

Elliot controlled his sigh as he glanced at his brother. 'No need. I'll call my mate, Jeff Mills. He'll come out later today or tomorrow.'

'That's the man I called,' said Belle.

'I'll get him to come sooner. You have my word,' said Elliot. He turned to the doctor. 'What should we do about...' He glanced at Belle, waiting for her to fill in the gap.

'Primrose. My sister's name is Primrose, but she gets called Rosie.'

'Rosie,' said Elliot.

Doctor Tully nodded towards the bedroom door. 'Just let her sleep. She'll be out for a couple of hours at least. When she wakes, give her something light to eat and then she can go home.'

Belle shook his hand before Ned led him downstairs.

Elliot could see the glare in her hazel eyes as they turned his way. 'It's up to you what you want to do. You can stick around here for a few hours or go home if you've got stuff to be getting on with. I'll have someone come get you when she wakes. Meanwhile, we've got a room full of kids downstairs celebrating my niece's sixth birthday, so we're quite busy here.'

*Oh, shut up, Elliot. You sound like you're trying to get rid of her. She hasn't done anything wrong. She's just worried about her sister. I'd be the same if it were Ned.*

Belle pointed at the bedroom door. 'May I just pop my head in to see her.'

'Of course. You don't need to ask.'

'I do. It's not my bedroom.'

Elliot gestured for her to step inside, then waited patiently on the landing for her to reappear.

'She looks settled. Is she wearing your dressing gown?'

His face flushed. 'My receptionist, Joy, changed her out of her wet clothes. I left the room. I had to have a hot shower.'

'Did you get wet too?'

'I jumped in and pulled her out. Her shoe was caught on the lawnmower.'

'Lawnmower?'

'I'll explain,' said Ned, appearing at the top of the stairs.

Elliot watched Belle's face harden when she looked at Ned.

'Not sure I want to talk to you, Gaston.'

Ned shook his head slightly. 'What? Who? I'm sorry, what did you just call me?'

A wave of embarrassment flashed across her hazel eyes so fast, Elliot wasn't sure if that was what he had seen after all.

'You remind me of him,' she mumbled.

'The bloke from Beauty and the Beast?'

'You know him?'

Ned rolled his bright eyes. 'Please! I have a six-year-old daughter. I know every Disney character that exists.'

Elliot interrupted them. 'Erm, this is my brother, Ned, and I'm Elliot. I feel we should be introduced properly. Although, I can see the resemblance to Gaston now that you've mentioned it.' He grinned at Ned. 'It's the muscles and good looks, right, Ned?'

Ned was grinning as Belle muttered, 'More like arrogance and entitlement.'

Elliot pulled in his lips as Ned stopped smiling.

'Well, this arrogant and entitled Disney character just arranged for your boiler to be fixed in the next hour. Jeff Mills is on his way to your place as we speak.'

Even Elliot was intrigued to know what her response would be to that.

It looked as though the words were trapped tightly in her throat, and it was taking an enormous amount of effort to free them.

'Thank you, Ned.'

She almost sounded sweet. Sweet enough to render Ned speechless for a few seconds. Elliot watched his brother's mouth flap open and then close quickly, and it did entertain him a touch. Their attempt at hating each other was very amusing to him, but he wished they would both leave, because he wanted to go back into his bedroom. Alone.

'I'll go home now,' said Belle. 'I'll leave my number with the lady at reception. When my sister wakes up, tell her that I'll bring her over some clothes and food.'

'You don't have to worry about food. We'll sort that,' said Elliot.

Ned smirked at her. 'We have a chef.'

Belle ignored him and started to make her way down the stairs.

'Erm, wait,' called out Elliot. 'What's your name?'

She stopped on the steps, her body just in front of his brother's, and her face so close. Elliot could see Ned's cheeks warm.

'Bluebell,' she replied. 'Most people call me Belle.'

Elliot held back the laugh that tried to escape his throat.

*Belle and Gaston. Priceless.*

He stood in his bedroom doorway and looked over at Primrose Trent wrapped in his dark-green dressing gown, fast asleep in his bed. Her long blonde hair was sprawled out across his pillow, and he wondered if Joy had taken the hairdryer to her wavy golden locks, as they looked almost dry. He stepped into the room and peered down at her face. There was a slight rosy tint in her raised cheekbones, and something almost tranquil about her presence. He laughed to himself as he remembered her calling him a merman.

*I wouldn't mind being Aquaman, or at least be able to swim as well as Ned. Bloody hell, I saved her life. What was she doing on that thing anyway? Who does the gardening in November? She looks peaceful. I hope she's okay when she wakes up. Kasey had a bad experience with Pepper River in October, and now she won't even go near the pool, so I can only imagine how this woman's feeling. Primrose. Rosie. She doesn't look as scary as her sister. I wonder if she'll hate us as well. I don't hate you Primrose Trent.*

Elliot went over to a large comfy chair in the corner of his room and sat down whilst pulling a small fold-away table over to his legs. He opened the laptop on it and got on with some work whilst he supervised her.

# 5

*Rosie*

A cool breeze and the faint smell of sweet flowers drifted over Rosie as she stirred from what seemed like a deep sleep. She stretched out her body beneath the warm quilt and rubbed her sleepy eyes. An oaky scent came from her shoulder, causing her to snuggle further into the softness of the material wrapped around her.

*Wait!*

She opened her eyes fully and glanced over her unfamiliar attire. She then wondered about her whereabouts. Her head lifted from the plump pillow, and her eyes scanned the bedroom she appeared to be in. It was a very nice room. Clean and decorated with light blues and soft whites and was definitely not the bedroom she had acquired in her new hotel. Her bedroom also didn't have a man in it. Dust, yes. Man, definitely no.

*Who on earth is he?*

She sat up slowly, feeling as though if she moved any faster it wouldn't be good for her. The quilt was clenched tightly in her hands as her eyes peered over at the sleeping man in the large squashy chair in the corner of the room. There was a laptop open on a table in front of him and a pair of dark glasses resting next to it.

*Goodness, he's hot, whoever he is.*

Her eyes rolled over his strong arms, taking in his tattoos, and then up to his peaceful, chiselled face. His dark hair was flopped to one side, revealing dark eyebrows and a few lines upon his forehead.

*I have to say something. I think. Should I? Maybe I should just leave. Not sure I want to. I can't keep staring at him. Can I? I can. I am. Say something. Find out what's happening. I need to know where I am.*

'Hello,' she whispered, wanting to wake him, but at the same time not wanting to disturb him. 'Hellooo.' She found herself enjoying the view, but she also wanted to know who he was and where she was, even though something told her that she was perfectly safe. She wrapped her arms around herself, hugging her elbows, hugging the dressing gown, and she wondered where her clothes had disappeared to. She couldn't see them anywhere. Suddenly, the memory of being dragged under the water hit her, and she gasped loudly, slapping one hand to her mouth.

The man in the chair stirred. His sleepy eyes peered over at her, and his body straightened. He didn't speak, and neither did she.

*Is he the… merman?*

He spoke first. 'How are you feeling?' His voice was soft and low, and it filled her with unexpected warmth.

'I'm a bit confused at the moment.' She sounded slightly hoarse so swallowed hard to help quench her dry throat.

He stood, revealing the fullness of his height and build, and Rosie was sure she was dreaming as Triton came closer to the bed.

'You fell in my swimming pool,' he said gently.

'I've just remembered that much.'

'I brought you up here to my room to rest. I had a female member of staff help you out of your wet clothes. She put you in my dressing gown. The doctor came and gave you something to help you sleep for a bit because you were anxious. And your sister has been too. She's going to bring you some clothes when you're ready to leave. The doctor said you were to eat something light before going home.'

Rosie felt a wave of emotion rush over her and before she could control her actions, she started to cry.

'Hey, hey, it's okay,' Elliot said, sitting down on the bed by her side, holding her hands in his.

*Flipping heck, Rosie.*

'I'm sorry. I don't mean to cry.'

'You have every right to. What happened to you was scary.'

She closed her eyes and took a deep breath as his hand gently brushed back her hair from her face. It felt warm and so soothing, and she wanted to just rest on his chest and fall back to sleep and pretend that none of the disasters in her life had ever happened.

*Why me? Why did this happen to me? What a fool. What a nightmare. Oh, I don't feel very well. I want my mum. Why can't my mum be here? I miss her. I need her to hold me. She always made everything better.*

As if he could read her mind, he leant towards her and gently guided her body onto his own. His arms wrapped around her, and she had never felt so safe before. Perhaps it was the drugs still in her system, or maybe she really was still asleep. Either way, she didn't care. It felt nice, and she was taking it.

His voice rumbled through her body. 'My name's Elliot, by the way. Your sister told me you are Primrose or Rosie. What would you prefer me to call you?'

'Rosie,' she mumbled into his solid chest.

'Rosie it is.'

*Oh goodness, I don't know who you are, Merman, but I really want to kiss you right now. Oh, what drugs have I been given? Wait...*

'Elliot, as in Elliot Renshaw?'

She was pretty sure she heard him swallow before he confirmed who he was. She had to move away now, but her body hadn't received the memo. His head must have lowered, as she could feel the warmth of his breath close to the back of her neck, and it felt so good. Way too good. Everything about Merman felt wonderful. There was no way she was moving away first. She would wait until he broke the hold. She waited, but he wasn't moving either.

*Why aren't you moving away from me? Maybe you don't know I'm a Trent. He must know. Why doesn't he care? Why doesn't he hate me? This is weird. Very odd and so relaxing. He smells nice, like this dressing gown. I'm wearing his nightclothes. He feels good on me. I like his arms. I like how they're holding me. He's still holding me. I need to let go. I don't want to. I can't. Oh, this feels so nice.*

'How are you feeling now?' he asked quietly. 'Are you hungry yet? It's gone lunchtime.'

*I like your voice, Merman. You sound caring. Gentle. I like your voice on my neck. I don't want your mouth to move away from my neck. I'm definitely high on something. I'm probably still dreaming. Oh well, it's a lovely dream. Let's see how long it lasts. What did he ask me? Oh, yeah.*

'My stomach feels empty, but I still feel a bit tired and would rather go back to sleep, if I'm honest.'

She went to tell him that she should go so that she could have another nap at home, knowing that would be the normal response in that type of situation. But he lowered her back down to the soft pillow, showing his own response. His arms stayed with her all the way, which gave her a sense of security.

Aquamarine eyes peered down into hers as his face came to a stop directly over hers.

*Flipping heck! I so want to snog him senseless right now. Is he going to kiss me? He looks like he might. I'm going to let him if he goes for it. What are you waiting for, Merman? You can kiss me. Oh, I'm so tired. I need to keep my eyes open. I have to look at him. His eyes. So…*

Elliot released his arms from her body and went to pull away, but Rosie weakly held on, causing him to still. His bright eyes hit her straight in the heart.

'Please don't leave me,' she whispered, then wondered if she had said that out loud.

'I wasn't going to. I haven't all the time you've been sleeping. I was just going to go back to my laptop and get on with some work while you went back to sleep.'

Rosie loosened her grip on him.

*I don't want you to go back to work. I want to watch you. I want to sleep.*

'Will you just sit here with me until I drift off?'

Something woke slightly inside her brain, stirring her from her trance with him. She was about to mention that she was being silly, and also tell herself off for acting weird, as that had only just registered. But then Elliot slowly adjusted his position so that he was lying down by her side, facing her.

*Oh. He's right there.*

'Good enough?' he asked.

*I wasn't expecting that. Why is he being so lovely? He's a Renshaw. Why does he make me feel safe? Probably because he saved me. What the hell am I going to do about the lawnmower? That thing must have cost a fortune. Great! Belle's going to have a fit. I'm surprised she left me here. I'm in Elliot Renshaw's bed, wearing his dressing gown, and he's staring at me. Wow, his eyes are the colour of tropical waters. He's gorgeous. I wonder what he's thinking. Why am I so tired? Was I going to say something? I need to sleep. I need to see him. I like his eyes. I want to…*

'Go to sleep,' he whispered.

Rosie closed her sleepy eyes, and the corners of her mouth curled all by themselves as Elliot's hand came to rest on hers. 'Thank you, Merman.'

'I'm not really a merman,' he said, so softly, she barely heard him.

# 6

*Ned*

'Look at the state of this place,' mumbled Ned, standing in the foyer of the Inn on the Right. The only thing of colour was the orange sticky note stuck to the broken reception desk that Suzie had left for Belle, telling her that Rosie had fallen in the pool and was next door. His nose twitched as it met with the dust particles floating in the air, and he somehow managed to hold off a sneeze.

*It would be great to buy this place and re-join the hotels again. Then we can name it Pepper River Inn. Let's hope they sell. It will cost them a fortune to do this place up. Surely, they haven't got that much money. If they have, I'm certain they wouldn't waste it here. No one in their right mind would. Mind you, I'm not sure how stable these sisters are. Now I'm wondering just how sane we are wanting to take this place on. At least we know what we're doing. I just know these two don't have a clue.*

He looked around whilst no one was about, poking his nose in every available doorway to see how the Trents had designed their half. Not much impressed him nor worried him. In fact, he felt relieved now that he had the time to really see for himself just how bad the other side was. There was little chance of competition. Not anytime soon anyway. He saw a stairway leading downstairs and assumed that's where the kitchen was, if his own hotel was anything to go by.

He called down the steps as he walked to the bottom. 'Hello?'

Belle's voice echoed towards him. 'Down here.'

He felt himself smile and quickly wiped that expression from his face.

*There will be no smiling at this woman.*

He stopped as he entered the kitchen and stared over at her backside that was poking up in the air. His head tilted, and his smile had returned, blatantly defying him. 'What are you doing?'

Belle removed herself from the inside of a bottom cupboard, banging her head in the process, which caused Ned to bite his lip to stop the laughter that was about to erupt. He had no idea why he was being so polite. She didn't deserve his best behaviour. She didn't deserve any form of respect from him. She was, after all, a Trent, and one that liked to scowl at him a lot. No, there was no way he was going to be nice to her.

'I'm cleaning,' she replied, straightening to see who the voice belonged to. 'Oh, it's you. What are you doing here? Spying, no doubt.'

He looked around the kitchen, with mock amusement. 'Oh, yeah, there's so much to spy on. Wish I brought my camera now. Never mind. Next time.'

'You're not invited for a next time, mate. In fact, you weren't invited this time either, so what are you doing in my hotel?'

He snorted out a laugh, which appeared to make the corners of her mouth curl up for all but a second. 'Hotel is hardly the word I would use.'

'Nobody here cares what word you would use.'

He widened his bright eyes to gaze around the large, cold room again. 'You're the only one here.'

'Not true. There's Rodney.'

'Who?'

Belle pointed at the stone floor. 'The rat.'

He quickly scanned the floor. 'Oh my God, you have rats?'

She laughed and held a smugness in her eyes. 'You're afraid of rats?'

Ned knew that his expression had clearly given the game away. There was no turning back now. He hated rodents, with a passion. Kasey wasn't even allowed a hamster, which was a long-drawn-out conversation that took place one Sunday morning during the hangover from hell. 'You need to get rid of them. They're not hygienic, and if I so much as spot one rat over at my place, I'll have this place boarded up before you get a chance to leave.'

'Oh, shut up, you big baby. Why would any decent rat want to live at your place? You're there, for a start.'

'You can't have rats,' he snapped.

'I can do what I want, thank you very much, Edward Renshaw. You can sod off.'

'Oh, that's charming. Do you kiss your mother with that mouth?'

Belle's eyes dropped to the floor, and Ned felt as though she had just punched him in the gut.

'I wish I could kiss my mum again,' she mumbled.

*Oh crap. She's lost her mum.*

He knew how that felt. The last time he kissed his mum, he was five, and she was dying in a hospital bed, and that was his only memory of her. 'I lost my mum when I was a kid.'

'I was thirteen.'

'Five.'

A moment of silence filled the air, then a big, fluffy, ginger cat came from nowhere and slowly mooched its way across the cold floor to curl its body around Ned's legs.

Belle's eyes widened. 'Did you bring your cat with you?'

'Actually, he's your cat.'

'I don't have a cat.'

'He belonged to your uncle, but since no one has been here to look after him, he has been wandering over to ours every day. My daughter, Kasey, has adopted him. I don't know how he gets in and out of places, but he does. He does his own thing. We just feed him. Well, my daughter does.'

'What's his name?'

'We don't know. He has no tag, but Kasey calls him Tinks.'

'Tinks.'

'You can feed him from now on. He's your responsibility.'

Belle was clearly dumbstruck, but she nodded. 'I would have, had I known about him.'

'Maybe he can help with your rat problem. Though, I doubt it. Tinks doesn't seem to like to move very fast, as you will see for yourself over time.'

'Erm… I'll try and stop him coming over to yours,' she mumbled.

'Please don't. Kasey will miss him. They're quite close. Some nights I find him asleep on her bed.'

'Oh. Okay. She can keep him if she wants.'

'Don't push your responsibilities onto us.'

Belle shook her head and frowned. 'I wasn't. I was being nice.'

Coldness loomed, and it wasn't due to the weather.

Ned suddenly gestured towards the boiler. 'Did Jeff fix the problem?'

'No. We need a new one. It should be here in a few days.'

'No wonder it's so cold in here.' He watched her hug herself and had the strangest notion to help her with that action. Perhaps it was because he was also cold and would appreciate some body heat. 'Do you have any hot water?'

*Don't get involved, Ned.*

'We have electric showers and I can boil a kettle.'

*Don't say it. Don't say it.*

'You're welcome to stay at ours until your boiler is fixed. We have spare rooms at the moment, as our Christmas guests don't check-in till the week before the big day. It's pretty quiet at the moment.'

He could see her mulling it over. He was too. Why the hell had he suggested that? Where did that even come from? Elliot was starting to rub off on him.

'Thank you, but we'll be fine. It's just a few days. I'm sure we can rough it. Besides, it's only the heating.'

Ned had witnessed the state of the place. He was pretty sure it wasn't only the lack of heating that was causing them to rough it. There was dust galore, and rats. He saw broken furniture and a cracked toilet in the small bathroom in the foyer. He dread to think how the upstairs was shaping up, but still, if she wanted to stay put, it was no skin off his nose. He still couldn't believe he asked.

Her hazel eyes had softened, which brought a pleasantness to her features. The clump of knotted cobweb on the top of her blonde hair added to her frazzled look, which he thought was both funny and cute. He just hoped a spider didn't crawl out from the tangle, as there was no way he was going to intervene with that crawly mess. He wasn't really a fan of anything smaller than a rabbit, and even those he was wary of.

'Your sister's awake.'

Belle's face lit up as though someone had flicked a Christmas tree light switch. 'I'll fetch her clothes.'

He moved to one side as she brushed past him. Their arms touching caused them both to still for a second. Even with the dust on her, he could smell a faint hint of something fruity coming from her clothes. As though moving by itself, his head leaned closer towards her, and she seemed to lean his way.

'I...' He swallowed hard, dropping his gaze and stepping to one side.

Belle slowly approached the stairway and then turned unexpectedly, bumping straight into him, as he was close behind her. His arms shot out to steady her, then quickly released his hold as though her skin had burned him.

She went to speak, but he got in first.

'Watch it!' he snapped, taking a step back.

'Sorry, I didn't know you were right there. I was just going to ask how Rosie was, but I can find out for myself in a minute. I don't need to get into a conversation with you. I'll be right over. You can leave now.'

*How rude is she? I come all the way over here to give her the news when I could have just called her phone, and does she appreciate it? No.*

'I'll show myself out, shall I?'

She marched off up the stairs, with him stomping behind her. Her sharp voice shooting down so fast it could have cut his skin. 'That would be great.'

Ned reached the foyer to see her jog up to the next level, no doubt to Rosie's room. He stood there for a moment, lingering, with so much more to say to the infuriating woman. He wasn't quite sure what exactly it was that he wanted to say, but there was something bothering him, if not everything.

# 7

## Belle

*Oh my goodness, that man irritates me so much, and why on earth was he inviting us to stay at his poxy hotel? Like we'd want to stay there. Okay, so Rosie has already had a sleepover, of sorts, but she was drugged and forced to stay so that doesn't count. No doubt they have fed her by now too. Why are they being so nice? What are they after? This place, I guess. Think they can butter us up and we'll just down tools and hand over the lot. Well, think again, Renshaws. We're here for the long haul. Oh, why the flipping hell did Rosie have to go and waterbomb their pool with our mower? What was she thinking?*

Belle flopped her body backwards on Rosie's bed and sighed loudly, knowing no one could hear her, not that she cared about sounding dramatic. She hoped Gaston had gone home. 'What a cheek he's got, coming over here and just walking in like he owns the place.'

*I suppose I'd better get up and get on with rescuing Rosie from their evil clutches. If I find out they've said anything horrible to her, I'll have their guts for garters.*

She took a long calming breath and hauled herself off the springy mattress to gather some of Rosie's loungewear, as she figured her sister would be in a slouchy mood.

Tinks was following her around in the foyer and then went with her outside. Belle glanced down at the plump cat, who looked well and truly looked after.

'You know you're a traitor, right?'

Tinks was slouching along like it was a summer's day.

49

'You're a Trent cat. Please try to remember that.'

Tinks made a murmur.

'Oh, you've got something to say about that, have you? Well, I guess you have a right. If no one was around to care for you, you had little choice. Anyway, you did good to find the nice Renshaw. Kasey's the only one, I bet. An innocent child stuck with the likes of him. Feel free to sleep on her bed anytime you like, and feel free to piddle on Ned's, if ever in need.'

Belle walked into the warmth of the Inn on the Left, and this time she took in her surroundings. Tinks wandered off to who knows where, and she didn't feel the need to call him back. She was occupied with how Christmassy and welcoming the foyer looked. She tried not to smile at the large brick-built fireplace, alive and kicking, and she hid the delight in her eyes at the sight of the Christmas tree standing at the bottom of the wide, curved stairway that had a rust-red carpet. Twinkling lights were wrapped around a large, decorated, hanging garland above the reception, looking stylish and homely. She moved over to the tree to have a better look at the handmade wooden decorations that sat in amongst red, white, and gold ornaments and red and white berry lights.

*Oh, this tree is beautiful. I love a woodland theme. We need a tree, and a working fireplace, and... well, everything, really, but a tree would be a great start to getting us in the spirit. Right now, it doesn't feel like Christmas is around the corner at all.*

She walked over to the open arched doorway the other side of the long, beautifully carved reception desk that looked as though it had been shipped down from somewhere Nordic. She peered inside the dining room to see round tables dotted about, covered in white tablecloths, each topped with a Christmas candle. Another tree, much slimmer than the foyer one, sat in one corner, filled with more wooden decorations. A bar took up another corner and held its own set of fairy lights. The thought of a gin, or two, encouraged her to take a step closer to the polished surface.

*Nothing in this place looks like it came from Argos. Viking boat makers, more like. Ragnar and his crew turned up one day on the Isle of Wight and made friends with the Renshaws. It wouldn't surprise me. They seem like the jammy sort. It is a beautiful hotel. Maybe we should stay here for a few days. We could get some ideas. No. We can't copy them. I don't think we could afford to copy them. If we want any sort of custom, we're going to have to come up with something completely opposite to them. The haunted house is sounding better by the hour.*

She let out a strangled scream as Ned appeared from who knows where.

'See anything you like?' he asked, his voice filled with sarcasm.

She wasn't about to let him see her embarrassment for getting caught snooping. She gestured towards the bar. 'Gin.'

His face broke out into that powerful, sexy smile he had that completely annoyed her because it was so inviting. He moved behind the bar and pointed behind him. 'Which one would you like, Miss Trent?'

His friendly demeanour floored her momentarily. She browsed the bottles behind him, then picked a cherry flavoured one. He raised his brow and placed the bottle on the bar and pulled up two glasses. 'Think I'll join you. After hosting a Little Mermaid birthday party, I'm in need of one.'

Belle scoffed before she had time to think. 'More like her mother did all the work.'

He stopped mid-pour for a second, then continued. 'I thought you might have researched us Renshaws before you moved here.'

*I did, but why is he saying that?*

'Erm, I did look at your hotel website. I didn't delve into your DNA or anything though. Why?'

'If you had delved deeper, you might have seen an old local news article about a car crash that I was involved in when my daughter was barely one. My girlfriend, Kasey's mother, died that day. Kasey was unharmed, and I have been left with a permanent limp. Not that I need that to remind me of that night.'

Belle had no idea that her hand was resting on his on the bar. 'I'm so sorry, Ned. Really, I am. I would have never mentioned your daughter's mother had I known. I'm not that cruel.' She felt his hand slip away from under hers and that was when she realised her automatic caring action. Unsure what to do next, she swigged some of her drink, then placed both of her hands on her lap, out of harm's way.

'Okay,' he said quietly. 'Well, I'm glad that's cleared up.'

*I didn't even notice he limped. Oh, why did I have to mention Kasey's mum? Flipping heck, he looks so sad now, and he's just poured a second measure for himself. Great work, Belle. I know I don't like the man, but I would never stoop so low. I bet he thinks I knew all along and was just being cruel. I want to make him believe me, but I don't know how.*

'I really didn't know,' she whispered, but only because her voice broke.

His aquamarine eyes flashed her way. 'I believe you.'

Belle quickly finished her drink. 'I'm going to see my sister.'

He pointed at the ceiling. 'You know the way.'

*Right.*

She picked up her bag from the floor and left the room. She stopped once more at the Christmas tree by the stairs to take another look. Belle loved anything to do with Christmas, but the trees were always her favourite.

'It's a magic tree,' said a tiny voice from behind her.

Belle looked over her shoulder, then downwards to the little girl standing behind her, smiling at the mermaid costume she was happily swaying in. Her long, red, plaited hair was looped over one shoulder and bounced slightly as the girl moved from side to side whilst humming 'Part of Your World'.

'Oh, hello. You must be Ariel.'

The child giggled and sat down on the stairs. 'Today I am, but tomorrow I will be Kasey again.'

Belle sat down on the steps below Kasey so they were face to face. 'Well, my name is Belle.'

Kasey's face lit up with excitement, revealing her missing front teeth. 'Like Belle from Beauty and the Beast?'

Belle smiled. 'Actually, my full name is Bluebell, but most people call me Belle.'

Kasey mouthed the name, 'Bluebell.' Her bright eyes were the same colour as her dad's. 'Bluebell is a pretty name. You sound like a fairy.'

'I wish I was a fairy.'

Kasey sighed. 'Me too.'

Belle nodded towards the tree. 'Why is your tree magical?'

Kasey followed her eyes. 'It makes everyone smile.'

'That really is very magical.'

'Can you make people smile, Bluebell Belle?'

The girl's face was very serious, so Belle thought it best not to laugh. 'I'm not sure. Some people smile when I sing.'

'You can sing? I love to sing.'

'I was in a choir where I used to live, and we'd go around to different places and sing to people to help bring some cheer.'

'Do you know any Disney songs?'

'As a matter of fact, I do. We once dressed up as Disney characters and sang songs from the films.'

'Were you Belle?'

Belle smiled widely at Kasey's hopeful face. She nodded, and Kasey clapped her hands.

'Can I sing one with you? Please, Belle.'

*Oh crumbs, really? How am I supposed to get out of this?*

'Erm, okay, but just a little bit, and quietly, okay?'

'Okay,' Kasey whispered, placing a finger to her lips.

No one was about, so Belle felt she was getting off lightly. She had no embarrassment about singing in front of anyone, but performing on the stairs inside the Inn on the Left felt beyond weird and wrong on so many levels. What would her grandfather think, for a start. Very quietly, she began to sing 'Part of Your World', and just as quietly, Kasey joined in. They held hands and their voices went up a notch as they forgot about their quiet promise as they got lost in their enjoyment of the song. Belle and Kasey were smiling widely at each other, and Kasey had started to sway Belle's hands in the air. They giggled as they finished and both jumped when they heard clapping.

Belle stood sharply as Ned approached.

'Daddy, did you hear us?'

His face held an expression that Belle had not seen before. It was so gentle and filled with love.

'I did, and you were so good.'

'Belle too?'

Belle prayed she didn't blush as his eyes flashed her way. She could feel the heat hit her cheeks and was ready to blame it on the nearby fire crackling away.

'Belle too,' he replied, not moving his gaze.

Belle's stomach flipped, and she knew she had to flee the scene.

Kasey stood and placed her tiny hand into Belle's, which caused both adults to stare down in surprise at the linked fingers. 'Belle is magical. She has a Disney name and a fairy name. That makes her magical, doesn't it, Daddy?'

Belle glanced his way, but his eyes were on his daughter.

'Yes, it does,' he replied softly.

'Can she stay to watch one of my films, Daddy?'

'Erm, no, sorry. Belle is here to see her sister.'

Kasey tugged on Belle's hand, gaining her full attention. 'Is she the one who fell in the swimming pool?'

Belle nodded. 'Yes. I have some dry clothes for her, so I'm just going to pop upstairs and see her now. Okay?'

Kasey let her hand slip from her grip. 'Okay.' Her voice was sad and hit Belle straight in the heart.

'But, I'm sure I can watch one of your films another time. I know my sister would love that too, if she's allowed.'

Kasey beamed happily. 'Yes, she can come.' She trotted down to stand by her father. 'Can't she, Daddy?'

Ned's lips seemed pursed. 'Why not? The more the merrier.'

'You can come too, Daddy,' she added quietly.

He glanced down at her and smiled. 'Wouldn't miss it for the world.'

'Belle and her sister can have dinner with us tonight, Daddy, and then we can all watch a film.'

*I'm not saying anything. He can deal with that fallout.*

'Sure, why not?' was his reply. He faced Belle. 'You'll have to ask your sister what she thinks and get back to us.'

Belle found herself nodding against her will.

Kasey let out a small cheer. 'Yay, we have a date.'

Belle and Ned quickly looked at each other. 'It's not a date,' they said in unison.

Belle headed up the stairs before anything else was said.

# 8

*Rosie*

A rush of guilt hit her when Rosie noticed Belle standing in Elliot's bedroom doorway. Elliot had been listening to her telling him about how unpredictable her little car could be and when it got stuck in the snow on a hill last winter. He was smiling and fully engrossed in her story, and she was fully engrossed in him.

Rosie had woken on his chest, with his strong arms wrapped around her as if that was the only place they should be. She had smiled to herself at how surreal the situation was. He was a stranger, and she questioned why he didn't feel like one. She felt as though she'd woken in his arms many times before, and each time felt just as good as the last. It was completely blowing her mind. He had smiled at her when she glanced up at him, and when he got up, her body felt cold and lonely, which only freaked her out some more.

Belle had obviously seen them chatting, smiling, and enjoying each other's company, and Rosie knew she wasn't supposed to act that way with a Renshaw. What would her grandfather say, or Uncle Frank? She felt trapped between two families that didn't feel like hers. It wasn't her argument, and Elliot wasn't as nasty as she was led to believe. In fact, he was lovely and kind. He had held her when she cried and saved her from drowning, all of which she was pretty sure an enemy wouldn't do.

'How are you, Rosie?' Belle asked, entering.

Rosie felt uncomfortable. She was sitting at a table, eating lunch with Elliot, looking perfectly happy, and she wasn't sure what Belle's first impression of that setup was.

Elliot had arranged for a table to be brought to his room. It was dressed with a cream tablecloth, shiny silverware, and afternoon tea. Rosie knew full well it looked as though she were on some sort of date.

'I feel okay,' she replied.

Belle waggled the black holdall she was carrying. 'I brought clothes.'

Rosie missed Elliot's dressing gown already. 'Oh, thanks, Belle. Erm… about the lawnmower.'

Elliot interrupted. 'We've had it removed from the pool. It's back in your garden at the moment. Not sure it's ever going to work again.'

Belle looked at him. Her face revealing no clear expression. 'Thank you. You can send us the bill.'

'No need,' said Elliot.

'There is every need,' said Belle, her tone filled with authority.

Elliot didn't respond, and Rosie felt even more uncomfortable. She decided it was best to just get up and head off somewhere to get changed so that they could go home.

Elliot pointed to a door in his room. 'You can use my bathroom. Feel free to have a shower or bath before you get changed, if you want. Everything you might need is in there.'

The thought of having a long hot soak in the tub was making Rosie smile. She wondered if she dared. Would Belle mind? Her eyes rolled over to her sister.

Belle appeared to be studying her. 'You might as well, Rosie. We both know how much you love a bath, and we've got no boiler for the next few days.'

Elliot looked concerned. 'Didn't Jeff fix it?'

'It's knackered, apparently. He's ordered a new one.'

Elliot turned to Rosie. 'The doctor said you need to stay warm.'

Belle scoffed, gaining attention. 'She fell into a swimming pool. She's dry now. She won't freeze.'

Rosie shrugged. 'She's right. I'm fine now.'

'Sorry.' Elliot shook his head slightly as he stood. 'Of course you're fine. I was just following doctor's orders.'

'You've done a good job too.' Rosie felt the need to praise him. 'You saved me, kept me warm and dry, comforted me and fed me, and now you're offering me use of your bath. I think we can safely say that you did more than was asked of you.'

Belle dropped the bag on the floor, creating a thump. 'Yes, thank you for saving my sister, and for looking after her.'

Elliot's bright eyes twinkled at Rosie. 'My pleasure. I'll leave you to it.'

Rosie could feel a twang of disappointment as he left the room. Her eyes quickly shot to Belle's as Belle plonked herself down where Elliot had just been sitting.

'What the bloody hell, Rosie?'

'What?'

'Erm, let me see. How about, everything.'

*Where to start?*

'The gardening seemed like a good idea at the time, and between that and waking up here, it's all a bit fuzzy, if I'm honest. I guess I freaked out. I know I passed out. I might have even thrown up, but that hasn't been confirmed.

Although, there is a wet patch on the carpet over the other side of the bed, and it smells very sweet as though it's just been cleaned, so it's quite possible that's where vomit-gate took place.'

Belle pointed over to the bedroom door. 'And what about him?' Her voice was low and filled with contempt.

'He jumped in and pulled me out. You know that much.'

'That's not what I'm talking about, and you know that much.'

Rosie shrugged nonchalantly. 'He was kind to me. There's nothing else to add.'

Belle leaned over the fruit scones. 'He's a Renshaw, Rosie. Just remember that.'

'He was nothing but nice, so I don't care what his name is. I'm judging him on what he is like.'

Belle sat back, glanced once more at the door, and then shook her head. 'I'm sure he felt bad that you nearly drowned, but now that you are okay, he will go back to being a horrible Renshaw. They can't be trusted.'

Rosie nodded, even though she was struggling to see Elliot as horrible. 'What's this about the boiler?'

Belled gestured towards the doorway. 'They arranged for that boiler man who we called to come out today. Costs a small fortune to buy a new boiler, you know. I had no idea they cost that much, and we won't be able to afford another one of those ride-on mowers, so don't even think about that. Oh, and Ned Renshaw said we can stay here until we've got heating. I turned him down, of course.'

Rosie kept a straight face. 'Those Renshaws sound terrible.'

'They're not all terrible. I met Ned's daughter. She's six today, and she got me singing a Disney song with her on the stairs. She's so sweet, but she's only gone and invited us for dinner here tonight. She wants us to watch a Disney film with her afterwards as well. I didn't know what to say.'

'I hope you said yes. It's her birthday, after all. Plus, we love a sing-along.'

'Speaking of which, I went to the library when I was in Sandly earlier. I found us a choir we can join. It was up on the notice board. I called the choirmaster, and we're meeting him tomorrow to showcase our voices. He said we're just in time to get ready for the Christmas show.'

That cheered Rosie up. 'Fantastic. I really miss singing with our old group.'

'Yes, it'll be good to make some new friends and be part of the community.'

'I think we've already made some new friends, Belle. I know they're Renshaws, but Elliot was so nice. I don't want to snub him.'

Belle huffed back into her chair. 'You fancy him, don't you? Unbelievable, Rosie. I thought you weren't going to bother with men ever again, and if you are going to get back in the saddle, you can do a lot better than him. Of all people, Rosie. Come on. You can't allow yourself to have feelings for that man. In fact, you haven't. You're just feeling grateful because he saved you. That's the psychology of the situation. Some sort of Florence Nightingale effect you two have going on or a trauma bond or something. I don't know.'

Rosie picked up the bag and headed for the bathroom. 'Why don't you finish off that lunch while I have a bath. I can still smell the pool water in my hair, and I don't like it.'

'You can leave the door open, Rosie. No one will come in. I'll make sure of that. Well, Tinks might. Apparently, he goes where he wants.'

Rosie smiled to herself as she went to enter the bathroom. Her sister knew that baths and showers made her feel claustrophobic, so she didn't like the door closed.

*Hang on a minute, what?*

She turned back to Belle. 'Who is Tinks?'

'Our cat.'

'We have a cat?'

'He was Uncle Frank's, but Kasey's sort of adopted him. Big fluffy ginger thing. Reminds me of Garfield. Lazy with a sarcastic face.'

Rosie was looking forward to meeting him, especially as he had been described as sarcastic. She entered the bathroom to get ready.

*Flipping heck!*

Her mouth gaped at the stunning room before her. It was rustic and best suited to a log cabin somewhere in the mountains. Dark wood and crisp white worked side by side, creating warmth and light. There were wooden beams on the ceiling and a log burner opposite the bath. Some green plants lined the wide windowsill in front of an arched window, and candles in storm lamps sat below.

Hot water flowed from curved copper taps, filling the large white bath, bringing an instant smile to Rosie's face. She swirled the water with one hand, adding some cold till it reached her desired temperature.

Navy towels, a creamy shower gel, and shampoo that smelled like freshy cut grapefruit was what she removed from the cupboard, not before having a quick sniff of Elliot's oaky aftershave.

Rosie lowered herself into his bath, relaxing instantly. All thoughts were of them holding each other in bed. Her beneath the covers. Him to her side. She wished he had been under the quilt with her, preferably naked. She giggled to herself at the thought and at the madness of it all.

*Pops must hate me right now, not to mention Uncle Frank. Oh, why did it have to be me who let the family down? Why is Elliot Renshaw so flipping nice? And how is anyone that good-looking? His eyes, that smile, and that body. Good grief, it's ridiculous. I'm ridiculous. I'm in his bath. I wish I could stay here longer, but Belle will be chomping on her fingernails by now. She hates this place, and the Renshaws, but what if I could get her to change her mind? I know there was chemistry between me and Elliot. I could see it in his eyes. He likes me. I'm pretty sure he does. We worked well together, like old friends. I want to get to know him. I need to find a way to break down the wall between our families, but Belle, and probably Ned, won't make it easy.*

Rosie started to sing 'Part of Your World', and sounded just as good as Ariel herself. Her smile widened when she heard her sister join in from the bedroom.

Rosie had an opening. The little girl had invited them for dinner and a film tonight, and it was polite to accept, especially as it was the child's birthday. And after everything Elliot had done, it would seem rude to say no. If she played it smart, maybe, just maybe, they could stay overnight, perhaps even until they had heating. It would only be a few days, and it was offered. Belle would hate it, but it would be a great opportunity for Belle to get to know the Renshaws for who they really were. The family stories had filled them with nothing but contempt and dread, but those stories were about people in the past, not the owners of the divided Pepper River Inn of today. What if she could break the cycle? What if she and Elliot were the first ones to make peace? And what if, against all the odds, Belle and Ned Renshaw became friends?

'It's worth a try.'

# 9

*Elliot*

'Everyone's gone home early,' said Ned. 'Might as well, we've got no guests till next week, and that's only our anniversary couple who come this time every year for a few days.'

Elliot didn't mind. He knew they were fully booked for two weeks over Christmas. It was nice to have a bit of peace and quiet before the madness hit. He couldn't remember a Christmas when he wasn't looking after others. His thoughts drifted to the woman upstairs in his bathroom. He had done way more than look after her, and he had enjoyed every second of it. How bizarre. He moved over the other side of the kitchen to switch the coffee machine on. 'Do you want a coffee, Ned?'

'Yeah, go on then.' Ned tied up another black bag filled with party leftovers. 'Kasey had a good day today, and the Trent woman didn't drown in our pool, so not a bad day in all.'

The two men looked at each other and laughed.

Ned shook his head dramatically. 'What a day!'

'You can say that again. I was dressed as a merman saving someone from drowning.'

Ned flashed him a smile. 'Mermen are helpful like that. Might want to watch out for those sirens though.'

Elliot's eyes followed his brother's finger to the ceiling. 'Sirens?'

Ned lowered his voice. 'Those two up there.'

'You view them as singing creatures about to lure us to our death?'

'Exactly that.'

Elliot had to laugh.

'Oh,' added Ned, 'and Kasey has only gone and bloody well invited them for dinner tonight.'

Elliot felt something stir in his stomach. He liked that idea and was proud of Kasey for being so thoughtful. He knew his brother wasn't feeling the same love, as Ned's finger was wagging his way.

'Don't even think about it, Elliot. I've already had one of them singing on the stairs, sounding all Disney as well. See, siren. The other one probably wasn't really drowning at all. She just made it look that way so you'd be a mug and jump in to save her. Sneaky tactics. We can't put anything past them. Trents, remember.'

'Well, if we are living next door to a couple of mythical creatures, Kasey will be pleased.'

'It's not funny. Even I got sucked in at one point.'

'What do you mean?'

'I said they could stay here until their heating came back on. Don't laugh. I know. I don't know what I was thinking. I had a moment of weakness. I felt sorry for the girl, that's all. She turned down the offer, so that's a relief. But now I don't know if they're staying for dinner, and, get this part, Kasey wants them to watch a film with her afterwards.'

'Well, at least Kasey is showing them that Renshaws are nice.'

'We can't make ourselves vulnerable, Elliot.'

'Ned, it's dinner and a film, hardly showing them what's in the safe.'

'The only reason they would stick around here is to steal all our hotel ideas. They'll try and copy us and take our guests. You mark my words. You can take your eye off the ball, but I'm watching them.'

'That's good. You can continue to watch them tonight when they stay for dinner. I'll cook.'

Ned scraped his hand through his mop of dark hair. 'Bloody hell, Elliot, don't tell me you like that woman you saved. You've only known her five minutes, and she's a Trent.'

'What is this, West Side Story?'

Ned sighed loudly. 'Stay away from her. No good will come of it. The Renshaws and Trents have a long history filled with hate. We can't be the ones who go soft. That family tried to destroy ours, and those two up there will be no different.'

'Ned, it's an old conflict that really has nothing to do with us. We didn't start it. We don't even know what started it, and I don't actually care anymore. I'm not a spiteful person. I'm not going to go around hating, and Rosie hasn't given me any reason to hate her.'

'Oh, Rosie is it? Well, give her time. She will. You might want to throw the towel in, but they won't be thinking that way.'

'I'm going upstairs after this coffee, and I'm going to let them know that they are invited for dinner and a film, and they can stay here till their boiler is fixed if they want.'

'So, I don't get a say in it?'

'Not today, no. It's Kasey's birthday. It's what she wants. Plus, you invited them to stay here.'

'Don't use her as an excuse, and I've retracted my offer.'

'Tough!'

*He's right, we don't know them, but that has to change. I want to take the risk. I want to see if Rosie is as nice as I think she is. I'm fed up already with this stupid old argument. It has nothing to do with me. We've only just met them. Their derelict hotel is hardly going to knock us off our feet, and... I know there was a spark between me and Primrose Trent.*

'One step at a time, Ned. Let's just get to know them. Figure it out from there.'

'Okay. Best to keep your enemies close, I guess.'

\* \* \*

Dinner was homemade pizzas and eaten in the private living room at the back of the hotel far off in the left-hand side of the building. And Beauty and the Beast was on the telly. Elliot secretly found it highly amusing that Kasey had sat herself in between Belle and Rosie on the large brown sofa, and even more amusing that his niece had placed Ned next to Belle. He was glad he was left out of the mix. The armchair suited him just fine. He was sitting close to Rosie, enjoying hearing her sing along with her sister and his niece. He suppressed a grin when Ned gave him a look that said, *sirens*, whilst tapping his foot in time to the music.

Rosie smiled his way from time to time, making his heart warm and the family feud fade even faster. As much as he loved his niece and brother, he did wish it was just him and Rosie sharing the night. Homemade pizza and a Disney movie wasn't exactly his idea of a date, but after the day they'd had, it was nice to just sit back and relax. He was pleased to see Rosie so settled too, and Kasey was like a pig in mud. Ned, however, not so much. His arm was squashed next to his nemesis, and his face only broke out into a smile whenever Kasey smiled his way. Elliot had to bite his lip to stop himself from laughing, especially at the Gaston and Belle moments.

Elliot had always been a people watcher. His dad had taught him it was a good way of finding out what the guests required before they spoke. Body language played a big part, and right there and then everyone's body in front of him had something different to say.

Ned stretched out his arm, clearly numbed by the overcrowded sofa situation. He placed it along the back of the sofa, without the thought of how it looked. It was as though he had put it around Belle's shoulders. His fingers were certainly close enough to touch her. Belle obviously had the same thought. Her face reddened slightly, and she shifted in her seat, moving further into Kasey.

'You all have great voices,' said Elliot, filling the silence as the film finished. He ignored Ned's raised eyebrows and concentrated on his niece instead.

'Belle is magical, that's why. Daddy thinks that too.'

Rosie held the biggest smile at that comment, but it was Ned who caught Elliot's eye.

*Oh my word, Ned just blushed. Ha! Oh, that is beyond funny.*

'We have to go home now,' Belle told Kasey, whilst struggling to unglue herself from the soft sofa.

Rosie groaned. 'Do we have to? It's so cold over there.'

Elliot could see that Ned wasn't about to offer any warmth, and as concern for Rosie had rushed over him like a tidal wave at her comment, he felt the need to speak. 'We have spare rooms, if you want to stay the night.'

Kasey bounced her legs. 'Please stay. I've never had fairy friends before.'

Rosie turned to her. 'We're not real fairies.'

Kasey's shoulders slumped. 'I know, but you have pretty fairy names. I wish I had a pretty name or a pretty face like you both have.'

Ned went to speak, but Belle got in first. 'Your name is pretty and so are you. You're beautiful, just like a Disney princess.'

Kasey seemed satisfied with the compliment, and Ned seemed surprised.

Rosie was looking at her sister, awaiting confirmation of a sleepover, and Elliot really wanted that sleepover to be in his bed. He knew that wouldn't happen, and he had to get a grip, but it was still a nice thought. One that warmed him, if not tormented him a touch.

'The rooms are all made up, ready for guests. You can stay here every night until you have heating. The offer is there,' said Elliot, leaning forward in his chair, gravitating towards Rosie.

'We'll need to go back and get some overnight bits,' said Rosie quietly, sounding unsure about speaking at all.

Kasey squealed. 'Can I stay up late, Daddy?'

'No. You've had a big day. Time for your PJs and bed.'

Kasey moaned as she stood. 'Can Belle read me a story?'

'No,' was Ned's speedy reply. 'She has to go home and pack a bag.'

Was that his way of agreeing to their sleepover after all? Elliot wasn't sure. Ned's tone was moody, and he was pretty sure that was the last he would see of him for the night.

Ned lifted his daughter and carried her away. 'Say goodnight.'

Kasey looked over his shoulder and told everyone that she hoped they had sweet dreams.

Elliot's eyes met Rosie's.

'Thanks for this,' she said.

'Do you need any help with your bags?'

Belle stepped between them. 'No, we can manage. Thanks.'

Elliot followed them outside and watched them leave through the main entrance. He moved over to the fireplace to see that the fire had almost died, then he made his way to the bar.

*Oh, Elliot, what are you playing at? Is Ned right? Should I be getting involved with a Trent? Oh, this is ridiculous. Don't overthink things. One step at a time.*

# 10

*Ned*

Ned stood in the doorway of his kitchen, watching Belle opening cupboards and nosing inside. His lack of trust towards her was practically waving in his face. He didn't like her, and he kept telling himself that. There was something about her that was niggling at him, but he couldn't quite put his finger on what it was. It wasn't just because she was a Trent. There was something else about her that bothered him. Kasey had fallen in love with her, and that irritated all of him, from his bones to his blood. Fairy. Magical. Pretty.

*Okay, so she is pretty. I'll give her that one, but the only thing magical about her is the fact that she would no doubt happily feed me a poisoned apple.*

'Can I help you with something?'

Belle jumped and spun around. She looked jittery, and it amused him.

*Good. Be afraid. Be very afraid, because I've got your number, missy.*

'I was looking for teabags.'

*Oh, okay. Hardly worthy of Crimewatch.*

'I always have a cuppa before bed,' she added, not a trace of a smile on her full lips. She straightened to her full height of five-five as though ready for a fight.

Ned thought he'd try a different tactic. He pulled back the smirk that dared to twitch at the side of his mouth, then made his way towards her. She didn't budge, even when he stood toe to toe with her. He slowly leaned into her body and reached one arm up over her head. He opened a cupboard, fully aware that her nose was touching his chest, and pulled down a glass jar filled with teabags. He straightened and handed her the item, then stepped back. She turned to face the worktop, and he allowed the smile to crawl onto his lips, hoping he had achieved perhaps a small fluttering in her heart. There was one going on inside his chest, but he was sure that was just a remnant from his hectic day.

'Anything else I can do for you?' he asked, using his best husky voice. He would have added a smouldering look but she hadn't turned back to him yet.

*Let's see if I've got you hot and flustered. Just exactly how composed are you, Bluebell Trent? Can I weaken your knees? Make your heart skip a beat? Have I won here?*

He listened to the chinking noise of the teaspoon in the cup and started to become impatient.

*How long does it take to make a bloody cup of tea?*

'We're going to Sandly tomorrow.' Her voice was delicate all of a sudden, and it wafted around him, confusing him. 'Would you happen to know where we could buy a real Christmas tree around here?'

'Yeah. Will you be driving?'

*And are you ever going to turn around?*

'Yes. We have my sister's car.'

'In that case, on your way back, just as you see the river, take Silver Wish Road. There's a farm at the end that sells them. It's where we buy ours.'

She turned, hugging her tea, and smiled softly as though unsure she should. 'Thanks.'

*She's smiling at me. Why? She doesn't look flustered. Just... sweet. She's trying to beat me at my own game. She thinks I'm stupid.*

'I would have thought Christmas trees would be the last thing on your mind.'

'It's Christmas soon. It will be cheery to have a tree up.' She glanced over her shoulder. 'Do you want a cup of tea?'

Ned shook his head. 'No, ta.' He watched her take a sip. 'Would you like a biscuit with that? I happen to know where the stash of chocolate Hobnobs are.'

*And just exactly why did you say that, Ned? Jeez!*

'No, thanks. I try not to have a lot of sugar. Took me a long time to lose all my weight. I'm not keen on putting it back.'

Ned could see that she wasn't as slim as her sister, but he couldn't imagine her on the large side. 'I'll let the chef know you're on a diet.'

'I'm not on a diet. I just eat healthier now than I used to. I cut a lot of things out, and other things down. Plus, I run most mornings. It all worked for me.'

'I run.'

*Why did I mention that? What am I even doing in the conversation? I only came in here for a bottle of water to take to bed.*

She gave a slight shrug of one shoulder. 'Probably see you out there some mornings.'

*Not if I can help it.*

'Probably.'

'I'd like to run of a night, but it's a bit scary. If I knew for sure I'd be safe, that would be my preferred time to run.'

'You think about safety when running?'

Belle nodded and gazed down at her cup.

For some reason, he now wanted her to run whenever she felt like it, just like he did. 'Fancy a run now?'

She looked up with amused confusion in her eyes, and he flashed her his genuine smile so that she knew he meant his words.

'With you?' she asked, sounding wary.

He shrugged. 'If you think you can keep up.'

'I haven't got my running gear here.'

'That's okay. I'll just get mine on, and then we'll head over to yours and you can get changed, and then I'll show you my favourite route.'

Belle placed her tea on the side and nodded. 'Okay.'

He left the kitchen and headed straight for his room, changed into his running clothes, and then popped his head into Elliot's room to tell him that he was off for a run, and to listen out in case Kasey woke at all. He was surprised to see Rosie sitting in the bedroom with his brother, but at the same time nothing about the day was surprising him anymore, especially the part where he had just asked Belle out for a night-time run. As soon as she mentioned it, he had to make it happen for her. Why shouldn't she run of a night? He did at times, and he felt perfectly safe. If she needed a night-time running buddy to make her feel safe, he was happy to take up the role. He just wasn't quite sure why he was happy to be that person.

Belle led him into the cold, dark foyer of her hotel and told him to find somewhere clean to sit. There wasn't much on offer, so he just got on with some warmup exercises instead. She didn't take long, and they were soon on the pathway around the back of the inns.

'That's Wishing Point up there,' he told her, nodding towards a huge, grassy, sloping field. 'Normally filled with dandelions. We'll run around the base, then over to the track that runs parallel with the road that leads down to Sandly. There's a viewing point over there.'

Belle handed him one of her earphones. 'Do you want to run to my playlist?' She fumbled with the strap on her arm that was holding her phone.

*Should be interesting. Let's see what music she runs to.*

'Sure.' He put the earphone in and laughed as he heard Alice Cooper singing 'Poison'. 'Really?'

Her smile widened, bringing her whole face alive with warmth under the glow of the clear night, and something deep within him stilled for a moment.

She tapped his elbow. 'Come on.'

He joined her in a slow and steady pace that he wasn't used to running at, and after five minutes he could see she wanted to say something. 'What?'

'I don't normally run this slow.'

He grinned. 'Neither do I.'

'I was worried about speeding up, because you said you have a limp.'

'Have you noticed it?'

She shook her head.

'In that case, shall we up the pace?'

She nodded and moved in front. He caught up and matched her, feeling much better about their run. She was a lot better than he had expected. He reminded himself not to underestimate her.

Ned pulled her to a stop at the viewing area. 'Sandly.' He pointed down at the lights over the seaside town below them. 'Pretty, right?'

Belle's eyes were twinkling just as much as the town as she seemed to lean towards him. 'Oh, that's lovely. There's so much I have to see here.'

He gravitated closer to her. 'Have you been to Pepper Lane yet?'

'No, but I know it's just up the road from us.'

'You'll like it there. It's full of chocolate box cottages and quaint shops. You and Rosie will love Edith's Tearoom, and perhaps one day we can get a drink and something to eat in The Ugly Duckling. It's a lovely family pub.'

'Sounds nice.' The sparkle in her eyes didn't go unnoticed. They were gazing up at him, and he found himself staring back.

He lowered his head a touch and controlled his breathing.

*You're staring, Ned. Stop. Look away. Why can't I look away? Say something.*

'Didn't you ever come here for a holiday?'

'No. When my dad left, he left. I think he hated the inn. He watched his own dad have so much stress over the place, especially with the old man next...'

Silence loomed for a few seconds.

'We should head back,' said Ned, stepping away. He waited for Belle to agree, then they jogged back the way they had come. This time, in silence.

# 11

*Belle*

Belle had slept like a log all night, and she really appreciated waking in a warm and cosy room. The Renshaws sure knew how to decorate a hotel. She couldn't find anything to silently complain about. Breakfast had been a quiet affair, mostly by her. And the enquiring looks coming from Rosie across the breakfast table didn't go unnoticed. Due to her unexpected late-night run, which she found secretly exhilarating, she skipped her morning run and was happy to jump straight in the car with her sister and head off to Sandly.

'What is wrong with you today, Belle?'

'Nothing. It was such a weird day yesterday. I think it's only just hitting me.'

'Well, let it go now. Yesterday has gone. Today, we've got a choir audition. As soon as we can find this place.'

'I told you to use the satnav.'

'It's around here somewhere. Ooh, look, a car park. Let's park up and walk. By the way, did you go out last night with Ned? He told Elliot he was going for a run, and, well, I wasn't sure…'

'Yes. I went.'

'Does that mean you've decided to make peace with him?'

'Nope.'

They got out the car and spotted a small brown hut over by a muddy piece of grass. A worn sign held the faded words, *Rainbow Hut*, and the sisters knew they had arrived at their destination.

Inside was a cheery middle-aged man sitting at a shiny upright piano. He had thick white hair, pale skin, and rosy cheeks, giving off a Santa vibe. He was talking to a young lady and man in their twenties, who looked just like each other, showing the world they were most definitely siblings. They shared the same dark skin tone and big brown eyes, and those eyes sparkled happily as soon as they saw the newcomers enter the hut.

'Ah, you must be Bluebell and Primrose Trent,' said the man at the piano. 'Come in. Come in. Meet my children, Kristen and Kris. I'm Sean. Come closer to the piano. Now, tell me all about your singing experiences, if you have any.'

Belle nodded. 'We do. We were in a choir where we used to live. We loved it so much. That's why we wanted to find one here.'

Sean's fluffy white beard bounced slightly as he nodded. His whole persona was jolly. 'Wonderful. Wonderful.'

Kristen beamed at the sisters. 'That's good. Dad's always on the lookout for new members.'

'And new ideas,' said Kris, rolling his eyes at his dad. 'We really need some fresh material around here.'

'Yes, all right, all right,' said Sean. 'I hear you loud and clear.'

'Well, if it's any help,' said Rosie, 'we once dressed up as Disney characters for our Christmas show and sang songs from the films. It went down really well and was such a laugh.'

Kris started to sing 'A Whole New World', sounding perfect.

Sean clapped his hands together. 'My, my, that does sound like fun. What do you think, kids?'

'Firstly, stop calling us kids,' said Kristen. 'Secondly, I love a Disney film. Who doesn't?' She turned to Belle. 'We have a lady who works on our costumes. She's fab. I'm sure she can rustle us up some Disney costumes. Maybe the fancy dress shop will loan us some for free, seeing how it's for charity. We have buckets for money donations whenever we sing. The money goes to the local donkey rescue centre. Normally, at Christmas, we dress in old Victorian clothes and sing a lot of *fa la la la*. It would be great to shake things up a bit this year.'

'We do a Christmas show on Christmas Eve outside the town hall if it's dry, inside otherwise,' said Kris.

Sean flapped his hands. 'Well, come along, ladies. Let's hear what you've got in you first. Do you want to do a Disney song now?'

They both laughed and nodded.

'Funnily enough, we had some practice last night,' said Rosie, nudging Belle's arm.

'Who wants to go first?' asked Sean. 'Bluebell or Primrose? Such pretty names.'

'We go by Belle and Rosie,' said Belle.

'Delightful,' he sang out. 'Well, Belle, what do you have?'

'I can sing "A Whole New World" with Kris, if you like, Kris?'

Kris nodded, happy to accompany her.

By the end of the song, Sean's glowing expression revealed just how excited he was to have Belle's amazing voice join his choir, and after Rosie finished a perfect rendition of 'Let It Go', he was practically salivating at the mouth.

'My goodness, you have been gifted, ladies, and now you're on our team. Wonderful.'

Rosie glanced around the empty hut. 'How many are there in the choir?'

Sean was mentally adding up whilst tapping each of his fingers. 'With you two, that makes sixteen of us.'

'And we're all fantastic,' said Kris, grinning widely.

Kristen nodded. 'People always say we are wasted on the Isle of Wight, but Dad says this is where we're needed, and it's good to spread cheer everywhere.'

Rosie agreed. 'You're not wrong there, Sean.'

Sean handed them each a sheet of paper containing their rehearsals and weekly subs information. The money helped pay for the hall hire and material for costumes. 'And if you can get any sponsors, that would be great. Costumes drink most of our money, and if we're to have new ones made in time for Christmas, it might cost a little extra.'

'We're pretty new here, but I can ask the people we've already met,' said Rosie.

Belle shot her a warning look.

*Oh no, she wouldn't, would she?*

Sean shook hands with them both as he ushered them out of the hut, obviously not wanting to pay any more hourly rates than he had to. 'I'll see you both on Wednesday evening, then you can meet the rest of the gang, and we'll talk Disney. How exciting. What a treat meeting you two.'

Belle and Rosie said their goodbyes and made their way back to the car.

Rosie smiled happily. 'That went really well.'

Belle was purposely boring her eyes into her sister.

'What?'

'Are you thinking of asking the Renshaws to sponsor our new choir?'

Rosie pulled out of the car park. 'They have a small business that's…'

'Our competition. Do you really want to advertise the Inn on the Left and help put them on the map?'

Rosie sighed. 'I think they're already on the map, Belle. We, however, aren't even a dot on the landscape. Another way to look at it is, it will mean they owe us one.'

'No, they won't. They'll be doing us a favour by forking out.'

'I think Elliot will be happy to help.'

'Oh goodness, really, Rosie! You've known this man all of five minutes and you're already obsessed.'

'Slight exaggeration.'

'Okay, you've known him almost two days.'

'Why don't we just focus on buying a Christmas tree now.'

Belle also knew it was wise to change the subject. Anything to do with the Renshaws seemed to rattle her, and it was starting to get on her nerves. 'I'm just thinking that selling everything we owned to start fresh here wasn't the best idea. We should have saved our Christmas decorations at least.'

'I saved some of the old bits that belonged to Mum and Dad.'

Belle's heart filled with warm memories of their childhood Christmases. 'Oh, I'm glad you did that. They're definitely going on the tree.'

'Are you sure you want a real one? Won't it be dead in a couple of weeks?'

'They last a bit longer than two weeks, Rosie, and, yes, we need a real one. Did you check out the trees next door? They were so beautiful. I'd like to know where they got their wooden ornaments from.'

'You could try asking.'

Belle folded her arms across her lap. 'No chance. Even something as simple as that will bring Ned Renshaw's smug grin to the surface. I'm not giving him the satisfaction of asking him for anything ever again.'

'Again? What did you last ask for?'

'Well, I did ask where we could get a tree around here, but it was late, and I wasn't thinking clearly. I had bed head.'

'Bed head?'

'Yeah, you know. When it's late and your brain changes.'

Rosie laughed. 'Thought you meant like bed hair for a moment. Thought something else might have taken place between you and Ned.'

Belle scoffed, even though the thought of a naked Ned giving her bed hair wasn't the worst thought she'd ever had. Nope, that thought had to go. He could keep his naked body well and truly away from hers, and whilst he was at it, he could take his sexy smile and gorgeous eyes away too.

*And how bloody dare he lean over me like that just to get the teabags. He could have just told me where they were, but no, he had to make a whole show of it. He smelled so good, and my nose touched his chest. Under any other circumstances, I might have poked out my tongue and tasted his neck.*

Belle pulled in her lips so that she didn't laugh at her thoughts.

*He thinks he's all that. I've seen his type before, and he's a liar. Reckons he's got a limp, but how true is that? He can run all right. Okay, so maybe I did see a slight limp that I lied about seeing, but I wouldn't have even noticed that if he didn't point it out. Oh, why did I have to meet him? Why did I have to meet any Renshaws? Why did Pops have to have a fight with his best mate in the first place? I'd love to know what that was over. I bet it was a woman.*

'Silver Wish Road,' announced Rosie, bringing Belle back to the present.

Belle stared out of the window at the rows of Christmas trees for sale as they entered a place called Silver Wish Farm. 'Oh, look, Rosie, it's Christmas.'

# 12

*Elliot*

Watching the Trent sisters remove a rather large Christmas tree from the roof of Rosie's small car was the funniest thing Elliot had seen in ages. He stood behind the window, peering down at them, knowing full well he should go and offer his help, but he was enjoying the spectacle far too much to interrupt. Plus, something told him that he would not be welcome. It looked like something they wanted to do together. They seemed happy enough. There was laughter and needle fights, and their love for each other shone through the hazy day. He decided to give them a few minutes before he headed over there to let them know that lunch was available if they wanted it.

He went down to his office and opened the safe. There was something on his mind that he wanted to clear up, mainly with himself. He sat back in his chair and scanned the document in his hand.

Back when his grandfather had fallen out with Conway Trent, the two men had made up a contract between them, stating what neither of them was allowed to do with their half of the inn. Some of the rules had been passed down to his father and Frank Trent by mouth, but it wasn't something Elliot and Ned had really thought too much about. Their father had kept to their side, and Frank to his, and they did everything they could to keep the hate alive, everything except break any of the rules. Now, Elliot wanted to know if the contract was still valid. The owners of the contract were long gone, so did the document still mean anything?

'No flowers are to grow over three-foot high. What?'

He continued to browse the list.

'There shall be no different outside bins. Seriously, Gramps? What the actual... Christmas Day must be taken in turns. What does that even mean? No Renshaw and Trent marriages allowed. Ever. Wow! They just looked to the future with that one. No crossing over onto each other's property. Whoops. Maybe I should add, no driving of lawnmowers into each other's swimming pools.' Elliot laughed loudly. 'This is nuts.'

'What's nuts?' asked Ned, poking his head around the door.

Elliot waved the document. 'This. It's like Romeo and Juliet shit. I think our grandfather must have lost the plot.'

Ned entered the room, widening his eyes. 'Is that the contract about the inns? Why have you got that out?'

'I wanted to see if it's legit or not. I'm thinking of taking it to Montgomery to find out.'

'A solicitor?'

Elliot shrugged. 'Why not? We've got serious competition now that Rosie and Belle have taken over. They're determined to get that place up and running. We need to be on top form with this stuff.' He waggled the paper. 'You should read some of this stuff. It's beyond ridiculous. I know you don't think much of Belle, but if you did, you wouldn't be allowed to marry her.'

A thin line appeared between Ned's brow. 'What? Show me that.'

'It's true. Says so right there.'

Ned was grinning whilst reading. 'No one's allowed to plant trees. So, that explains why we don't have any on our land. Oh dear, I think we've broken the fence rule. Ours is way too high.'

'How high should it be?'

'Three-foot.'

Elliot laughed.

Ned's face turned serious. 'Hey, it says here that neither party is allowed to sell their half of the inn to the other.' He slapped the document down on the desk. 'Great! There goes our plan to re-join the hotels. I wanted to give it back its original name too.'

'You need something magical to break the curse,' said Kasey, standing in the doorway, fiddling with a pink fairy wand.

Elliot looked at Ned. 'She's not wrong. It feels like a curse, and we do need to break it.' He placed his hand over the contract. 'I'm calling the solicitor in the morning. Right now, I'm going to trespass to invite the dreaded Trents over for lunch.'

Kasey giggled as he ruffled her hair on passing.

Walking onto their property felt daring and illegal, and Elliot had to tell himself to stop being stupid. He was just knocking at his neighbour's door to invite them for lunch. What was wrong with that? He half expected dogs from hell to leap out at him and chase him out of the non-existent gates. He stopped and took a moment to study the building.

*Wow, this place will cost a fortune to put right. I wonder if they know that. Surely, they must have the funds. Why else would they take on a project like this? Ned's right. This place would be great back together again with ours.*

Laughter echoed out to the doorstep where Elliot dithered. The door was wide open, and he could hear Rosie and Belle quite clearly talking about tree decorations, then the hotel. He knew he shouldn't eavesdrop but found he couldn't help himself.

'We need to get more cleaning done today after this,' said Rosie.

'Tree. Lunch, Cleaning,' said Belle.

'Wouldn't it be lovely to have our inn looking as wonderful as next door.'

'We can't copy them, Rosie.'

'I don't mean that. It was just so nice over there, and I wanted to stay.'

'Only because they have heating.'

'No, Belle. They made us feel welcome.'

'You mean Elliot made you feel welcome. Ned's an arse.'

Elliot's eyes widened at the comment. He didn't feel he could argue the case, as Ned could be a great big fat arse when he wanted to be. He made allowances for his brother's moods most of the time, because he knew that ever since Ned lost Penny he had become angry with the world. Ned didn't expect anyone else to understand that, but Elliot knew. He also knew the old Ned. How playful he used to be before the accident happened.

'We'll see how it goes with them,' said Rosie. 'Who knows what will happen. We've only just met them. If they do turn out to be horrible people, we'll just stay away.'

'It's a bit tricky when they're right next door and are our archenemies.'

He heard Rosie laugh. He liked her laugh. He liked her smile.

'Belle, lots of people have neighbours they hardly see. We have hotels to run. We'll all be too busy to bother each other.'

*You're right about that.*

Rosie wasn't finished. 'I think they might surprise us. Elliot is nothing like I expected. You know, going on the rumours.'

Elliot frowned.

*What rumours?*

'You just want to snog him senseless, that's why you want us to play happy families.'

Elliot strained his ears. He was desperate to hear the response to that comment.

'He's super-gorgeous, Belle, and he was so kind to me. I've never experienced anything like it before.'

Elliot smiled widely, feeling rather pleased with himself.

Belle lowered her voice. 'Anyone would seem kind to you after that thing you were living with before, Rosie. You just be careful. It took us ages to get him arrested in the end. You've been afraid of men ever since he hurt you, which does make me wonder about Elliot. I am surprised how quickly you've taken to him.'

Elliot could feel his blood boiling at the thought of some man hurting Rosie.

Rosie cleared her throat. 'Elliot made me feel safe, Belle. I don't know how to explain it. I just wasn't afraid of him.'

Elliot lowered his head and took a silent, steady breath. He wasn't sure how to feel. All he did know was that he wanted Rosie to know that she would always be safe with him. He was just as amazed as Belle, now that he knew that snippet of information about her past.

*Poor Rosie. It sounds like she's really been through the mill when it comes to trauma. She won't be getting any stress here from me, or Ned. I'll make sure of that. It must be another reason why they came here. A fresh start. The last thing she needs is a family war.*

'I'm glad you feel safe with a man again, Rosie. I really am, but why did it have to be him?'

Elliot raised his head.

'I don't know, Belle. I just know he feels familiar, like I've known him for ages. I know it doesn't make any sense.'

'Look, Rosie, if you really like him that much, I won't stand in your way. I promise. I'm just worried about who they are, that's all. I'm worried about what Pops would have made of it, or Uncle Frank.'

'I don't think there's that much to worry about. It's not like Elliot's asked me out or anything. Maybe he was just being kind to me. He might not like me back.'

*I do.*

'I have no idea what he thinks of me after I destroyed his pool with a lawnmower.'

Elliot laughed to himself as Belle laughed out loud.

'Oh, I forgot to ask you, Rosie. How did you sleep? Any nightmares? I was worried they might come back. If they do, we'll nip it in the bud. We'll ask that doctor to recommend a therapist.'

'I thought that too, but so far so good. I slept really well last night. I was supposed to be in the room below Elliot's, but we were talking late into the night, and I guess I fell asleep. When I woke up in the morning, I was in his bed, and he was asleep in the big chair he has in the corner of his room.'

*And I have the backache to prove it.*

'I've missed him all day today,' added Rosie.

Her voice was so soft, it melted his heart. He knew how she felt, because he had thought about her all morning. How lovely she looked sleeping in his bed. And how he wanted to be by her side with his arms wrapped around her all night.

Rosie giggled. 'When I woke up, I just wanted to go over to him and curl up on his lap.'

*You should have.*

'Aww, Rosie, that's actually quite sweet.'

Rosie snorted out a laugh. 'It's not that sweet. I also wanted to strip him naked and squeeze that gorgeous bum of his.'

Elliot's eyes widened along with his grin.

'Uncle Elliot,' called out Kasey, running towards him.

Elliot's face flushed.

*Oh shit, they're gonna know I'm out here now.*

Belle poked her head around the door at the same time that Elliot jumped the five steps and scooped Kasey up into his arms. He swung his head around to see Rosie peer over the top of her sister's shoulder. Her face looked every bit as alarmed as his.

'Hello,' he said, trying for casual. 'We were wondering if you would like some lunch with us?'

'We have a curse to break,' added Kasey, waving her wand and knocking Elliot's head in the process.

'Ned's cooked pork for lunch. All the trimmings. It'll be ready in about half an hour. Totally up to you.' He watched them turn to each other. Some mumbling took place, then Belle accepted the invite as Rosie gave a thumbs-up sign in the background.

'Right. Good. Great. See you in a bit,' he called out, quickly turning away.

# 13

*Rosie*

Rosie wasn't sure which moment of her time with Elliot was the most embarrassing. She felt mortified that he had overheard her say she wanted to sink her fingernails into him, or to be precise, his bottom. Belle had assured her that he couldn't have heard, because he wasn't at the door, but she wasn't so sure. He looked rattled when she saw him outside, and he rushed off as if he had just seen a ghost. She had no idea why she had decided to give him a thumbs-up sign either. None of this was in her masterplan when she decided to move to Pepper Bay. Elliot Renshaw was definitely a surprise.

Lunch was lovely but quiet, and Kasey made sure they were sleeping over again by blatantly asking and stating that they should, and she secured a bedtime story from Belle before Ned had a chance to protest. Rosie liked her. She reminded her of Belle when she was little.

Rosie knew they should head back, as they still had so much to clean. It seemed like a never-ending task, but they had managed two bedrooms, one bathroom, and the kitchen so far, but the thick dust was still clogging her lungs. She was so grateful for her time spent next door. The warmth. The food. The firm mattress of Elliot's bed. Elliot.

Her stomach flipped when he asked her if he could talk to her in private up in his room. She left her sister behind in the dining room, colouring in picture books with Kasey and Ned, and both Belle and Ned gave the impression they were even competing at that. She left them to it, praying they wouldn't fight, and followed Elliot into his now so familiar bedroom.

There was a hint of his oaky cologne lingering in the air, and it made her smile to herself. A lightheaded feeling took hold, which she didn't mind, as it wasn't making her faint, just relaxed, as though his presence alone was sedating her.

She enjoyed his company so much already, and his bedroom even more. It felt as though it was their special place. Their own secret hideaway where the world no longer existed. Where the family feud definitely didn't exist.

'Sit on the bed a minute, Rosie. I have something I want to say.'

She did, and he sat next to her, facing her way. She couldn't help but gaze into his beautiful eyes. They were so mesmerising.

*Please don't say anything that will spoil whatever this is we have. I know we have a connection. It's real. I can feel it. You can too. Can't you?*

'Is there something wrong, Elliot? Is this because I fell asleep in your bed again. It's becoming a bit of a habit, isn't it? I'm sorry. You should have woken me.'

He shook his head slightly and ran his fingers through his mop of dark hair. Rosie watched it fall back into place as though it hadn't been touched. It was all she could do to stop herself from reaching up and playing with the short strands.

*I want to touch your hair, Elliot. I want to touch you. Run my fingers all over your body. Get totally lost in you. What would you say if you could read my mind?*

'Okay, this is going to sound nuts.' He was nervous, that much was obvious. 'I don't know where to start.'

'Best to just spit it out, I say.'

His bright eyes rolled up and the bashfulness disappeared, causing Rosie's heart to skip a beat. There was something in the way he was looking at her that filled her with even more desire. She glanced down at his full lips, and he noticed, but she didn't care. It was all too much. His close proximity. His bed. His scent. The way his stare darkened slightly.

*Sod it.*

She leaned forward and pressed her lips gently onto his and waited. She didn't have to wait long. It was all the invitation he needed. He kissed her back. Softly at first, then hard, causing one hundred butterflies to do acrobats in her stomach.

His hands reached up to cup her face, entwining with her golden locks that were half tied back and half down. A small moan of need came from his mouth, and Rosie took that signal to push him backwards onto the bed. She climbed on top of him and proceeded to kiss his mouth, then his neck, and she didn't feel as though it was possible for her to stop kissing him.

He didn't complain, but he did flip her over and kiss her along her collarbone.

'Elliot,' she whispered, barely able to speak at all.

Their hands tangled in each other's hair. Gripping, holding, then stroking softly. Her leg slid up his, and he took her ankle in his palm before moving his hand all the way up to caress her thigh.

'Elliot.' Her breathy voice filled the air. She rolled her head deeper into the pillow and arched her back. He whispered her name in her ear as soon as his face met hers again.

All thought was lost to feeling as Rosie melted into his hold. It was as though she was drugged again. A tingling sensation filled her whilst rendering her weak. He had all the power over her, and she was happy for it to be that way. Fizzing excitement consumed her. She had less energy than him, it would seem, judging by the way he was kissing her.

A beat later, she came back into the moment. Finding the use of her own mouth. Meeting his. Joining in. Pulling him closer.

The noise that left him sounded both needy and surprised. He lowered his head and took small nibbles of her neck, swirling the tip of his nose along her skin.

'Elliot, please.' She realised she just pleaded, but that wasn't what she meant. She gulped a mouthful of air and swallowed what tasted like him.

His mouth met hers again for a moment before pulling back to look at her. His eyes were smiling but still filled with need. 'Are you trying to speak, Rosie?'

'What did you bring me up here for?'

He grinned, and she couldn't help but smile back. His sexy smile encouraging her to do so. 'This.' He kissed her again, and she let him. Falling further into his world once more. She couldn't stop. For all eternity, she could kiss this man.

He moved his mouth, giving them both room to breathe for less than a second, and then headed back in for another long, lingering, heated kiss.

'You wanted to say something to me,' she mumbled on his lips.

He pulled back again and took a deep breath. 'I wanted to tell you how much I like you, but it would seem you got there first.'

Rosie giggled. 'I couldn't help myself.'

His mouth was on her shoulder, sliding her top to one side with his nose. 'I'm glad your self-control is so weak.'

She cupped his face so that he was forced to look her way, and she lost her smile for a moment. 'I want you to know that I don't normally act this way, but…'

He turned his face in her palm and placed her fingertips into his mouth. 'But what?'

She was melting beneath him, so scrunched one shoulder up to her neck in an attempt to bring some sort of normality into the mix. 'I don't know, really. It's all a bit new to me. This. Us. How I feel when I'm with you.'

Elliot released her fingers and bent to give her a soft peck on the mouth. She was ready to take more. To give more. But he slowly pulled her up to a sitting position in front of him. 'It's new for me too, Rosie.' The softness in his voice warmed her heart. 'We like each other. We've made that clear. It's happened so fast, it's surprised us both, so we can slow it down. Go at a pace that you feel comfortable with. I'm not going anywhere.'

She smiled and held his hands.

'And you can grab my bum anytime you like,' he added.

*Oh God!*

She groaned as she lowered her face so that her forehead was resting on his shoulder. 'You did hear.' She felt him kiss her head.

'I really like you, Primrose Trent,' he mumbled into her hair. He lifted her head to look into her eyes. 'But just so you know, I can never marry you. It says so in the contract.'

Rosie burst out laughing. 'Blooming heck. Does that thing really exist?'

'Yes, but it doesn't say we can't kiss, or do other things.'

'Do you want to do other things with me, Mr Renshaw?'

He tugged her onto his lap and stroked his nose against hers. 'Oh yeah.'

They smiled at each other, and Rosie tenderly kissed his cheek.

'But only when you're ready,' he added. 'There's no rush.'

'I'm ready now.' She didn't care how desperate she sounded. After that kiss, she was more than ready for him. Something had to give. There was no way she could move on with her life with that hanging in the balance. She wanted more from him now. Another kiss just like that. Another experience like that. She'd never known a kiss like it. It would stay with her forever, even if he decided not to.

He breathed out a laugh. 'You want to do stuff now?'

*You have no idea, but I can't. I know we can't, but bloody hell, I so want to.*

'I do, but I won't. My sister is downstairs, and your niece could walk in at any moment. We have to be sensible.'

His hand slowly moved over her thigh. 'I'll lock the door.' He pressed his warm lips onto her neck, groaning quietly against her skin.

Rosie pushed her body closer to his. Tilting her head back whilst drawing breath. 'I'm sleeping over again tonight. I'll be in the room beneath you.'

'You won't,' he said knowingly.

She shook her head and breathed out a laugh. 'No, probably not.'

'I'm looking forward to tonight, but meanwhile...' He curled his fingers around the back of her head and brought her face closer to his.

Their kiss deepened, and Rosie was once more transported to his realm. Time stopped and nothing existed except for her heightened senses. She could hear his heartbeat. Taste his scent. Feel his need for her.

Rosie could kiss him all day and night. He felt so good, and she felt so connected to him already. It was quite surreal and absolutely wonderful. She wrapped her arms and legs tighter around his body, feeling his muscles press against her. His warm lips were peppering kisses along her neck, and she wondered how exactly she was going to be able to hold off till nightfall.

'Elliot, take me to the bathroom and lock the door. I can't wait.'

His smile pressed against her cheekbone. 'Yes, you can, Rosie. I need you to.'

'Please, Elliot. I want you now.'

A puff of warm air from his mouth tingled her skin.

'I don't want to rush this, Rosie. I want to explore you. I'm going to need more time. Give me the whole night. It still won't be enough, but I'm hoping I'll manage with that.'

She held her mouth inches from his. 'Can't you manage a little bit now in the bathroom?'

He flashed her a smile that weakened her jelly legs even more. 'I'll do whatever you want me to do, but, please, let me just have this. Just give me more time with you. No hard floors. No bathtubs. Just my bed. Just hours and hours in my bed.'

Rosie was lost for words. She closed her eyes as he gently kissed her lips, parting them slowly, asking for permission. 'Okay.'

# 14

*Belle*

Monday morning was fresh and bright, thanks to the sun lighting the sky and a mild late-November breeze. A slight farmyard smell wafted over the small, arched, wooden bridge that crossed over Pepper River, filling Belle's nostrils as she played Poohsticks by herself. The water in that section of the river was dark and deep, but the edges that soaked into the bank were shallow and almost clear, revealing small stones in various shades of brown, dark weeds, and teeny-tiny silver fish. As soon as she had spotted the picturesque crossing, a huge smile lifted her face. If only she could paint, she would happily sit right there and create the prettiest picture she could to give the old bridge the justice it deserved.

A calm flow of dead leaves floated towards her, joining the two small sticks she had just thrown down. She quickly moved to the other side of the bridge to see which stick won the race.

'You know, that game is better when you have competition,' said Ned, approaching from out of nowhere and making her jump.

Belle rested one arm on the bridge, not trusting its old wood completely but wanting to look relaxed and unfazed by Ned's sudden appearance. 'Do you want a race?'

He shrugged nonchalantly. 'Sure.'

She left the bridge to forage around by him to find what she believed to be a good stick. She could see his amused expression out of the corner of her eye, but she didn't care.

If she wanted to take her stick-choosing seriously, then that was up to her.

*Let him pick the rubbish stick that goes nowhere fast. He might take the race more seriously himself next time. If you're going to be in a competition, then your aim is to win. What's the point otherwise? Rosie would say, joining in is fun. Don't take it too seriously, Belle, blah, blah, blah, Belle. Well, Rosie, I am taking it seriously, because look who wants to race me. He's not winning. Not even at Poohsticks.*

Belle smiled smugly to herself as she straightened from the ground with her champion stick, which she held proudly aloft as though it had just won. She gave Ned a deadpan stare, as he was clearly fighting back a grin at her behaviour. She lowered her arm. 'Are you going to pick a stick?'

'When you're finished.'

'I have.'

'Are you sure?'

She huffed quietly and went back on the bridge to stand where she thought was a prime position. She peered over her shoulder, without making it obvious, to see him grab the first stick he saw. She quickly looked back down at the water as he approached.

'Ready, Bluebell?'

She refused to move her head, but her eyes rolled his way all by themselves. His mouth was curled up to one side, and his stupid Disney hair was flopped over his forehead, and it was so unfair that he had the ability to look extra-cute every time he annoyed her, which was pretty much every time she saw him. He was pressing his arm against hers, which she was sure was his attempt at distraction. She silently sighed and held her arm out over the side.

'Ready when you are, Edward.'

He stretched out his arm. The stick ready to go. 'After three.'

Before he had a chance to count, Belle got in first. 'One, two, three.'

They dropped their sticks and made their way over to the other side of the bridge. Belle concentrating way more than Ned, who was taking it all in his stride.

*Oh, come on, come on. Please don't let him win.*

A moment later, the two sticks reappeared. Ned's in first place.

*Oh, pants to you, Winnie-the-Pooh.*

Ned turned slowly, with the obvious intention to show off his full beam. He offered no smug words, and that only wound Belle up even further.

'Where were you heading?' she asked, knowing full well she had avoided any sort of congratulations.

*Now what, you sarky git? Go on, call me out on my change of subject. Rub my nose in the fact that you just beat me at something.*

'Edith's Tearoom in Pepper Lane. Were you off somewhere or just hanging about here?'

*He's being polite. Why?*

'I was attempting to find my way down to the shops in Pepper Lane. I heard there is a shortcut around here. A bridge, a farm, something about a walk walk. I wasn't sure if I could cross the tramline though. I know it runs the length of the river from Sandly to Pepper Bay. I thought I'd see how far I could get. Pick up some freshly made pastries for after lunch. We've got a lot of cleaning to do, when my sister can tear herself away from your brother, that is.'

'Yes, they seem to have formed an attachment.'

'That's one word for it,' she mumbled.

Ned gestured to the other side of the bridge. 'I can show you the way, if you like, seeing how I'm going that way anyway. It's up to you.'

*I suppose that would be the sensible thing.*

'Okay. Ta.'

They left the bridge and headed over towards a patch of evergreen trees. On the other side was an earthy pathway and a tram crossing. There was no gate or barrier, which Belle quickly pointed out.

'You just use your Green Cross Code,' said Ned.

She didn't like the way he was looking at her, as if she didn't know what he was talking about. 'It's still feels unsafe.'

'A tram won't come at you like a train. You just, stop, look, listen. Check both ways again, and when it's all clear, you can cross.'

'Yes, thank you, Dad.'

'If it helps, I know the tram's timetable, and it isn't due to pass by for another two hours.'

'Oh, that's a long while.'

'It's not a regular bus.'

Belle checked before crossing anyway and hurried to catch up to him, as he had marched off. 'I'm going to go on the tram when the weather turns nice.'

Ned pointed over to their left. 'It runs across a bridge further down there where the river curves, then it's on the other side of the riverbank all the way to Pepper Lane. The water is much deeper at the curve. The tram fell in the river once, maybe twice. It was updated in the summer, thanks to a local resident, so it's much safer now.'

Belle's planned tram ride suddenly didn't feel like a good plan at all. 'Where are we now?'

'This land belongs to the Sheridan family. They own Dreamcatcher Farm.'

She followed his finger stretching out to their right.

'It goes way back over there. They have a fruit field and a vegetable one the other side of the farmhouse. It's where we get all our produce from. They also own the post office shop too, aptly named, The Post Office Shop, which you'll see in a minute. It's only a small shop, but it's handy for a few essentials like milk, eggs, loo roll, that sort of thing. They even sell your basic first aid bits and pieces. Saves you a trip to Sandly at times. You can get fresh bread there too, if you go early, and I mean early. Otherwise, you're out of luck. They don't bake many each morning, but what is baked is sought after.'

Belle could almost taste it. 'Sounds yummy. Who doesn't love freshly baked bread.'

They approached a wide dirt track that had deep tractor-tyre marks that appeared to have been ground-in many moons ago and never quite recovered.

'This track is called Walk Walk Road,' said Ned, guiding her left onto its hard ground.

'Doesn't look much like a road. Why is it called Walk Walk?'

He shrugged and apologised after wobbling on the uneven ground and accidentally bumping into her shoulder. 'At the other end is Pepper Lane.'

Belle swallowed hard, as her throat had dried up after Ned had touched her. Obviously, it was from the dusty road beneath her feet. 'Thanks for showing me. It's quite an easy route.' She paused for a second as her eyes met with a small cottage-style house. 'That's the shop?'

Ned breathed out a laugh. 'It's much bigger on the inside. You can't really see how far back it goes from this side.'

Belle smiled with affection at the hand-painted sign lining the top of the shop. Pretty brushstrokes looked to be the newest part. A red post box was built into the wall, and a pick-up truck sat out front, almost hiding one of the small square windows. 'I like that shop already.'

Ned nodded his agreement. 'It's got character, hasn't it?'

Belle looked behind her as they carried on down the track. A large farmhouse sat in the near distance, looking just as welcoming as the shop. 'The Sheridans have a lot of land.'

'Most farmers do.'

'I wonder if you can go fruit picking over there?'

He nodded. 'They hire people when needed, and they let others come for a bit of fun during the summer.'

'Wait till I tell Rosie. She'll love that.'

When they reached the end of the road, Ned gestured left. 'This is Pepper Lane.' He stopped her on the grassy verge and pointed uphill. 'It goes all the way up to the cliff, but you can veer off the other way to head towards Sandly. It's known as the long way. That's why most people jump on the tram. It's quicker. Plus, you don't have to worry about parking. No cars are allowed to park in Pepper Lane, but there's a small car park by the tram stop.'

Belle's eyes were alight with delight. 'Wow! Look at all the cottages. How beautiful are they.'

'The last cottage, up the top there, is Starlight Cottage, and the one right at the bottom is Honeybee Cottage, then you have a variety in between.'

Belle pointed over the road at a gorgeous lemon thatched cottage. 'I think I'm in love with that one.'

Ned smiled. 'That's Lemon Drop Cottage.' He nudged her arm, sending a slight shiver through her body. 'Come on, we turn right here, downhill, that's where the shops are, and there is a small shingle beach at the bottom.'

Belle skipped into step at his side. It was the happiest she felt since arriving on the Isle of Wight. She was so pleased to be part of such a beautiful place, even if her home was letting the side down. She started to wonder if the Inn on the Right was the talk of the bay. What must they think of the state of her place? Her eyes scanned all of the cottages she could see on her walk to the shops. 'My dad grew up here and left. I don't know why anyone would want to leave here.'

'Well, we don't have this view where we're situated.'

'We still have a nice view of the river, and this is on our doorstep.'

*We both need to stop saying we. It sounds like we live together.*

Ned came to a stop. 'As you can see, there aren't many shops down here. It's a tourist hotspot more than anything. Quaint, cute, and friendly.'

She looked over at the pub with the white-washed walls and dark wooden beams. 'The Ugly Duckling. That's a cute name.'

'The chef there is excellent. Wish he worked for us. Don't tell my chef I said that.'

'I'm definitely eating there then.'

'Edith's Tearoom is down towards the bottom, on the left. Shall we?'

Belle trailed behind him, taking in all of the pastel-coloured shops, one at a time. She made a mental note to pop into each one as soon as she came out of Edith's Tearoom.

The pastel-pink tea shop had bunting in the windows and pink gingham tablecloths on the tables inside. The smell of cake and coffee hit Belle straight away, and she appreciated the warmth of the cosy shop as well. She followed Ned over to the glass counter and eyed the goodies on display. She only came for pastries, and maybe a decent coffee, but now there were chocolate muffins and creamy fudge looking back at her. The giant cookies looked mouth-watering, as did the lemon drizzle cake, and the walnut loaf.

*Oh, how am I supposed to choose which little treat I'll allow myself?*

'Morning, Ned,' said the pretty blonde lady serving. 'Who have you brought with you today?'

'This is Bluebell Trent. The new owner of the Inn on the Right.'

Belle caught the look of surprise in the woman's face. She wasn't quite sure if things were about to get awkward, then it dawned on her that her walk down to the shops with Ned hadn't felt awkward at all.

The blonde lady snapped Belle out of her daydream. 'Pleased to meet you, Bluebell. I'm Joey. I'm one of the owners of this place.'

'Hello. Call me Belle. I love your shop. Everything looks so good. Do you make everything yourself?'

Joey nodded. Her taupe eyes beamed Belle's way. 'I do, with a couple of helpers.'

'Up at the crack of dawn, working so hard. That's our Joey,' said an old lady, who was sitting at a table by the window, cuddling a cup of tea.

Belle turned to see shrewd eyes boring into her.

'That's my gran, Josephine,' said Joey.

Belle gave a casual wave. 'Hello, I'm Belle.'

Josephine nodded. 'I know who you are, my lovely. I read Ned's tea leaves a long time ago. I saw you coming long before he did.'

Belle caught Ned rolling his eyes.

'Not that you had my permission to read my tea leaves, Josephine.'

She waved him away. 'Oh hush, child. Perhaps if you had listened to me back then, you'd be more prepared for the young lady now.'

Ned grinned. 'You know me, Josephine, always prepared for everything.'

Josephine cackled out a sore throat of a laugh. 'Bah! You didn't know what hit you when the flower girl turned up. I can tell you're still struggling with her now. I can feel your energy, Edward Renshaw, and energy doesn't lie.'

Belle muffled her laugh. Josephine was highly amusing, and so was the slight blush on Ned's face.

'Leave him alone, Gran,' called over Joey. She turned back to her customers. 'How's it going up there, Belle? The last time I saw the place, well, let's just say it needed some repairs, and that was when Frank owned the place.'

'He was my uncle. I don't think he had the money for repairs. Me and my sister are going to try our best to bring the old place back to life.'

Joey was looking just as sad as her grandmother. 'I didn't know Frank had family. Sorry for your loss. He used to be friends with my dad, years back.'

Belle felt the need to explain. 'My dad was Frank's brother, but because there was so much stress with the two inns, he decided to leave, and he never returned. That's why I've never been here before.'

'Frank and Clive were a couple of idiots,' said Josephine flatly.

Belle was sure Ned would say something, but he didn't. Maybe he thought that the family feud was uncalled for. Maybe he didn't agree with his dad and grandfather.

'Yes, thank you for your input, Gran,' said Joey. She looked at Ned. 'What can I get for you two before my grandmother insults any more members of your family?'

'I'll have the usual, please.'

Belle was still looking at the old lady. She turned to Joey when Ned nudged her arm. She wondered how many more times he was going to touch her today. 'I'll have a black coffee to go, and two slices of lemon drizzle, a cookie, one cinnamon swirl, and four pieces of fudge.' She looked at Ned's amused face. 'Most of that is for Rosie. She has a sweet tooth. I allow myself the odd slice of cake every so often.' She turned back to Joey, who was now busy with their order. 'Rosie is my sister.'

Joey smiled over her shoulder. 'I can't wait to meet her, and if you need an extra pair of hands for cleaning or anything, I finish at four. I can always pop over and help out.'

'She's pregnant. She's supposed to be taking it easy,' called over Josephine.

'Gran, I was talking about a bit of cleaning. I think I can manage to put a mop around the floor.'

Belle smiled warmly at Joey's stomach to see the slightest of bumps. 'That's kind of you, thanks, but we're taking things slowly. We did think we could open for Christmas, but that dream went out the window as soon as we saw the place.'

Joey smiled sympathetically. 'Oh dear.'

'She's got Ned to help, anyway,' said Josephine.

Ned scoffed loudly. 'I'm not helping the competition.'

Belle chastised herself for feeling her heart deflate at his sharp comment. He had every right not to help her, and she wasn't sure why she had suddenly forgot that they were sworn enemies. The walk down to Pepper Lane had felt so nice and natural, like two friends just mooching along, enjoying their day, but that wasn't the case at all. It was just a moment where the family feud didn't exist, simply because she had been distracted by the surrounding beauty. Plus, he was acting like a normal person for once. He hadn't been snarky, even when he won Poohsticks, and he had kindly shown her the way to the shops. His comment was a harsh reminder of exactly who he was.

'You won't be competition much longer,' said Josephine.

Ned breathed out a laugh. 'The Renshaws and Trents have always been in competition.'

'Yes, but your flower girl won't be a Trent for much longer.'

Belle frowned with confusion. 'What do you mean?'

Josephine rolled her eyes. 'What do you think I mean? I'm talking about when you two marry.'

Ned appeared to choke on air whilst Belle bit her lip to stop herself from laughing at the old lady, who seemed rather serious. She didn't want to offend her by telling her that she was mistaken.

Josephine wagged a finger. 'Don't you laugh at me, young flower. I see the truth. I know Ned's destiny. Seen it with my very own eyes, so I have.'

'You're not always right,' said Ned. 'This time, you're definitely not right.'

Belle felt like being a tease. She snapped her head his way. 'Why wouldn't you marry me? What's wrong with me?'

Ned went to speak but stopped, swallowed, and closed his mouth. All eyes were on him, watching his cogs frantically turn. Belle and Joey grinned at each other as Ned turned away for a second. His bright eyes were filled with mischief as he turned back.

Belle's stomach flipped as his gorgeous aquamarine eyes met hers.

'If you ever beat me at anything, I'll marry you, Belle, because then, and only then, will you be good enough to be my wife.'

Joey laughed out loud whilst Belle stood there gobsmacked at his big-headed response.

'Well, maybe you're not good enough for me,' Belle said, poking him in the chest.

Ned glanced down at her finger, and she quickly pulled it away.

'You're what Pepper River Inn needs,' said Josephine. 'You'll see.'

# 15

*Ned*

Ned watched Belle's eyes following the long narrow conduit that ran down the side of the pavement outside the shops on Edith's Tearoom's side. She glanced over at the shingle beach and smiled softly.

'I'm going to say hello to the sea.' Her eyes looked up at his with a warmth in them, but he wasn't sure if that was for him or the bay. Probably the bay.

'Would you like some company?'

She shrugged nonchalantly. 'I know my way back, if you have stuff to be getting on with.'

'What kind of husband would I be not walking my missus home?'

He waited to see if his comment and grin made her smile, but she simply turned towards the beach and walked away.

*She seems upset, I think. I'm not sure how she's feeling. That will be Josephine and her predictions. She's probably freaked the poor woman out. Flower girl, that's actually quite cute. I'll have to use that. Why am I even offering to hang out with her anyway? What's come over me today? I've actually had a nice morning. She's not so bad, when she's not scowling at me. She did poke me in the chest. I wanted her finger to stay there. For her hand to rest on my chest. I'm definitely losing the plot. I'm just going to be polite. It's not the Renshaws who are the rude family. Marriage, to her though. A Trent!*

Belle was sitting on a wall, staring out at the calm, cold, inky sea. She seemed relaxed as she sipped her coffee. Perhaps a million miles away. Ned knew that's how he felt whenever he sat there. He joined her. His arm touching hers, and he knew full well he had done that on purpose, because he wanted to touch her. He wanted to put his arm around her, but he couldn't, even if she was his future wife. He laughed on the inside and glanced at her face.

'It's nice down here,' she said, not looking at him.

'Wait till you come down in the summer.'

'Didn't think you'd want me to still be here by then.'

She had a point. He just didn't know how to respond. It would be everything he wanted if she sold her half of the inn to his family, but that would also mean never seeing her again, and he wasn't sure about that.

*Please don't tell me this woman is growing on me. I need to reel in my emotions. I'm not going to be like Elliot and his flower girl. I have to be the one with the clear head, because if Elliot falls in love, he'll probably give them our hotel out of pure stupidity.*

He quietly sipped his peppermint tea and tried not to shiver when a crisp breeze entered his hip-length brown coat.

She must have noticed because she made a comment about how it's always colder by the sea, then added, 'You should head back. When I've finished my drink, I plan to pop into each shop on my way home.'

'I'm happy to join you, but if you want to be alone, of course, I'll go.'

*Why am I even trying to stay? Oh, flipping heck! I'm starting to get on my own nerves now.*

Belle shrugged. 'I'm not fussed.'

*That's noncommittal. I like her style. It wasn't a flat no, so maybe it's a yes without embarrassment. I'll take her lack of a no as a yes. No, I won't. She needs to be clear.*

'I'll join you then, yes?'

She shrugged again, which only irritated him. 'Okay,' she finally said.

Ned glanced over his shoulder at the shops behind them. He didn't realise he was so close to her hair until he smelled his shampoo on her.

*Elliot must have supplied her with my things rather than his own or the hotel's. Cheek! She smells like me now, sort of. She's been sleeping in the room below mine, using my things, and reading with my daughter. Anyone would think she's part of the family. Why did she have to use my shampoo? I can't stop breathing her in. It's like she's in the shower with me. I can't think about that.*

He rolled his eyes down her cheek towards her mouth, then quickly looked back at the shops. 'You might like Pepper Pot Farm Shop. They sell cheese made at their farm, and eggs. There's jam made by Josephine in there. That might interest you. She's the owner's grandmother too. His name is Nate Walker. He's built like an American wrestler. He gets a lot of eyelashes fluttering his way.'

Belle smiled into her takeaway cup.

'He's married though,' he felt the need to add.

Belle slowly nodded her head. She still hadn't turned, and he wasn't sure if she would whilst his head was practically over her shoulder.

'There's a nice gift shop next door. Lots of handmade candles in there. The lady who owns the place is very talented. If you like books or art, there's The Book Gallery up the top, just opposite the pub. Lots of local artwork sold there. Originals and prints. We have some pictures in our inn, and Kasey loves going in there for story time and to buy a new book.' He turned back to the sea. 'Sometimes I think my daughter only reads to escape the real world.'

'I think that's why most people read. I think that's why we have the entertainment industry, and why we have so many creative people. Are you creative at all?'

Ned shook his head. 'No. Well, I like cooking, if that counts. I help our chef some days, when we're busy. Are you creative?'

'No. Our Rosie is the creative one. She makes the most beautiful pieces from pottery. She hasn't made any for a long while, and she sold all of her equipment too.'

'Why did she do that?'

Belle's silence made him think he had touched a nerve, and he didn't want to get involved.

'Sorry, none of my business.'

'It's okay. It's no secret. She had a right... I won't swear, let's just say her ex wasn't exactly nice to her, and bit by bit she just started to fade away. She lost all joy in life for a while back then.'

Ned felt terrible that Belle had shared that private information with him. He wasn't sure that was the kind of thing you told your enemy. 'I'm sorry that Rosie went through a tough time.'

'Me too,' Belle mumbled.

He shuffled his bum on the wall so that he was facing her. 'I just want you to know that you don't have to worry about Elliot in that way. He's so not like that. Too kind, in fact. Your sister is completely safe with him. He would never raise his hand to a woman. It's rare you hear him raise his voice to anyone. He's quite a calm person.'

'Good to know,' she said quietly. 'Rosie needs someone like that.'

'What type do you need?'

*And I asked that because...*

The sharpness in her hazel eyes as she turned to him hit him straight in the gut. 'I don't need anyone.'

*Right.*

'I don't suppose anyone needs anyone, really. It's just nice to have someone to hold you at times. Sometimes you can miss someone simply holding your hand. I miss Penny holding my hand.'

Belle's eyes softened. 'Kasey's mum?'

He nodded and smiled a smile that failed to reach his eyes.

'What was she like?'

'Imagine an older version of Kasey, and that's what she looked like. She was a confident person, very feisty, and loads of fun. She always made me laugh. If she were here right now, she'd have her boots and socks off and paddle in the freezing cold water.'

Belle laughed. 'Have you ever done that?'

'Nope. November is not the time for a paddle.'

'Coward.'

He grinned as she playfully nudged his arm.

'Come on, let's go for it. We can winter paddle in Penny's honour.'

Ned pointed down at the shoreline. The cold water lapped so calmly against the shingles, it almost invited him to step forward. 'I'm not going in there.'

Belle was already untying the laces on her walking boots. 'I'll race you in.' She stopped and laughed. 'You know what it means if I beat you at something?'

*Oh shit!*

Ned kicked off his black boots so fast, he stumbled into her lap.

Belle laughed and pushed him off. 'No cheating, trying to pin me down.'

He laughed. 'I wasn't, but you can eat my socks.' He threw them her way as he ran across the uncomfortable stones whilst tugging the bottom of his jeans up, and he just about managed to beat her into the sea.

Belle pushed his shoulder as she joined him. 'Wow, you really don't want to marry me.'

Ned went to laugh but held his breath as an icy wave reached above his ankles. 'Ooh, that's freezing.'

Belle obviously felt the same chill and bounced her feet in an attempt to warm them, but she stumbled on a stone and wobbled into him.

He caught her by the arm and quickly steadied her body, not realising for a few seconds that as his hand slipped down to pass her wrist, she caught his fingers, entwined them with her own, and gently held on.

Her small hand in his felt so nice, he forgot who she was. He sighed inwardly at just how much he wanted to stay like that. He had to let go. What would Penny say? What would his father say? Why did she have to go and do that? It was all Josephine Walker's fault. Going on about marriage and destiny. A part of his brain had got carried away.

*Get a grip, Ned.*

It took all of his willpower to slip his hand out of hers, and he immediately regretted his action. He felt even colder and so alone. Every part of him ached with a need to turn to her and just hold her, and he hated that he was feeling that way. 'I'm going back up. Come on, it's too cold. Let's warm up in the shops.'

He glanced over his shoulder to see if she followed him and was pleased to see her heading his way. Not so pleased to see that the big smile she had on her rosy face whilst in the sea had disappeared. She looked just as sad as he now felt. He figured she was probably cold, not sad.

*Why would she be sad?*

# 16

Rosie popped her head around Elliot's office doorway. 'The boiler man just called. Our new boiler is being fitted tomorrow.'

Elliot knew they were both thinking the same thing. No more sharing a bed. No more holding each other through the night. No more waking to each other's smile. He shuffled in his chair, resting his arms on the desk. 'That's good. At least you'll be warm now.'

'I've been nice and warm, thanks to you.'

He felt his heart smile.

Rosie tucked her hair behind her ear and tilted her head so that it pressed against the doorframe. 'Not sure what I can do to repay you.'

'You don't have to do anything.'

She straightened. 'How about if we take you, Ned, and Kasey out to dinner tomorrow night. How does that sound?'

'Sounds lovely. Thank you. I'll have to check with Ned when he gets back.'

There was a moment of silence, and Elliot knew it was because neither of them wanted to say goodbye and go about their day.

Rosie sighed quietly. 'I suppose I'd better go home. I've got lots of cleaning to do. We'll get there one day.'

He stood and made his way over to her. 'Do you want some help?' He liked her smile, but the one she was showing was filled with uncertainty, and he didn't know what to make of it. Did she think he was joking? Was she thinking up a polite excuse to get rid of him? Thankfully, she put him out of his misery.

'You're not supposed to help me.'

He brushed his hand down the side of her hair and leaned in closer to her face. 'I'm not supposed to do a lot of things with you, but that doesn't stop me.'

The feel of her lips on his brought a stirring in his stomach that no other woman had ever created. She tasted so good, and he couldn't get enough of her. She started to kiss him harder, moving the back of his head so that he was closer to her. Elliot slammed the door shut with one hand and blindly found the lock.

Rosie's hands were on the zip of his jeans, and one of her legs wrapped around him. He grabbed her thighs and lifted her, pressing her back against the door. Her mouth was trailing along his neck, and his need for her was through the roof. Her breathing was heavy and close to his ear as he felt his jeans slip over his hips.

'I want you, Elliot,' she whispered.

The desire in her soft voice almost sent him over the edge.

'Just like last night, and this morning, and in the shower, I want you again,' she added.

Elliot could hardly contain himself. He met her mouth and kissed her again. 'Don't leave me, Rosie.' His voice was a trembling whisper that caused her to still.

She pulled back and looked at him. The warmth in her eyes settled his racing heart, but only slightly.

'I'm not going anywhere, Elliot. I'll only be next door. We'll still see each other all the time.' She gently kissed his lips and then his nose.

He went to say something but a tapping sound on the door interrupted.

'Mr Renshaw,' said Joy, somewhat meekly. 'You should be leaving now for your appointment with Mr James.'

Elliot kept his eyes on Rosie. 'Yes, thank you, Joy.'

Rosie climbed down from his body and pulled his jeans up for him. Her head leaned forward to rest on his.

He took a deep breath and kissed her temple, then stepped back and tidied his clothes whilst she did the same.

Rosie giggled. 'Do you think she heard us?'

*I hope not.*

He shrugged and pulled her back into his arms and peppered kisses down her neck.

'We'll never get anything done at this rate,' she mumbled.

'I want to finish what we started.'

'I do too, but you have an appointment, and I have a hotel to tidy.'

Elliot groaned as she stepped away. 'Rosie, you're killing me.'

She breathed out a laugh and kissed him on the cheek. 'I'll be back tonight for my last sleepover.'

He felt his heart deflate, and she must have realised what she had just said.

'Obviously, it won't be our last, but you know what I mean,' she quickly added.

He reached out, held her hand, lowered his head, and struggled to steady his emotions. 'Rosie, can I put a label on this?'

She raised their links fingers and kissed his knuckles. 'What do you mean?'

He took a step closer and looked her in the eyes. 'I want you to be my girlfriend. I want us to be a couple, not just two people fooling around together. I want you to know how serious I am about you. That's what I mean by label.'

'I'll be your label, I mean girlfriend. I'd like that.'

For some strange reason, Elliot really didn't expect her to agree. He was pleasantly surprised by her happy attitude to the request.

'But I'd like a clause added,' she said.

'A clause? What do you mean?'

'A get-out clause. Basically, if I no longer want to be your girlfriend, I can just leave.'

The lines on his head crinkled. 'I think you'll find that's what everyone does. You don't need a clause for breaking up. You just leave.'

She shook her head slightly. 'No, you don't. Not always. Sometimes the other person doesn't allow you to leave. They harass you, constantly knock at your door, ring your phone, turn up where you work. Threaten you, even.'

Elliot scoffed. 'Yeah, because that'll win back their heart.' Her hand slipped from his as she took a step away, and he sighed inwardly at the sadness he could see overtaking her. 'Look, Rosie, I don't understand people who do all that stuff. I know they might be hurting, but at the end of the day, you cannot make someone love you, and if their heart has buggered off, it's buggered off. I promise you, if at any time you want out of our relationship, I will not try to stop you, and I certainly won't harass you. I'll be far too busy crying in the corner.' He pointed behind him and hoped she would smile.

She looked up and offered a weak smile and a whole heap of psychological scars.

*Sod it. I don't care how early into this we are. I'm telling her. I'm telling her everything.*

'I love you, Primrose Trent. Yes, already. I won't ever do anything to hurt you, and I will prove to you every single day that you are safe with me.'

She stepped forward and wrapped her arms around him. 'I'm sorry for being wary…'

'Hey, look at me.' He gently lifted her chin. 'You don't have anything to be sorry about. You're still healing from your past, and that's okay. It takes as long as it takes, and I'll be with you every step of the way. Whatever it takes, Rosie. I'll help you.'

Her soft lips on his filled him with warmth when all he wanted to do was cry for her, and also find her ex and punch him in the face.

'Hey, Rosie, why don't you come out with me today. I'm off to Sandly to see a friend of mine. He's a solicitor, and I'm going there to ask about the contract between our inns. I want to see if it is still valid. I actually want to just throw it in the bin. He'll let me know if I can do that.'

She seemed to perk up. 'Oh, that's interesting. Yes, I'd like to come. I'll just get my coat and meet you outside.'

He pulled her back as she turned to walk away and gave her a slow, lingering kiss that he poured all of his heart into. 'I love that I met you.'

She kissed him back, stepped away, unlocked the office door, turned to him with a big smile and said, 'I love that I met you too, Merman.'

Elliot secretly loved it when she called him that. He watched her leave, then picked up his coat and his copy of the contract and made his way outside to his car.

The sun was still shining, but the air was turning colder. He threw his coat and paperwork on the back seat of his dark-blue Land Rover and started the engine so that it would be nice and warm inside for Rosie. He switched the radio off and waited, with only his thoughts for company.

*Why couldn't I have met Rosie years ago? I wish she had grown up here. Although, it probably wouldn't have worked out for us that way. We would have been forced to hate each other. What a bloody mess. Cheers, Grandad.*

He watched Rosie practically skip across the driveway towards his car, and every single part of him smiled. She tossed her coat and handbag on the back seat, climbed in next to him, leaned over, and kissed his cheek.

'How's it going, beautiful?' he asked, grinning sideways at her as he pulled the car away.

'It's going wonderfully, thank you very much.'

He reached over and held her hand. 'Good.'

'Stop grinning at me with that sexy smile of yours, Elliot Renshaw, else I won't be able to hold myself back from sliding over there to sit on your lap, then we'll get arrested for car shenanigans in broad daylight.'

He burst out laughing. 'We could pull in among some trees and jump in the back.'

'No, let's be sensible. Anyway, we've already made love twice this morning. I'm sure that's enough for you for one day.'

Elliot shook his head. 'I'm pretty sure it's not.'

She raised his hand and kissed his knuckles. 'Blame your receptionist for interrupting us in your office.'

'Joy is very efficient. She mans the desk, sorts my diary, and hires and fires. She's an all-rounder, really. We'd be lost without her. You will need good management. I know there's you and Belle, but you need your staff to be at the top of their game. Hire people who have passion. Who want to make the best of their job. Also, make them part of your hotel's family. Have them work with you, rather than feeling they work for you. Everyone knows their place. They'll still know you're the boss, but you become approachable, and a good work colleague.'

Rosie smiled his way. 'Thanks for the advice. Not going to lie, I need all the help I can get.'

'Have you ever done this sort of thing before?'

'Nope.'

'Do you have any business training at all?'

'Nope.'

Elliot breathed out a laugh. 'What did you do before this life, Primrose Trent?'

'Well, I made plates, mugs, that sort of thing, from pottery, and I sold my work online and in a gift shop in Dorset. It wasn't my shop, but the owner saw my work online one day and asked if she could sell some pieces in her shop.'

'So, beautiful and talented. Aren't you the lucky one. I'd like to be able to do something with my hands.'

'Trust me, Elliot, you do plenty with your hands. I have the warm flushes of memory entering my body every five minutes to prove it.'

He laughed, really wanting to make some more warm flushes for her. 'So, when do I get to see your pottery work?' He could see out of his peripheral vision that she was no longer smiling. He squeezed her hand lightly. 'Hey?'

'I don't have any pieces to show you, I'm afraid. I haven't made anything for some time now.'

'You don't enjoy it anymore?'

She turned to face him, and he glanced her way for a second.

'I do,' she replied. 'I love it so much, but I gave up on everything a while back, and now I have the inn to worry about, so I doubt I'll be making any new pieces anytime soon. Anyway, I sold all my equipment. On to pastures new now.'

'What are you hoping for with the hotel? Now that you've seen it, I mean. And, no, I'm not trying to buy you out, but it is something I have wanted. I don't want to lie to you about that. I would love to reunite the two inns again and give it back its original name. It's something to think about if you decide in the end that the hotel game isn't for you. It's not for everyone.'

'Well, I guess someone would have to buy the place if we can't make a business out of it. It's not like we can renovate it into a big house and just live there. Although, it would make a lovely big house, but it would cost a fortune in bills.'

'Do you mind if I ask if you have a mortgage on the place, or if you were left with any debts?'

She shook her head. 'I don't mind telling my boyfriend, but Belle would say you're just being a cunning Renshaw, trying to dig for dirt.'

Elliot grinned widely. 'I'm just trying to see if there is any way I can help you, and that is to keep or sell the place. If you want to make a successful hotel, I will teach you everything I know.'

'Ned's going to have a fit when he hears that.'

He sighed heavily. 'Tell me about it.'

'We don't have a mortgage or debts, just a family feud, a curious contract, a new cat, and a few ghosts probably trying to haunt me right about now for sleeping with you.'

'I really wish I knew why our grandfathers fell out. They were best friends once, by all accounts.'

He pulled up on a small parking bay outside James and Son Solicitors. They got out and entered the glass-fronted renovated house.

Montgomery James was a smartly dressed man around Elliot's age, who welcomed them into his office at the back of the building.

Elliot stared out of the window behind the solicitor as he sat down. The small garden was neatly trimmed and had evergreen shrubs as borders. He held Rosie's hand as soon as she sat in the green velvet chair to his side. He had introduced her as his girlfriend, but didn't really care if he hadn't. He was still going to hold her hand whenever he wanted, regardless of their company.

Monty scanned the paperwork on his desk. 'Wait, Trent?'

Elliot and Rosie nodded.

'That's right, Monty. Rosie owns the Inn on the Right.'

'And we really want to know if this stupid contract is legal,' said Rosie, shifting forward.

Monty looked at Elliot. 'Have you read it all?'

'No. I gave up after I read that no one's allowed to plant sunflowers.'

Rosie giggled.

Elliot waved his copy, and Rosie pinched it to take a peek. 'It's beyond ridiculous, Monty. I think they were both drunk when they wrote out their rules, but I don't see why we have to abide by them. It even states that Renshaws and Trents aren't ever allowed to marry. They can't make that law. Can they?'

Rosie's eyes peered over the top of the paper she held. 'Your fence is too high.'

He grinned. 'Yeah, sorry about that, but Frank started pelting our windows with rotten tomatoes, and we didn't know what else to do. We thought it might help, and he didn't say anything about the fence, and, in all honesty, we didn't actually know about that rule at the time. We only did the front. He'd already put up large panels at the back years ago. We didn't think anything of it.'

Rosie looked at Monty. 'So, can I sue him?' She gestured towards Elliot, making him laugh.

'I'll give you fifty pence.'

'Each,' she said quickly. 'One for me, and one for Belle.'

He scrunched his face. 'Ooh, you drive a hard bargain, Miss Trent.'

Monty smiled at them. 'I'm glad to see you two getting along.'

Elliot waved his free hand in the air. 'This is to be laughed at. Our grandparents were clearly insane. Nobody slices a hotel in half, for a start. What were they thinking? Come on, Monty, tell us about this stupid contract. Get us out of it, please.'

'Well, after you called me, I asked my dad. We actually have the original contract here. It would appear your grandfathers wrote it all down together and then brought it to my grandfather. Now, I will agree, it is daft in a lot of places. Most places, actually, but their agreement on their business is a different matter altogether.'

Elliot felt Rosie's hand tighten in his.

Monty pointed to a section on the contract. 'However, you see this line here.'

They both peered over the dark-wood desk.

'This line means that this contract died at the same time your grandfathers did,' he added.

Elliot rolled his eyes up. 'You mean, we don't have to abide by their petty rules?'

'I can plant sunflowers?' asked Rosie.

Elliot laughed, and she tugged his hand.

'What? I like sunflowers.'

'Then, we'll have rows of them.'

'I'm glad this makes you happy,' said Monty, 'but please remember one thing. All the pettiness is no longer haunting you, but you both still have the same business right next door to each other and either party can now make changes that you might have been holding off on. For example, ownership of the original name. You could face different issues now. Conflict. There's nothing to stop either of you doing what you want with your inn. In some ways, that contract, for all that it was worth to the living, did you some favours. Now, it's open season. Now, it's down to you to do the right thing by each other.'

Elliot knew that Rosie was probably thinking the same thing as him.

*Ned and Belle.*

# 17

*Rosie*

Rosie was on her knees, scrubbing the skirting board beneath the window in one of the guest bedrooms when Belle walked in.

'I've just put on another wash. Those old drapes are coming up a treat. I'm glad we decided to give them a go, rather than toss them out. We made a good call there, Rosie. Hey, do you think we should take up the offer of help from the residents in Pepper Lane? How nice was it for them to offer to help clean this place. Maybe we should have a cleaning open day. We could offer lunch or something.'

'Speaking of which. I told Elliot we'd take them out for dinner tomorrow night to say thank you for letting us stay.'

'Okay. We can go to that lovely pub, The Ugly Duckling.'

'I just have to wait and see if it's okay with Ned.' Rosie sat up and huffed. 'Maybe a cleaning party would be a good idea.'

'I'll spread the word. There was a lady in the cheese farm shop called Tessie, and she added me to the Pepper Bay WhatsApp group. I can ask on there. We have choir practice Wednesday night, so maybe Thursday will be okay. The shops in Pepper Lane close at four, so what about if I ask them to come up after that for a couple of hours, and we can supply them with dinner afterwards.'

'It'll have to be something basic. We don't have a chef.'

'Hiring staff is way in the distance for us, Rosie.' Belle breathed out a whoosh of air as she lowered her eyes to the floorboards. 'Sometimes this place overwhelms me.'

Rosie flopped her cloth into a nearby red bucket and brushed back a piece of hair that was stuck like cooked spaghetti to her sweaty forehead. 'Once all the cleaning is done, we'll get on with some repairs before painting.'

Belle's eyes drifted around the large room. 'It's going to take a lot of paint.'

'Belle, do you really want to take this business on? We could sell, or make this our home. Although, it will cost a bit in bills, but still. It's worth thinking about. We don't have to have a hotel just because that's what it originally was.' Rosie could see the suspicion in her sister's face, and she knew Belle had every right to feel that way. She hadn't told her about Elliot's offer, nor had she told her about her trip to see Monty that morning. 'I'm just asking, Belle. No need for that look.'

Belle leaned on the splintered doorframe. 'It's just, we agreed to this. This would be our new life.'

'I know, but we weren't expecting this disaster. Plus, neither of us know anything about hotels or business.'

'You had an online business.'

Rosie flapped one arm. 'It hardly makes me Karren Brady.'

'Do you want to quit, Rosie?'

'It's not quitting. It's about us doing something that makes us happy.'

Belle scoffed. 'That's rich, coming from you.'

'What does that mean?'

'You love pottery, but you're not doing that for a living anymore.'

'No. I'm scrubbing skirting boards instead. See. I bet you miss working in a nursery. You love working with kids.'

'That's my old life, Rosie. This is the new one. I committed. I thought you did too. What's changed?'

'My heart's not in it, Belle, but I'll still give it a go. I know it's early days, and I've got a lot to learn. Elliot said he'll teach me everything I need to know about hotels.'

Belle huffed. 'That's big of him. Why would he do that?'

Rosie couldn't fight back the smile erupting on her face. 'Because he loves me.'

Belle sat down on the floor in front of her as she laughed. 'You sure about that?'

'He told me.'

Belle stopped laughing. 'Really? He told you that he loves you?'

Rosie nodded. Her heart was filled with happiness, and the butterflies in her stomach were sitting down nicely having afternoon tea or something equally pleasant.

'And how do you feel about him?' asked Belle.

'I love him too, but I didn't tell him. I was too scared.'

'Why were you scared? Did he do something to make you afraid?'

Rosie reached forward and gently tapped Belle's knee. 'No. He's so sweet. It wasn't about him. It was about me. I have all this trauma in my head from *you know who*, and I can feel it holding me back from Elliot.'

'There's nothing wrong with taking things slowly, Rosie. You've only known him a few days. It's all moved too quickly for you two.'

'I know. It's so strange, but I feel like I've known him forever. He makes me feel safe, and yet, I'm still wary, and

I know it's because of my past. I know not all men are like my ex. There are loads of lovely men in this world, but I can't seem to help it. I still feel apprehensive. I even asked for a get-out clause in our relationship.'

'You're calling it a relationship now? Hang on a minute, a clause?'

'That if I want to leave, I can.'

'Of course you can. It's what people do when they break up. You don't need a contract for that.'

Rosie started to twiddle with the bottom of her torn tee-shirt. 'I know. I sounded like an idiot, but I got flustered and didn't know what to say when he asked me to be his girlfriend.'

'Hey, you don't have to be his girlfriend just because you're sleeping with him. You can still be a free agent, Rosie.'

Rosie looked at her worried sister and smiled. 'I know, but I kind of like being called his girlfriend.' She paused and took a deep breath. 'There's something I haven't told you yet.'

'I don't want details on your sex life.'

Rosie laughed. The memory of Elliot's strong body leaning over hers on his bed caused her butterflies' tranquil tea party to end abruptly as music started to play and they took to dancing the jive instead. 'No, it's not that. I went to see a solicitor this morning whilst you were out. Elliot took me. We went over the contract between the two inns. Turns out, it died along with Pops. We don't have to abide by their mad rules after all.'

Belle's beaming face caused alarm bells for Rosie. She really hoped her sister wasn't about to turn into Uncle Frank and start doing crazy things to next door.

'So, I can be a real boy now?'

132

Rosie shook her head. 'Yes, your strings have been well and truly cut, but we're not hostile people, Belle. We're going to be good neighbours. Not egg-throwing, fence-planting, name-stealing crazy...'

'Name stealing? We can have the original name?'

'I think it's best if both sides agree not to go down that road. We've just got rid of the barriers. Why create more?'

'We still hate each other.'

'Do we? I happen to love Elliot, and I'm not about to take part in anything that will hurt him or destroy what we have only just started.'

Belle huffed as she stood. 'You make Pops so proud.'

Rosie frowned as she creaked to her feet. 'Hey, that's not fair. Pops and his ex-best friend are long gone, and neither of them are going to dictate what I do with my life. I don't care who hates me from now on, and that includes you, Belle. So if you want to fall out with me for loving Elliot, you best say so now. Let's hear it.'

Belle looked both astonished and deeply wounded. 'You'd choose him over me?'

Rosie sighed on the inside. 'I'm not choosing anyone. I'm just trying to have a normal life. One that doesn't include ghosts telling me what to do. I expect you to support me. Surely, you don't hate the Renshaws that much. You like Kasey.'

'She's a kid.'

'Belle, I don't want to fight with them, nor do I want to fight with you. Can we just concentrate on this place, and our new choir?'

Belle twisted her lips to one side, clearly considering the proposal, and then nodded. 'Okay.'

'Now, tell me about your morning. Did you find Pepper Lane easily enough, or did you get a bit lost in places?'

The fact that Belle swallowed hard didn't go unnoticed, and Rosie wondered what her sister was hiding from her. There were some serious tell-tale signs creeping onto Belle's slightly flushed face.

*Hmm!*

'Actually, Ned showed me the way,' Belle said sheepishly.

'Ned?'

'I bumped into him on the cutest little bridge you will ever see in your life. I can't wait to show you, Rosie. You'll love it.'

'So, how did you two get on?'

Belle laughed. 'So-so.'

'Did you fight?'

'No. We were okay. He introduced me to everyone we met. They all know each other around here.' Belle laughed again. 'There was this old lady in the tea shop... Oh, I brought you back some sweet treats, by the way. They're in the kitchen, if the rat hasn't eaten them, or the cat. I don't think that cat likes me, you know.'

'Erm, back to your story.'

'Oh, yeah. So, this old lady reckons she's a fortune teller. Guess what she told me?'

Rosie shrugged with amusement. She really wanted to meet the old lady herself now. She loved a bit of fortune telling.

Belle giggled, then composed herself. 'That I'm going to marry Ned.'

Rosie choked on air. 'Well, now the contract's null and void, I guess you can.'

'Don't be daft. Edward Renshaw, of all people. She's way off. Belle does not end up with Gaston.'

'Wait till I tell Elliot. He will laugh his head off.'

'Yes, thank you. It's bad enough Ned doesn't think I'm good enough for him.'

'What? Were you actually offended?'

Belle scrunched her nose. 'Well, you should have seen his face. Anyone would have thought he'd been told he was to marry a swamp monster or something. He'd be lucky to have someone like me by his side.'

Rosie controlled the sarcastic grin trying to make an appearance. 'Yes, yes, he would.'

'The point is, he could have been politer about his facial expression.'

'What did you expect? You hate each other, supposedly. Now, I'm not so sure.'

Belle's shoulders slumped. She pulled out her phone and directed her attention to that. 'I don't hate him. Okay.'

Rosie smiled to herself. 'Do you like him?' She watched Belle's cheeks redden a touch and already knew the answer, but she felt like being a tease. She wanted to make her sister admit out loud that Ned Renshaw wasn't the monster she first thought.

Belle glanced up from her screen. 'There, I've sent the message about our clean-up party, for want of a better phrase.'

'Do you like him?'

'Really? You're going to hassle me about this?'

Rosie nodded.

'He's all right, but I don't fancy him, if that's what you're getting at. Sometimes he can be… nice. Sometimes, he can still be a right horrible sod.'

Rosie sighed loudly. 'Well, it's a start, I guess. Now, how about some lunch?'

'Ooh, good plan.'

# 18

*Ned*

Ned sat alone at the dining table nearest the bar. A glass of brandy was to one side of his game of solitaire. He flipped over a card and stared absentmindedly at the queen of hearts. He was tired, but not in body. Spending the morning with Belle had drained him. He didn't want her inside his head, and he certainly didn't want her anywhere near his heart.

There had been moments where he forgot himself. When he forgot Penny. He couldn't allow that memory to disappear. Penny must always stay with him. Why did Belle have to make him smile on the inside? Why her? Why now?

*Bloody Josephine, getting inside my head too. That woman really doesn't care. She just blurts out whatever she wants to say and sod the rest of us. Well, cheers, Mrs Walker.*

He raised his glass and toasted the air, took a sip, and then put it back on the table in the exact same spot. He picked up a card and twiddled it between his finger and thumb.

Belle was upstairs, sleeping probably. It was late, and he was pretty sure he was the only one awake. He was glad the Trent sisters weren't going to be sleeping in his hotel anymore after tonight. He was going to toast the boiler repair man but decided he couldn't be bothered.

Ned wanted space. Space from his life, his thoughts, and especially Bluebell Trent. At least tomorrow he would get a rest from seeing her, and if he were lucky, he wouldn't see her the day after that either. He had fat chance later in the week, thanks to Belle's WhatsApp post asking for some sort of cleaning party, and Elliot agreeing to attend with him and offering a free dinner to all helpers. Rosie had insisted they feed everyone, then Elliot had insisted, and that battle went on for a while, bored the crap out of him, and almost caused him to leave the group altogether.

He sighed deeply and rested his head on his hand, the two of clubs tapping against his hair. Ned had never felt this way before, and he wasn't a hundred percent sure what exactly it was that he was feeling. He just knew it was taking up too much brain power and sapping his energy. The presence of someone behind him caused him to stir.

'Is it okay if I sit in here with my tea?' asked Belle quietly.

Ned raised one hand up and gestured for her to enter his lonely domain. He didn't expect her to plop herself down opposite him. He rolled his bloodshot eyes up to watch her blue mug almost touch his brandy glass. He removed his head from his hand. 'I thought everyone was asleep.'

'Maybe everyone else is. I'm wide awake.'

He pulled in his lips as he slowly bobbed his head.

'Your eyes looked tired,' she mumbled.

'Thanks.'

'I didn't mean anything by it. You just look like you need a good kip, that's all.' She pointed down at a row of cards to let him know where to place the one he was still holding.

He put the card in place and picked up another one to stare mindlessly at.

Belle sipped her tea, and Ned found his eyes wander to her lips. He looked down at the white tablecloth.

'Have you got stuff on your mind that you'd like to talk about?' she asked.

His brow wrinkled. 'What?'

'You look as though you have the weight of the world on your shoulders.'

'What if I have? What's that got to do with you?'

He shouldn't have snapped and was surprised when she didn't bite back. Her hazel eyes were staring at the cards, and her silence was worse than her bark.

*What's wrong with her?*

'Why haven't you snapped back at me?'

She gave a half-shrug and took another mouthful of tea. 'I can't be bothered. I'm tired.'

A moment of silence lingered between them.

*You're tired. I'm tired. Must be something in the air. She looks sad. Don't know why she's sitting with me. It's not like I can do anything to help lift her mood. I can't even lift my own.*

'I'm sorry for biting your head off.'

She shrugged again and gave a despondent glance his way, which hit him straight in the heart, much to his annoyance. She tapped at a row of cards, and he placed down the one he was holding.

'You know this is a game for one player, right?'

The corner of her mouth twitched. 'Sorry.'

Ned folded his arms in a strop. 'Okay, what's wrong with you? And don't say you're tired. A minute ago, you were wide awake.'

'I'm not sleepy tired, just, you know.'

He did know.

'Is there anything you would like to talk about?' He kind of hoped there wasn't but still felt the need to ask because she had asked him.

'No, I'm okay. I'm just in a quiet mood.'

'That's because it's late. You should go to bed.'

Belle went back to staring at the cards. 'Are you coming out to dinner with us tomorrow night? Rosie said Elliot was coming. We're going to that pub in Pepper Lane. Did he mention it to you?'

*Yep, and I said no.*

'Hmm, we'll be there.'

'I didn't think you'd go.'

He tilted his head. 'Free meal. Free booze. Why not?'

She placed her cup back down next to his brandy. 'Do you drink every night?'

He breathed out a laugh. 'No. You worried I'm a drunk?'

She shook her head. 'Why would I be worried?'

'Because you're looking at your future husband. It might be a concern.'

Her smile was wide and that pleased him. She had a pretty smile that revealed a slightly crooked tooth to one side that he thought gave her character. He had already worked out that only her genuine smile revealed that particular tooth.

'I'm going to bed.' She stood and appeared to be waiting. 'Are you coming with me?'

His mind replayed the sentence, as that couldn't be right.

She shook her head in disbelief. 'Oh goodness, no, that's not what I meant. Sorry. Ignore me. I just wondered if you were also going to bed. Not with me. Your bed. Separate beds. Alone.'

Her rambling amused him and suddenly warmed him more than the brandy. He stood, leaving his cards and drink untouched. 'I'll walk you up.'

It wasn't clear if he was doing it or her, but their arms kept brushing against each other's as they made their way up the stairs. He didn't care. Her bare arm poking out of her pink tee-shirt sleeve felt nice, and he found himself wanting to touch more of her at every step they silently climbed.

Belle's bedroom was just to the left at the top of the stairs. She dithered in her doorway, taking turns to look between him and the dark-red carpet.

Ned knew his eyes had darkened, because he could feel the exact emotion rushing through his body. He just had to figure out what he was going to do about it. A deep desire was taking over, and it was all he could do to stop his hand from wandering into her long blonde hair. The brandy was clouding his judgment. Maybe it was a simple case of sleep deprivation. Something was taking over his tired mind.

*Just say goodnight. Be done. Over. Just goodnight. You can do it, Ned. Nice and easy.*

He stepped forward and lowered his head and gently kissed her cheek, staying in that position for a moment longer than a peck on the cheek took. He went to move his face away but her mouth suddenly brushed across his, causing his stomach to flip.

The feeling of Belle's fingers entwined in the hair around the back of his head made him kiss her harder. She stumbled into the door, and he caught her waist and steadied her. His heart was racing, and his need had accelerated. Her warm tongue was in his mouth, and her other hand at the base of his spine. She pulled him inside the bedroom, and he closed and locked the door.

Belle stepped back and appeared to be studying him. She then took him by the hand and guided him to the bed. 'I feel lonely tonight, Ned, that's all.'

He nodded. 'I understand.'

*You have no idea how much I understand. How alone I feel. How you've made me recognise that.*

'It will just be a one-off. Do you still want to stay?' she asked softly.

'Yes.'

'I'd rather keep my top on, and I don't want you to touch my stomach.' Her voice was quiet and calm as though that line had been rehearsed.

'May I ask why?'

Belle sat on the bed and gestured for him to join her. 'I just have some scars in that area.'

Ned was none the wiser. 'Do they hurt?'

She breathed out a laugh through her nose. 'No, they're just scars.'

'Ah, you just don't want me to see them.'

'Only because they can be a turn-off.'

He frowned in annoyance. 'Says who?'

'Let's just say I've been told.'

He scoffed, waving one hand behind him as though waving someone away. 'By an idiot. Scars are just a part of someone. We've all got at least one somewhere.' He stood. 'Let me show you mine.' He quickly stripped off down to his black boxers, and the look of lust in her eyes at his lean torso didn't go unnoticed, which made him smile on the inside.

Belle bent forward, examining his body in the dull light of the bedside table lamp.

'Right, where shall we start?' He twisted his waist. 'So, here's the big one that runs along my hipline. See.' He lowered his finger to his thigh as he turned away from her. 'There's a long thin one down my leg. It reminds me of Pepper River.'

Belle muffled a laugh as he turned back to face her. He raised his arm to reveal the wide scar underneath his biceps and then sat down to let her have a closer look at the one next to his heart. He twisted away and nodded down at the one just below his shoulder.

'Oh my goodness, Ned. Have you been to war?'

'Car crash,' he said casually. 'The car rolled and was hit again, twice. Firefighters had to cut us out.' He turned back to see tears sitting in her eyes.

'I'm sorry, I forgot for a moment. This is the accident that killed Penny.'

He nodded and gazed down at his chest. 'We all have scars, Bluebell Trent.' He raised his eyes. 'There's no shame in that.'

Belle's hand rested on his heart as a lone tear escaped her eye.

He wiped her cheek and kissed her lips briefly. 'Hey, don't cry for me.'

'What caused the accident? Do you know?'

'Winter. Black ice. Drunk driver. Speeding. Take your pick.' He caught the enquiry in her expression. 'I wasn't the speed-freak or the drunk. I was just on my way home with my family from a weekend away.'

'What a nightmare,' she whispered.

'Yeah, it was. So, what's your story? Can your scars outdo my scars?'

Belle giggled. 'What is this, Jaws?'

He smiled widely. 'I love that scene.' He watched her hand stroke over her stomach, and he wondered if he should change the subject. Maybe sit in bed and watch Jaws. He was just about to suggest that when she slowly lifted her tee-shirt to reveal, what he considered, three rather neat scars.

'Looks like your seamstress did a better job than mine.'

Her worried eyes rolled up to meet his, and he struggled to feel her concerns.

He hovered his hand over her stomach. 'May I?'

She placed her hand over his and guided it to her skin. He stroked her with his thumb whilst looking in her eyes.

'They're just scars, Flower Girl,' he whispered.

She smiled and another teardrop escaped.

'You're beautiful, Belle. Don't listen to anyone who says otherwise.'

She tightened her grip on his hand, and a flurry of something delightful washed through him.

'You even beat me at scars, Ned.'

He breathed out a laugh. 'Hey, what can I say. I'm good at everything.'

Belle's chest lifted and dropped heavily. 'We've had a bit of a day today, you and me, haven't we?'

'Something like that. Shall we just get in bed and watch a film, have a cuddle, and go to sleep for a bit?'

'Sounds perfect.'

'I can't stay all night. I don't want Kasey to come into my room in the morning to find I'm not there.'

'That's understandable.'

He nodded over at the plump white pillows. 'Okay. Pick a side, Mrs Renshaw.'

She nudged his arm and climbed in the side nearest to them whilst he turned the telly on and grabbed the remote.

'We have stored films on here.' He glanced at her and smiled as he snuggled down next to her. 'We've got Jaws.'

'Oh, brilliant. You have to put that on now.'

He started the movie, then put his arm around her, and she wriggled into place against his chest. It felt so normal, as though they had been snuggling up to each other for years. He kissed her head and smiled.

Belle cleared her throat. 'I was born with complications, and I had to have a couple of operations throughout my childhood years, and when I was older, my womb was removed.'

That was the last thing he expected to hear. He lifted her from his chest so that he could see her face. 'I'm so sorry, Belle.'

She smiled softly. 'Now we know each other's scars story.'

He took a steady breath. 'Yeah, I guess we do.'

She settled back into his arms, and he kissed her head once more. 'So, does that Pepper River scar run all the way up to your bum?'

He laughed quietly. 'You can find that out another time. Watch the film.'

*Belle*

The Ugly Duckling was a family pub that served food made by a local chef, Freddy Morland. It was the only pub in Pepper Bay and was every bit picture-worthy as the rest of Pepper Lane. Chalky white walls and dark-wood beams made the front, and inside was an open log fire, a long dark-wood bar, tables to one side, and a large Christmas tree twinkling brightly. Two of the Victorian street lamps from the beer garden out the back had been brought inside and placed either side of the back door, and a large garland draped across the top frame.

One of the owners, Elaine Sparrow, who everyone thought resembled Annie Lennox, showed the Trents and Renshaws to a table over by the fireplace and handed out menus.

Ned handed his back. 'I think we know what you serve here off by heart.'

Elaine took the menu and tapped him on the head with it. 'Cheeky sod. I'll have you know, Freddy has been working on some new creations lately.'

'Can I still have fish fingers?' asked Kasey.

Elaine reached down and stroked her head. 'Of course you can. You can have whatever you want.'

Kasey beamed widely. 'May I please have my colouring book too?'

Belle's eyes widened as she glanced at Elaine. 'Kasey has her own colouring book here?'

Elaine nodded. 'I don't see why not. Some of the older gentlemen here have their own beer tankard behind the bar, so why not Kasey's colouring book as well?'

Rosie clasped her hands together in front of her heart. 'Aww, that's so sweet.'

'We do aim to please,' said Elaine. 'We're a small community here, and we're friendly to one another.' She twisted the side of her mouth whilst looking at Ned. 'Hmm, so Renshaws and Trents having dinner together. That's a first under my watch. Nice though. I'm glad you're all getting along.' She took their drinks order and walked away.

Belle felt a tad awkward when Elliot's hand reached over and held Rosie's on the table.

'Why are you holding Rosie's hand?' asked Kasey.

Elliot grinned. 'Because I love her.'

Ned rolling his eyes didn't go unnoticed, except by his daughter. Kasey reached out her hands and placed one into her dad's and the other into Belle's, who was sitting the other side of her.

Belle felt slightly gobsmacked by the gesture of love from the little girl, and it was quite clear that Ned felt the same way. She chanced a glance his way and caught a slight smile tugging at the corner of his mouth. She wondered what exactly he was thinking, especially about her and the night they shared watching telly in bed together. She had woken in the wee small hours of the morning when she felt movement next to her, and she had peeped through sleepy eyes at the figure leaving her room. He had pulled the cover up over her shoulder and kissed her head, or maybe that part was a dream. Maybe it was all a weird dream. He hadn't mentioned the unexpected night at all, but in his defence, she hadn't seen him all day.

Belle took a large gulp of her orange juice as soon as it arrived, needing something to occupy her, as Rosie dreamily gazing into Elliot's bright eyes told her she'd get no help from her.

Elaine gave Kasey her colouring book and pencils and Kasey got stuck in as Rosie and Elliot turned to gaze dreamily into the flickering flames of the fire instead.

Belle went to start picking at her fingernail but something tapped her shoulder. She looked up and over to her left to see Ned's arm stretched around Kasey's chair and his hand touching the edge of hers. She rolled her eyes to his face and he hit her with his sexy grin and an added wink. It took all her might to hold in the roar of laughter that was rolling around in her throat.

The cheeky glint in Ned's eyes warmed her, and just for a moment everyone in the pub disappeared, but then Rosie laughed loudly as she turned back to the table, causing Belle to come crashing back down to earth with a bump.

Ned redirected his attention to his daughter's picture and complimented her blue trees and pink grass.

Elliot leaned on the table. 'So, Belle, I hear you two are off to choir practice tomorrow night.'

She nodded and smiled at his attempt at polite conversation. 'Yes, our choirmaster already texted me a reminder. Plus, he said that the rest of the group have been told about our Disney songs idea, and they were over the moon. So, that will be our Christmas show.'

'You'll come, won't you?' Rosie asked Elliot.

'Try and stop me.'

Belle made a conscious effort not to roll her eyes. 'Have you asked him about sponsorship yet?'

'What's that about?' asked Elliot at the same time as Ned.

Belle let Rosie explain.

'The costumes cost a lot to make, so Sean, our choirmaster, is on the lookout for anyone willing to sponsor our choir. It's just to help pay for material. That sort of thing. And in return, we advertise the sponsor at the show.'

'Sure, we'll do it,' said Elliot, but Ned didn't look as excited about being roped in.

'Great. Thanks,' said Rosie, her face gleaming with far too much joy than seemed possible, in Belle's opinion. 'I'll tell Sean to call you.' She leaned over and kissed his cheek.

Belle glanced at Ned, wondering if he was expecting a thank you kiss too. He wasn't getting one. Not from her anyway. It wasn't as though he had agreed. Now the thought of kissing him was running through her mind. The sensation of his lips pressed against hers had been her companion all day. The tang of the brandy in his mouth. The heat from his tongue. The tingling beneath her skin. She was so glad he wasn't there at breakfast. She had held her breath on entering the dining room, even with her well-rehearsed *nothing happened last night* routine.

His fingertip poked her back as Rosie and Elliot decided what food to order. She wanted to ignore him teasing her, but it was so hard. She tried to control her mouth, but it was starting to look like she had a nervous twitch in her cheek. Her stomach would not settle, and she was sure she couldn't eat. Just that one small touch from him powered through her with the force of lightning. It was becoming unbearable. It was becoming addictive. She couldn't decide if she loved or loathed the finger resting on her back. Would it move again? Stroke her again? Did she really want it to?

Elaine took their order, and Belle opted for a chicken salad, knowing she could just pick at that if the queasiness

148

continued. Ned's appetite didn't seem affected, as he had ordered some sort of deluxe burger with a whole heap of chips and extra salad.

Kasey stretched her head up to look over at the bar. 'Elaine, can I play in the snow, please?'

Rosie giggled. 'There isn't any snow.'

Elaine pointed at the back door. 'I have a snow machine above the door. Helps make it look Christmassy in the beer garden. Not that many sit out there in this weather.'

Elliot smiled at his niece. 'It's too cold tonight, love.'

'I'm not cold,' she told him.

Belle jumped at the opportunity to have a bit of space from Ned's wandering fingers. 'I'll pop outside with her for five minutes.' She scuffed her chair back at the same time as Kasey.

'Coat,' said Elliot, pointing at Kasey.

Elaine walked to the end of the bar. 'Go on then. Just five minutes.'

Kasey cheered as she flung her red coat on and ran outside, with Belle in hot pursuit.

Belle smiled widely as the snow machine came to life, spraying small clumps of fake snow over their heads. She watched Kasey swirling around on the winding pathway whilst singing 'Once Upon a December', and she hummed along until she felt a presence over her shoulder. Ned's hand was on the small of her back, and the heat from his warm body was flowing directly into the back of her neck.

'Hello,' he whispered, and she was totally lost in him.

'Daddy, dance.'

Belle felt his hand slip into hers, and her body was slowly swirled around and forced to a stop in front of him.

'Shall we, Mrs Renshaw?'

His voice was low and husky, and his eyes were definitely saying *come to bed*. She was happy to oblige, and he spun her around and manoeuvred her further out into the beer garden.

Rows of glass jars filled with fake candles lined the grassy verge, giving off extra light. They matched the ones sitting upon the wooden tables that were darted around.

Kasey continued to swirl and sing 'Once Upon a December' as Ned guided Belle in a snowy waltz. His quiet voice joined in with the song, making both Belle and Kasey smile.

'You sing too, Belle,' Kasey added into her lyrics.

Ned's eyes were fixed on Belle's, and she tried for her performance face. She was never afraid to be on the stage with a thousand eyes watching her sing. She didn't care who watched or heard her. She could sing to the world, but to just sing to Ned felt slightly intimidating. She brushed away the new feeling and found her voice.

Ned's eyes stopped twinkling, appearing to concentrate on her every flawless note as they danced under the falling snow.

Belle could see what was happening. He wasn't hiding his feelings. A tenderness was right there, staring at her deeply. She lowered her face, and he nudged her back up with his nose. She allowed her eyes to smile as she sang into his, and she controlled her breathing as his mouth came to rest inches from her own.

Elaine's voice called out from inside the pub, telling them their food was ready, and Kasey ran straight in.

Belle had no more energy left. The control slipped as soon as she stopped singing. Ned had stopped them dancing and was just looking at her with that same astonished-meets-dreamy gaze. She raised herself and kissed him on the lips. He pulled back quickly, and, just for a moment, she felt mortified.

He placed his fingers in his mouth and pulled out a bit of fake snow. 'Poxy stuff gets everywhere.'

Belle swallowed hard. 'We should go eat.'

'Yeah, just one sec.'

Her heart fluttered as he pulled her closer and kissed her tenderly, placing one hand on her cheek and the other on her back. His thumb slowly traced over her face, so light, she barely felt him. She closed her eyes and drifted away to a snowy forest filled with decorated Christmas trees, twinkling lights, and a full moon low in the sky. Ice glistened beneath their feet whilst cool air drew them closer together.

He slowly pulled away and smiled, and Belle's breathing felt sedated. 'Now, that's what you call a starters, Flower Girl.'

She bit her lip to muffle a warm giggle trying to surface.

He frowned for a moment, looking deeply in her eyes. 'You know what, Mrs Renshaw, I might just miss you tonight.'

# 20

*Rosie*

Choir practice started off with lots of excitement over the newbies, talk about the Disney theme for the Christmas show, and a flying bottle of water that had escaped Belle's hand and met Sean's lap. Luckily, it was sealed, but it still caused the *oof* in his voice to go up a tad higher.

Kristen calmed the group and gave everyone a Disney character whilst Nora, the dressmaker, took notes and measurements, all in amongst the singing and overdramatic performances that kept spontaneously bursting to life.

The Sandly Choir took turns belting out whatever Disney song came to mind next whilst leaping about like the kids from Fame, and both Belle and Rosie happily joined in and were made to feel right at home. Under normal circumstances, as told by Kris, the choir would have welcomed them into the nest in the usual fashion by singing a chorus of 'Consider Yourself', with every member sounding every bit the Artful Dodger. However, Disney had cornered the market of the small, draughty hut, and so the newcomers got to dance along with the group, with Kris singing 'You've Got a Friend in Me'.

The conga line to 'Supercalifragilisticexpialidocious' completely whacked out Rosie and Belle. They flopped to the floor in the corner by Nora to take a breather.

Nora was sewing a piece of gold-coloured cloth, which looked like a cuff that possibly belonged to a prince. Her nimble old fingers worked effortlessly, sometimes in time to the music.

'How long have you been making costumes?' asked Rosie.

Nora glanced up from her lap. 'Ooh, I don't know. Thirty years, maybe.'

'They say you're brilliant,' said Belle. 'I can't wait to see my costume. How do you make them so fast?'

Nora's wrinkled eyes held a shrewd glint. 'I get some of my friends to help. I think they only come for the French Fancies and Ladyfingers I supply. Still, it gets them out for a few hours, and we have a good natter. Catch up on the gossip.'

Rosie and Belle shared a smile.

'What's the latest?' asked Belle, and Rosie nudged her.

Nora's beady bright blue eyes homed in on Belle. 'You two, if you want to know. You're front news at the moment. Everyone wants to know who you are, where you came from, and what you used to do before coming here. The Inn on the Right is causing the locals to stir.'

Belle scrunched her nose. 'We're not that exciting. We're from Surrey. Rosie made pottery pieces, and I was a nursery teacher.'

Nora's eyes widened. 'Ooh, that's handy.' She waved over a young lady called Daphne. 'Daph, Belle here is a nursery teacher.'

Daphne beamed a wide smile. 'Ooh, how's that for luck. I work in a local nursery, and we're just about to advertise for a teacher to start in the new year. If you're interested, Belle, I'll give you my number before you leave, and you could apply for the job.'

Belle smiled politely and nodded.

Rosie watched Daphne dance her way back off into the small group who were writing down as many Disney songs they could think of.

Belle turned back to Nora. 'You see, we're quite boring, really.'

Rosie laughed. 'There's not much going on at our place, I'm afraid, Nora. You can report back with that news.'

'You were seen hand in hand with Elliot Renshaw. That's something going on right there.'

Rosie nodded. 'Yes, we're a couple, but that's nothing to write home about.'

Nora scoffed and choked on some phlegm. She quickly cleared her clogged throat. 'He's a Renshaw and you're a Trent. That's big news, my lovely.'

Belle scrunched her nose. 'Does everyone know about our family feud?'

Nora raised her drawn-on eyebrows. 'A hotel was cut in half, dear. Everyone knows about that story and all the trouble over the years.'

Rosie gave a half-shrug. 'I suppose it's different.'

'More like madness,' said Nora.

Belle sipped her water and cuffed her mouth. 'We don't even know what caused the split. Our grandfathers were best friends, by all accounts. What makes someone fall out of love with their bezzie mate?'

Nora stuck the needle into the cloth and crossed her hands. 'Falling out of love with each other wasn't the problem, ladies. Falling in love with each other was.'

Rosie's mouth gaped whilst Belle choked on air.

Nora blinked a couple of times. 'I'm surprised you didn't know.'

Both women slowly shook their head from side to side. Their mouths were drooped, and their minds were filled with a hundred questions.

Rosie found her voice first. 'So, they were in love?'

Nora confirmed with a low groaning sound. 'One of their wives found out and that's when it all went to pot. It was the wives, you know, who caused all the animosity, not that you can blame them. They were a bit upset.'

'So they separated the hotels, not the men,' said Belle.

Nora's head bobbed. 'Mary Gentry was Helen Renshaw's best friend. That's how word got out. Mary Gentry was like the town crier. It all got hushed back down though, probably why you didn't know. I guess they kept it from their children.'

Rosie sat up on her knees and leaned forward. 'Did the affair stop then, or were they still secretly meeting up?'

'If they did carry on carrying on, then nothing else was said, but there was so much anger, I doubt their relationship was ever the same again.'

Rosie flopped back onto her heels. 'Not sure who I feel sorry for the most.'

'Messy business,' said Nora, looking over her needlework.

Rosie turned to Belle. 'Elliot doesn't know about this. I asked him. He and Ned were as clueless as us.'

Nora smiled. 'Aw, Elliot Renshaw. He's a good man now. Mind you, I'm not keen on those tattoos along his arms. I've never seen the point of them myself.'

'I want to get one,' said Belle, staring at her arm.

Rosie had something else on her mind. 'What did you mean when you said that Elliot is a good man now?'

Belle stopped staring at her arm to look at Nora. 'He wasn't always nice?'

Nora's wrinkled mouth tightened as she gave a quick shake of the head. 'No, not at all. He got into lots of trouble when he was young.'

Rosie shrugged nonchalantly. 'Lots of kids are naughty.'

Nora scoffed. 'He wasn't naughty. He was feral.'

Belle gasped. 'Bloody hell.'

'Well, he's not like that now,' said Rosie quickly. 'He's lovely.'

Nora agreed.

'When did he change?' asked Belle, staring only at Rosie.

Rosie knew that her sister was now worried that Elliot was some sort of secret ogre. Belle had a stern crinkling of the brow that matched the harsh look in her judging eyes, which pretty much said she wasn't about to let the subject drop until she was satisfied she had all the relevant information she felt was needed.

Nora's cogs were turning. 'Ooh, early twenties, I'd say. Not sure what changed him. Some say his father locked him up for a spell and that might have done the trick, but I don't think so. Prison didn't change him, so I don't see what being locked in his room would do. I think he met a lady. No one knows. He went missing for a while back then. No one saw him for ages, that's why they think he was locked up somewhere in the hotel.'

'Erm, back up a minute, please, Nora,' said Belle, with her index finger waggling in the air. 'Prison?'

'Hmm, when he was a teenager. Eighteen, I think. Got six months.'

'What for?' asked Belle. Her tone was filled more with annoyance than curiosity.

Rosie was a tad concerned about all the things about Elliot that she didn't know. Surely, he would have mentioned that kind of backstory. It was pretty huge. Elliot was starting to sound like he led a double life. She knew it was his past, and she didn't have a right to judge a person who no longer existed, but she had shared parts of herself with him, so fair's fair. She really wanted to know every part of Elliot's story, and more importantly, why he had hidden his past from her.

'Criminal damage,' said Nora. 'He'd done other things before along those lines, but he didn't get away with it that time.'

'Are we talking graffiti?' asked Rosie, knowing full well she sounded hopeful.

Nora tilted her head and sighed quietly. 'Sorry to be the one who tells you, but Elliot broke in to your hotel and trashed the dining room.'

Belle turned sharply to Rosie. 'Bet he didn't tell you that either.'

*Nope.*

Nora flapped one hand as though waving the comment away. 'Oh, it was a long time ago. He's a lovely person now. Does all sorts to help people. He was in with a bad lot back then. Plus, he had all that hate inside him, thanks to his father, and that was passed down to Clive from his own mother. Poor Elliot and Ned never stood much of a chance after their mum died. Their dad did nothing but pour hatred into them. Elliot was messed up because of that man, I know. We all saw it.'

'Poor Elliot,' whispered Rosie, and she saw her sister roll her eyes. 'Well, it does sound like he had psychological reasons behind his actions.'

Belle huffed and shook her head. She turned back to Nora. 'You vouch for him now, do you?'

Nora nodded. 'Ooh yes, my lovely. We can't be judged on our past. I'm not a fan of back-shaming. It teaches our children nothing. We need to show how people can learn and grow, and we must always praise change and personal development. Otherwise, what's the point? No one will bother to better themselves if they believe that they will only ever be judged on their past. I'm not the same person I was last year, let alone twenty, thirty years ago. We move on. We learn, we grow, we change. Well, most of us do.'

Rosie couldn't tell if Belle was willing to see Elliot for the man he was today. She accepted that her little sister would always worry about any man she was in a relationship with because of what happened with her vile ex, but she really wanted Belle to love Elliot and see how kind and loving he was. She also desperately wanted to know why he suddenly changed one day and where he did disappear to. There was no way she was going to brush it under the rug. An honest chat was on the cards, and it was happening as soon as she got home.

# 21

Elliot was sitting up in bed when his phone bleeped with a message from Rosie asking if she could come over. He wasn't quite sure whether she was asking to stay the night or not but told her to come over anyway. He was already missing her sleeping by his side and had secretly cursed her new boiler, more than once.

He removed his dark glasses and closed his book. He couldn't quite put his finger on it, but he had a sudden bad feeling. It was late, and he knew that Rosie had been home from choir practice for a couple of hours. She hadn't replied to his text asking how the night went, and he wondered if things really would change between them now that she was no longer staying at his.

*Stop overthinking. You're just creating problems for yourself. Worry when there's something to worry about.*

Elliot leaned down to the floor to retrieve his green tee-shirt and put it back on. He tapped his feet together beneath the quilt and waited patiently. The night wouldn't be about cuddles. His gut feelings were never wrong.

A gentle tapping sound hit his door, causing his head to jolt up. 'Come in.'

The door opened and Rosie's cheerful but tired face peered around the wood. 'Sorry, it's late, I know. But when I looked out the window and saw Ned standing outside, I figured you hadn't locked up.'

Elliot couldn't help the wave of happiness that filled him at seeing her. He loved this woman so much already. It was blowing his mind. Now she was in his bedroom in her pyjamas once again, he didn't want her to leave. He waved her inside, and she entered fully and closed the door.

'Lock it,' he whispered, then grinned as she smiled at him.

'I haven't come here for that.'

He gave a half-shrug. 'Just in case.' He flipped the covers to one side as an invitation.

Rosie removed her dressing gown and climbed in, and he immediately pulled her into his arms and kissed her mouth with so much need, he lost his breath for a moment. It didn't help that her hands were in his hair, tugging him closer to her face.

He pulled her lower and slid her body on top of his. He knew she had something to say, but he couldn't stop kissing her, and she clearly couldn't stop kissing him either. He didn't know where to touch first. He was losing control and had to get a grip.

*Slow down. Breathe.*

Her mouth was trailing kisses down his neck, and one of her hands was sitting in the waistline of his pyjama bottoms. He sat up, taking her with him, and placed his mouth back onto hers. Her legs wrapped around him, and he pulled her closer.

'Do you have more condoms in your drawer?' she mumbled against his mouth.

'Yes, but…'

'No buts, Elliot. I want to make love.'

He pulled his face away to look at her. She was flushed and smiling, but there was a slight sadness in her eyes, and he needed to know what was on her mind.

'I want that too, Rosie, but we both know that's not why you're here tonight.'

160

She lowered her head, and he kissed her hairline.

'I love you, Rosie. I'll make love you to anytime you want, you know that, but I get the feeling you want to talk.'

'It's true. I do, but then I saw you and... Well, let's just say I have no willpower.' She leaned forward and kissed him, and Elliot knew she wasn't the only one with a weakness.

He kissed her hard, and she pulled his top over his head before he had a chance to draw breath. His name was being mumbled over his collarbone, and it was so difficult for him to hold her off. No part of him wanted to, and any part that dared suggest it got battered down immediately.

Rosie sat back and crossed her legs in front of her. 'Okay, let's get this out the way, but just know that afterwards I'm going to ravish you, my beautiful merman.'

Elliot's stomach flipped. He kissed her hand that came up to stroke the side of his face, then placed it into his own on his lap. 'Talk to me, Rosie. What's wrong?'

'I was told about your past today, and I'm wondering why you didn't tell me.'

He sighed inwardly. 'What have you been told?'

She started to fidget slightly. 'Not sure what's true, but sounds like I've been told everything. Criminal damage to my place. Feral behaviour. Bad gang. Prison. That sort of thing.'

He glanced at their entwined fingers, wishing he was making love now instead. His past was exactly that, the past. It wasn't somewhere he visited often, so mostly he blanked it out of his life. He wasn't that person anymore, so why hang out with him again? He didn't want to show how deflated he felt about the subject, but he didn't want to act indifferent either.

*She has a right to know everything about me. She's putting her trust in me. Look at her eyes. They're not even judging me, just waiting patiently for me to explain what a horrible little shit I was.*

'I should have told you, Rosie, but I have wiped that life clean away. I'm not used to talking about it anymore, that's all. I wasn't trying to hide anything from you, and I'm sorry for all of the upset I caused your family when I was younger.'

'You were filled with a lot of hate.'

He breathed out a laugh though his nose. 'Isn't that the truth. I didn't know myself back then, Rosie. I was a mess. Something never felt right, and I was fighting myself more than I was the outside world. I was angry and filled with hate, yes, but I was also torn between the life I was living and a life I knew I should be living in.'

'Did prison change you?'

He shook his head and failed to smile her way. 'No. Made me worse.'

'But you changed.'

'Yeah, but that was a few years later.'

'I heard your dad might have locked you away, or that you met a woman who helped change you.'

Elliot had to laugh inwardly at the rumours about his life. He had heard them all back then. There was even one about a secret dungeon at the hotel, and he was trapped there, starved and beaten.

*In for a penny, in for a pound.*

'I overdosed, Rosie. I tried to take my own life.' Before he had a chance to finish his story, her arms flew around his neck and held him. He hugged her back and smiled. 'It's all right, babe. It was a long time ago.' He pulled her away and wiped away the tear that had escaped from her eye. 'Hey, it's all good.'

She nodded and sat back, pulling in her lips and lowering her eyes.

He continued with his story. 'I'd had enough of my life, so that's what happened. A few days later, my mum's stepsister came down from London to see me. She's a very spiritual person, and she taught me how to calm my thoughts. She stayed for a few months and taught me how to meditate, how to do yoga, and she signed me up to a local martial arts class too. Said it would help channel my energy. She taught me self-discipline, self-love, and self-worth. We used to talk for hours about life, energy, the universe, how to heal from the inside, stuff like that. She was so easy to listen to, and she was the one who changed my life.'

Rosie smiled. 'I like her.'

'She told me that the reason I was so conflicted inside was because there was a battle going on between two people. The me who my dad had created, and the me who was my authentic self. She helped me to see myself, my truth. She set me straight, Rosie. She set me free.'

Rosie clasped her hands together in front of her chest. 'Oh, I'd love to meet her, Elliot.'

'She wants to meet you too.'

'You've told her about me?'

He nodded and smiled at the surprise in her expression. 'She'll be here for Christmas. She comes every year the day after Yule and stays for a few days. I tell her to come earlier and stay longer, but she likes to celebrate Yule with her friends back home, so she comes up after that and then goes home to see in the new year with her friends.'

'So, I'll see her soon. I feel a bit nervous now.'

Elliot laughed. 'You'll be fine. She loves you already, you know.'

'Does she know I'm a Trent?'

'She's glad you are. If she could wipe out the family feud, she would have done it years ago.'

Rosie gasped, making him jump. 'Oh, I found out why the fallout happened between our grandads.'

'You found out a lot tonight.'

'I met a lady called Nora…'

'Oh, that explains that. So, she knows something, or was she just on the rumour wagon?'

Rosie shrugged and shuffled closer to him. 'She said our grandads were having an affair.'

'Both of them?'

'No, not like that. Together. They were in love with each other.'

The corners of his mouth were working all by themselves. They curled up into the biggest smile. 'Oh my God, I've heard it all now. Do you believe that?'

'Why not? It gives an explanation.'

He sighed deeply and grabbed her hands. 'It does, and if it's true, I don't know who to feel sorry for, my grandfather or grandmother.'

'That's what I said. Our poor grandfathers loved each other but couldn't be together, and our poor grandmothers were heartbroken for being cheated on. It must have been horrible for all of them.'

He kissed her knuckles, breathed in the faint smell of creamy lavender moisturiser on her hand, and pulled her back onto his lap. 'I don't care anymore about what happened. The fact that we're not at war is all that matters. We've broken the curse, as Kasey would say. We're not enemies. We love each other, don't we?'

*Why am I forcing her to tell me that she loves me? What am I doing?*

She nodded and kissed him, wiping all worries away. He kissed her back and desire filled him as her hold on him strengthened.

'Can we make love now?' she mumbled against his lips.

He could feel her mouth curl. 'That depends. Have you got any more gossip first?'

'No.'

He pulled her back and looked into her gentle gaze. 'Rosie, doesn't my past give you any issues with me?'

'I don't know that person, Elliot. I only know you. I forgive you for whatever you did to my family when you weren't in your right mind. It would appear you have learnt how to forgive yourself too. I want to concentrate on the here and now, and what we can do together to create happiness and peace again for Pepper River Inn.'

Every part of her beautiful soul warmed his heart. He couldn't believe how lucky he was to have met her and to have her as his partner.

'Just so you know, we haven't put in for the original name, even though Ned wants to. I don't want anything to cause trouble for us.'

'I wish we could both have it.'

He raised his brow in surprise. 'That would mean joining the hotels again.'

'I would do that with you.'

*Wow!*

'You know what, Primrose Trent, I would do that with you too, within a heartbeat.'

She flopped over his shoulder and sighed. 'I wish it was up to us. You'd make the place brilliant. You know what you're doing.'

He stroked her back and her hair, soothing his own soul with every light touch. 'Hey, I'm going to teach you everything about this gig.'

'My heart's not in it, Elliot.' Her voice sounded so broken, he felt her pain.

'I know.'

She pulled away and arched an eyebrow. 'You do?'

*Oh, Rosie. It's been written all over you since we met. I know you're trying. I really do. I wish I could help you find your true dream. I want you to live your best life. Make the right choices for yourself.*

He gave a slight nod and rested his head on hers.

'I don't know what to do, Elliot.'

'You can start by staying here the night with me.'

'I won't leave Belle alone over there.'

'In that case, I'm going to walk you home and climb into bed with you for the night, and we'll worry about this another time.' He felt her arms cling on to him tightly. 'It's going to be all right, Rosie. Everything will be okay.'

# 22

*Ned*

There was once a house-painting party that Ned went to, but he had never been to a house-cleaning party before. He wasn't entirely convinced he wanted to go at all, but it was Belle's home, and he hadn't seen her since their meal out at The Ugly Duckling. He wasn't sure if he was avoiding her or if it were the other way around.

A skip had arrived in the morning and was already filled with mattresses and broken kitchen cupboards. Ned glanced over the top as he passed it by in the driveway. A pile of mouldy shower curtains were strewn across a cracked sink and a rusty pipe. He looked around at the unloved front garden and let out a long breath.

*What I could do with this section alone.*

He glanced over at the rundown building. Its haunted house appeal was the only thing going for it.

*What a money pit.*

He could hear muffled voices coming from inside and figured he was the latecomer. He had an excuse. He didn't want to go, but he would use the excuse that his babysitter was running late, even though Suzie was already at the hotel, working.

Belle stepped outside to place a filled bin bag down to one side. He caught her eye and she waved. There was no turning back now. If he were to lie about why he turned around and went straight back home, it would have to be spectacular, and he couldn't think up that kind of lie that quickly. She was watching him, waiting. He swore under his breath and approached with a fake smile.

'Thought you weren't coming,' she said, wiping her hands down her baggy top.

'Yeah, sorry, babysitter was late.'

'Oh, okay. Come in. Grab a cloth or something.'

He followed her into the foyer and arched an eyebrow at how much better it looked since his last visit. He said hello to Joey as she passed him by with an empty mop bucket, then asked who else had turned up.

'Me, that's who,' said Josh, Joey's husband. 'I'm supervising my wife so she doesn't overexert herself.'

Ned smiled over at him before he disappeared down the stairway to the kitchen. He felt Belle's body lean on the back of his arm.

'How dreamy is Joey's husband,' she whispered.

He glanced over his shoulder at her and frowned. 'If you like that sort of thing.' He stilled as her hand rested on his back as though it belonged there, touching him, holding him. He took a step away and turned. 'Where do you want me?'

The twinkle in her eye didn't go unnoticed, and he had a sudden urge to take her upstairs to one of the bedrooms. She went to speak but was interrupted by Tessie Walker, a short red-headed woman with the cutest freckles and the biggest smile. She grabbed Ned and pulled him down so that she could kiss his cheek.

'About time you turned up, Renshaw.'

'Yes, yes, I'm here now, Tess. You on your own?'

She nodded, and her head of curls bounced. 'Girls have got homework, and Nate's asleep.' She turned to Belle. 'He gets up before dawn, so I didn't want to wake him. Life on our dairy farm is endless lately. I think we might have to hire some extra staff soon.' She shrugged casually. 'Our business just keeps on growing.'

'That's good to hear, Tess,' said Ned.

'Right, let's get on. I'm on dining room duty. We need to make sure Belle's business is booming one day soon too.'

Ned pursed his lips tightly as she walked away.

Belle tapped his arm. 'I think everyone forgets we're competition.'

He lowered his gaze to her small hand resting on his biceps and had to snap himself out of his hazy, faraway stare. 'Right. Tell me what to do.'

She looked around. 'Erm, Rosie and Elliot are upstairs in one of the bedrooms, hopefully cleaning it. Scott Harper is around here somewhere. Do you know him? He works with Anna in The Book Gallery, but he wasn't there that day we went inside, so I didn't get to meet him until about an hour ago. Joey brought him and his partner, Dolly. She's already been talking to Rosie about her gift shop in Pepper Lane. Told Rosie that if she starts making pottery pieces again, she can sell them there. That was nice of her, wasn't it?'

Ned nodded slowly whilst staring at the stairs.

Belle continued, 'I think Dolly and Scott are in the lounge area, or whatever you want to call that tip of a room.'

'Yes, by the way, I do know who Scott is. He's a local artist. We have some of his pictures in our inn. He's very good.'

Belle sighed out a laugh. 'I keep forgetting you lot all know each other around here. It's such a small place, really, isn't it?'

'Too small.'

He swallowed down a lump of dryness that had formed as Belle grabbed his hand so naturally and tugged him towards the stairs. 'Come on. You can help in one of the rooms. I'm about to start cleaning windows, but I'm going to have to hire someone to do the outside. I don't have a ladder that big.'

'Erm, I'll give you the number of our window cleaner.'

'Okay, thanks.'

For some reason, Ned felt like the pleasantries passing between them were forced. Well, they were from his end. Belle seemed to be oblivious to how awkward he was feeling around her. She was holding his hand, and she had kept touching him from the moment he stepped inside, and she was chatting away happily as though they were old friends, and she couldn't stop smiling at him.

She guided him into a bedroom on the first level. 'I was about to start in here, if you want to join me. The windows need doing and the bathroom, framework, and skirting. Basically, everything.

Ned stared at the white metal bedframe missing a mattress. It reminded him of a hospital bed, just double in size. 'Are you keeping that?'

'Yes, why?'

'It's not exactly… classy.'

'We thought it might make a bit of a rattle in the night, and as we've decided to go for a haunted hotel, it was fitting.'

'Haunted hotel?'

'Yes, well, look at the place. What would you do with it?'

Ned knew exactly what he would do with the place, because he had mulled over the idea with his brother many times throughout the years.

'Anyway,' said Belle. 'We wanted something that was so different to your place. That way, we won't really be your competition anymore. The people who would want to stay here wouldn't stay at yours and vice versa. That's the plan.'

She was studying his expression, he guessed for any signs of a truce, so he just nodded and made a low noncommittal sound. He went to look at what state the small side bathroom was in and turned his nose up immediately.

'Belle, you're going to need to rip this shower out and start again, and you can't keep that toilet either.'

'What's wrong with the loo,' she asked, approaching. She placed her hand on his arm again whilst she peered around him. 'Ooh, I see what you mean. Goodness, that's more money.'

His irritated emotion got the better of him. He spun around sharply, nearly knocking her over. 'Why do you keep touching me?'

She took a wobbly step back. 'I'm sorry. I didn't know I was.'

He swore under his breath at himself as she went back into the bedroom to clean a window.

'Erm, you don't have to clean in there. There's no point if we have to rip it out.' Her voice was quiet with a slight shake to her exhale.

He took a calming breath and found himself standing behind her. She didn't stop cleaning, so he raised his hand and placed it over hers to get her to stop.

'You're touching me now,' she said flatly.

He lowered his head to rest it on the back of hers. 'God, Belle, I'm such an arsehole. I'm so sorry. I'm just... I...'

She spun around so quickly, his arm fell down like a heavy weight. 'You're what, Ned?'

He jolted at her snap. Her eyes were filled with contempt, but he could also see the hurt he had just caused.

'Confused,' he admitted.

She pushed him in the chest to move him out of her way. 'Yeah, well, so am I, mate.'

'Belle, please don't leave.'

She stopped in the doorway, then walked back to him. She kept her voice steady and low. 'I get the feeling you don't want me near you.'

'I want you more than near me, Belle. That's the problem.' He waited for a response, but her opened mouth had closed again.

The taste of detergent was on his tongue, causing him to swallow down the chemical and reach for fresh air. He moved to open a window, drew breath, and faced her again.

'Something has grown between us, hasn't it?' he asked, feeling the words catch in his throat.

She nodded slowly and lowered her eyes to the dirty floorboards.

His jaw was tense with frustration. 'I've not been with anyone since Penny…'

'You don't have to explain, Ned.'

*I do.*

'Look at me, Belle.' He waited for her eyes to roll his way, then he stepped closer and placed one hand on her chin. 'I feel guilty for every touch, every look, and every feeling I get when I'm near you.'

'I understand,' she whispered.

'I don't know what to do, Belle.'

She turned her face into his hand and closed her eyes for a moment. 'I don't either.'

Ned stepped even closer and held her in his arms. Her face pressed into his chest, and her hands clasped his back as he silently fought back disappointment. He could feel her breathing against him and wondered if she could feel his racing heart. She softened further into his arms, and he lowered his head to rest his mouth on her hair. The smell of his shampoo was long gone and sorely missed.

She rolled her head up his body to look in his eyes, and he could tell she didn't want to express herself incorrectly, but she obviously had something to say. 'How about if you go home now. I'll tell the others that you didn't feel very well. Then, we can spend some more time apart. Maybe if we're not in each other's faces all the time, our brains will figure out how best to handle this situation.'

He avoided her eyes as he processed the idea. Part of him thought it sounded like a plan, and another part of him hated the idea.

*Argh! I want to rip my head off right now.*

'Do you want to do that?' he asked quietly, trying to keep some composure in amongst the growing madness.

She gave a half-shrug. 'I've never been in this situation before, Ned, so I don't know what to do for the best. All I know is that I have strong feelings for you and that I want to get to know you, and, right now, I just want to rip your clothes off and snog you until I get kaleidoscope eyes and need a defibrillator.'

Ned was fighting back a smile, but it surged through, giving a moment of respite to the shadow of disappointment that had covered his heart. He slowly traced one finger over her lips whilst controlling his breathing. He watched her eyes close and her chest rise, then relax. She was beautiful, and he wanted her so much, but she was right. They needed head space. Well, he did.

'Kiss me, Ned, before you go,' she whispered, still with her eyes closed and mouth facing his way.

His stomach flipped as agony entered his heart. Slowly, he dipped his head and tenderly kissed her mouth. He stayed there for a moment, then gently parted her lips, breathing in her warmth. She tasted like she'd not long eaten something sweet. He'd heard on the grapevine that Joey had a craving for Jelly Babies, so assumed they were floating around. The slight breaths they took in between kisses made his head light and his heart miss beats. Their tongues were gliding over each other's so softly, it relaxed his weary soul. There was nowhere he would rather be than right there in that dusty room, locked together in an embrace with Bluebell Trent. It took every ounce of a strength he never knew he had to pull away and leave.

# 23

*Belle*

As the days all seemed to roll over into one, Belle found herself pining for Ned more and more. It had been two weeks. December had arrived and snow had covered the ground, making everything outside the Inn on the Right look so much cleaner than it was, and even when Kasey had wandered onto their side with Tinks to build a snowman, Ned didn't appear with her.

Rosie was still seeing Elliot every day, but she wasn't sleeping over, not wanting to leave her sister alone, even though Belle told her that she didn't mind.

Belle kept herself occupied with lots of trips to the DIY shop, a bit of Christmas shopping, and choir practice. She had taken Daphne up on her job offer and had just got back from her interview.

'How did it go?' asked Rosie.

'Good. I think.' She walked across the foyer. 'I'm just going to pop to the loo, then I'm going for a walk to The Post Office Shop to get some stamps for our Christmas cards. They have one of those post boxes built into the wall there, so I'll post them at the same time. Do you fancy a walk?'

Rosie kicked off her yellow slippers. 'Ooh, yes. I've not been there yet.'

Belle got herself ready, had a glass of water, and ventured back outside.

Rosie was smiling at their wellies crunching in the snow. 'We're welly-wearing women now, Belle.'

'We're nice and warm and dry women.'

Rosie kicked some snow her way, then stopped to take in the picturesque scene of the small bridge where Belle had played Poohsticks with Ned. 'Oh, wow! How pretty is that.'

The memory of her day spent with Ned filled Belle's heart so much, she felt her cheeks warm. She wished she could go back to that day. She felt so helpless. There wasn't anything she could do about Ned. He was the one who needed to figure out what he wanted. If he could move forward with his life. Belle already knew she wanted to be with him. She knew how much her feelings for him had grown.

'Rosie, I need to tell you something,' she said, crossing the bridge.

'Oh?'

'It's about me and Ned.'

Rosie's happy smile disappeared. 'Oh no, what have you done?'

Belle's eye filled with humour. 'Hey, don't look at me like that. I haven't done anything. Well, maybe I have.'

Rosie slotted her arm through Belle's. 'I'm sure whatever it is, I can make things right again. I'll talk to Elliot, and we'll fix the problem between you and Ned. Did Ned start this issue?'

Belle shook her head. 'Rosie, it's not what you think. We haven't been at war or anything. We've just, well, we've, more like I've…'

'Spit it out, Belle. I'm losing the will to live here.'

'I think I might have fallen for him ever so slightly. A lot.'

Rosie's grip on her tightened as she released a quiet squeal.

Belle lowered her gaze to the snow beneath her wellies. 'Don't get excited. See. This is why I didn't tell you. I knew you'd go and buy a wedding hat.'

'Hey, I can get excited about my sister finally having a love life.'

Belle scoffed. 'I haven't got a love life. I just like someone. There's a difference.'

'Have you told him?'

'He knows.'

Rosie stopped talking for a moment to take in the view of Dreamcatcher Farm and The Post Office Shop. 'It's like stepping into a painting, isn't it?'

Belle nodded and smiled at the beauty of their surroundings. 'It really is. I'm glad we moved here, even though I might have to go back to work to help fund our new life.'

Rosie turned her way. 'Do you want me to start making pottery pieces again?'

'That's up to you. We're all right financially for a while, but it doesn't hurt to have some backup funds. You still have so many clients emailing you for new pieces. Your crockery is well loved, Rosie, but I only want you to do what makes you feel happy.'

A slow smile crept onto her face as though she couldn't hold it back. 'You and Ned make me happy. I would love that.'

Belle rolled her eyes. 'Yes, that's because you're a soppy old romantic.'

'So, what's Ned's take on this?' Rosie asked, tugging Belle's arm towards the shop.

'He hasn't had a relationship since his partner died, and he feels guilty about having feelings for me.'

Rosie pushed on the wooden door to the shop, trying not to disturb the precariously hanging Christmas wreath attached. 'Oh, that's quite sad. That's something only he can work out.'

Belle sighed quietly as she entered the shop. 'I know.'

They stood in the doorway and glanced around the farm shop that doubled up as a post office. There were a few aisles filled with food items, medical supplies, and household goods. Over to one side was a counter, with a grey till sitting on top and a few glass jars holding candy canes. Opposite was an area for freshly baked bread, organic farm eggs, and fresh fruit and veg. The shop felt cold, and the air smelled like a bakery. Dark wooden beams lined the low ceiling, and plain cream paint filled the walls. Twinkling fairy lights were haphazardly strewn across the wall behind the counter where a medium-built woman with dark hair, a pretty smile, and big chocolate eyes stood. She looked to be around the same age as the two sisters walking towards her.

'Good morning, or is it lunchtime yet?' She glanced at the thin gold watch attached to her right wrist.

'Almost twelve,' said Belle, checking her phone.

The woman looked back up. 'So it is. This morning has flown by. I hope you haven't come for any freshly baked bread. I didn't make many loaves this morning, and they've all gone already.'

Belle smiled at her friendly manner. 'Yes, I heard you have to get in quick.'

'Who told you that?'

'Ned Renshaw.'

The woman nodded. 'Aw, yes, well, he would know. He's one of my regulars. Hey, are you two the Trent sisters

I've been hearing about? I can see you look like each other. You have to be sisters.'

Rosie pulled out a wrapped candy cane from one of the jars. 'Yes, I'm Rosie and this is Belle, and I'm definitely buying one of these.'

Belle nudged her, telling her to pull out a few more to place on their Christmas tree.

'So pleased to finally put faces to the names. I'm Matilda Sheridan, but everyone calls me Tilly. My parents own Dreamcatcher Farm, and yes, I still live with my parents. Well, sort of. I live upstairs, but this is still owned by them.'

Belle breathed out a laugh. 'Don't worry, I lived with our dad for years. It helped me save a lot of my money. Maybe one day you can buy this place from them. It's a beautiful little cottage. I'd love a home like this.'

Tilly nodded. 'It's my favourite place in the world. Not that I've seen the world, but I reckon if I did go off and see the world, this would still be my favourite place.'

Rosie scrunched her nose as she pulled out her purse to pay for the candy canes. 'I've never had a favourite place.'

'Oh, didn't you fall in love with the Inn on the Right?' asked Tilly, taking the money and putting it in the till.

Rosie and Belle scoffed at the same time. 'No.'

Tilly held a sympathetic smile. 'Fair enough. It is a bit rundown. I guess it's more of an acquired taste.'

'You can say that again,' said Rosie, unwrapping her candy cane.

'Are you going to keep it as a hotel or just convert it into your forever home?' asked Tilly.

'We keep changing our mind,' said Belle, feeling there was no point sugar-coating it. 'We don't really know anything about the hotel world. I'm a nursery teacher and Rosie's a potter.'

'Ooh, I love pottery. I have the most wonderful crockery collection upstairs.'

'Then, you would love Rosie's work,' said Belle, smiling at her sister.

Tilly's big dark eyes widened. 'Wait a minute. Your name's Rosie Trent. My dinner set is Primrose Trent. Is there a connection here?'

Rosie smiled. 'That's me.'

Tilly went into fan mode. 'Oh, wow, your work is so beautiful. I always get compliments about my coffee mugs whenever someone stays for tea. I'm on your mailing list, and I have your online shop listed as my favourites.'

Rosie blushed slightly. 'Thank you so much for buying my work. I'm glad you like it. I haven't made anything new for a while now, so it's nice to know that my old stuff is still being appreciated.'

'Oh, please make some new pieces. I'd buy some.'

Rosie gave a noncommittal nod. 'I'll think about it. We have a lot on at the moment with the inn.'

'So, what can I do for you today, or have you just come for a browse?'

'Actually, I want to buy some stamps,' said Belle, reaching for her stack of Christmas cards and placing them on the counter. 'First class, please. I'm going to need twelve.'

Tilly opened the till and pulled out a book of stamps. 'I haven't sent mine off yet. I feel really behind this year. It's been a bit crazy round here lately. My head's not been in it.'

Rosie huffed. 'I know what you mean about not having your head in the game. We bought a Christmas tree a while back just to remind us what time of the year it is.'

'I used to put a tree up in here, but the baubles always get knocked, so I gave up with that idea in the end.'

'I like the one outside.' Rosie pointed to a small square window.

'Yeah, it's nice to have some twinkling lights outside. It can get a bit dark on the farm come nightfall, and Rory, that's my partner, is always tripping over, bless him. He's not been here long, so doesn't know all the holes yet, and there are no streetlamps along Walk Walk Road to help.'

'Why's it called that?' asked Rosie.

Tilly shrugged. 'Not sure.'

'Have you always lived here?' Belle asked.

Tilly held a proud smile. 'Yep. Born and bred. My mum had us all in the house.'

Rosie raised her brow. 'Goodness. I couldn't imagine having a baby at home.'

'Nor me,' said Tilly. 'Not something I have to worry about now at my age.'

Rosie scoffed. 'What! You're still young, Tilly.'

Tilly smiled widely. 'I'm older than I look. I'm fifty now.'

The two sisters did not hide their surprise.

'Wow, you look my age,' said Rosie. 'And I'm thirty-three.'

'Thanks. We have young genes in our family.'

'Do you have a big family, Tilly? It's only me and Belle in ours.'

'Yeah, there are a few of us. I just didn't get around to having any children of my own. Still, I have a lovely man that I get wrapped up in every night who completes my life.'

Rosie held a dreamy look. 'I love being wrapped up in my man's arms too.'

Belle stopped attaching stamps to her cards when Tilly's enquiring eyes turned her way. She knew exactly what she was about to be asked. 'No, I'm not wrapped up in anyone's arms. Ooh, let me quickly pick up some plasters while we're here.' She trotted off down one of the aisles. 'Nope, no one for me,' she called out. Then she mumbled to herself, 'No one wants me.'

'I know some single men,' called back Tilly.

Belle heard the smile in her voice and knew that Rosie would be grinning as though she's just read another one of her romance novels. The last thing Belle needed was to be set up with anyone, or worse, forced on a blind date. Nope, that would never do. There was no room for anyone else, for a start. Ned filled every part of her mind and heart. She would love to be wrapped up in him, but that wasn't something she was about to broadcast down the local shop.

'No, thanks, Tilly. I don't want a man, kids, relationships, responsibilities, or...' She stopped talking as she approached the counter to see Ned standing there. His eyes were on her, and Tilly was rolling hers sideways at him behind his back, trying to point out that there was an eligible bachelor standing right there in front of her.

Ned turned to Tilly whilst pulling out his wallet. 'Here's what we owe from yesterday. At least today I remembered my wallet.'

Tilly took the money from him and placed it in the till. 'That's the first time you've done that, Ned. Where's your head at lately?'

Belle closed her gaping mouth as Ned smiled politely at Tilly.

'It's Christmas,' he told her. 'There's always lots going on. Anyway, I'll see you tomorrow.'

Belle had no idea whether she should speak to him or not. He left the shop without saying another word, and she just knew that what he had overheard her say hurt him, if only a little bit. She dropped her shoulders and went to pay for the plasters. She felt like ripping open the box and sticking a large knee plaster straight over her big mouth.

# 24

*Elliot*

Elliot was pretty sure he heard a sniffle coming from his brother's bedroom as he passed it by. He stopped walking and listened for a moment. There. He knew he heard something. He thought that Ned was out on a late-night run, and he knew Kasey was fast asleep, because he had read her a bedtime story and tucked her in, so he slowly opened the door to see who was inside.

Ned was sitting on the bed, with his back facing Elliot. He had his head buried into his hands and was quietly crying. Elliot quickly entered and closed the door, causing Ned to jump and glance over his shoulder.

*He doesn't look good at all.*

'Hey, Ned, what's happened?'

Ned turned away, and Elliot sat by his side and put his arm around him.

'Talk to me, Ned. Have we just had bad news?'

Ned shook his head slowly. 'No. Nothing like that. No one's died. I'm just having a moment, that's all.'

*I think you've been having a lot of those lately.*

Elliot pulled him closer and kissed the side of his head. 'What's caused this?'

Ned's gaze was firmly on his lap as he wiped his eyes. 'I'm tired, Elliot.'

'Yeah, I can see, but why, Ned? I need you to talk to me.'

Ned straightened and wiped his nose with the tissue that was scrunched in his hand. 'I'm just messing everything up.'

'What have you done?'

Ned breathed out a long and steady sigh. 'I have a situation that I don't know how to deal with.'

'Okay. Well, a problem shared and all that.'

Ned glanced at him. 'I don't think you can help with this one, mate.'

*I'll do anything for you. You're my little brother. I'll find a way to help. I promise.*

Elliot smiled warmly. If there was one thing life had taught him, it was to talk over thoughts and feelings and not bottle things up. He had regular chats with his aunt, and he always felt refreshed afterwards. He wasn't about to let Ned shut up shop. Talking wasn't for everyone, and Ned wasn't much of a fan, but Elliot needed his little brother's shoulders to drop the heavy weight that was clearly holding him down.

'Try me, Ned.'

Ned chewed on his lip for a moment, then raised his head a touch and shuffled around to face his brother.

Elliot's eyes widened along with his kind smile. 'Come on. Whatever it is, we'll figure it out.'

'I've gone and fallen for Bluebell Trent.'

*Thank God. I was starting to worry he'd done something stupid.*

Elliot pursed his lips, then slowly nodded. 'Okay.'

'She likes me too.'

'Well, that's good.'

Ned arched an eyebrow. 'I can't go there, Elliot.'

Elliot huffed out a loud sigh. 'Come on, Ned. You can't let this stupid family feud affect you. I'm sure as hell not allowing it to interfere in my life. I love Rosie. She's the best thing that's happened to me in a long while. I'm not about to let her go because the Ghost of Pepper River Inn said so.'

Ned muffled his laugh. 'It's not that ghost.' He stopped smiling. 'It's another ghost.'

'Ah, Penny.'

'Yeah.'

'You feel guilty for liking someone.'

Ned nodded. 'Yep.'

'I don't know what to say, Ned. I think that Penny wouldn't expect you to never fall in love again. You can't stop living because she died. Your life still goes on. I know it's not fair, but what else is anyone supposed to do?' He moved his arm from Ned's shoulder and tapped his hand. 'You survived. You have to live your life.'

Ned sighed. 'Sometimes I wish it wasn't me who survived.'

*I remember. I'll never forget that look in your eyes when I had to break the news of her death to you. It will haunt me forever. But you can't be haunted forever. I won't let that happen to you. You need to feel free. To live. You can't carry a guilt that isn't yours to carry. I won't allow this to ruin your life. I want you to want to live, to feel, to love again. I want you to enjoy life.*

'I read somewhere once that a lot of survivors feel that way, Ned. It's quite common.'

'I don't want this in my life, Elliot. I was happy before she came along. I was doing all right. I've been fine all these years on my own. Why now? Why her? Why anyone? I don't want anyone.'

'Clearly, you do.'

*I think you always have. We all want someone to hold our hand from time to time. You're no different. You've just been ignoring the feeling. Distracting yourself from your thoughts. You're having to face yourself right now. That's your problem. Finally, you're looking straight at the subject. No more hiding, Ned. Time to face life again.*

Ned stood and approached the window. 'I'm just going to shake it off. It's not my fault I've got feelings. That just happens without our input, but I can choose not to act on those feelings.'

'And how's that working out for you?'

Ned turned with a suppressed smile. He pointed towards his sore eyes and sighed. 'My brain feels so fried right now.'

'Have you spoken to Belle about any of this?'

'Not really. She knows it's about Penny, not her, but I don't expect her to understand. I don't want a deep and meaningful with her, anyway. I've been avoiding her, but I saw her this morning in The Post Office Shop. She was telling Tilly how happy she is to be single, blah, blah, blah. I couldn't even look at her. I knew she was lying through her teeth, but that wasn't the problem. Seeing her was like a punch straight in the solar plexus. Do you know how hard it is not to be able to put your arms around the person you want to hold so much?'

Elliot nodded. 'I've been there.'

Ned sat back down. 'What would you do if this was your situation?'

'It's tricky to answer because I haven't got the emotional attachment that you have. I've never lost a partner, so I can't say how that would make me feel in the long run. I just know that, as harsh at it is, life goes on, and we have to move forward with it. Of course, you can choose to stay single forever. There aren't any rules, but you do have to do what feels right for you. If you really want this woman in your life, you'll only feel miserable without her. If I'm honest, Ned, I think you've already made your mind up that you want to give it a go, and that's why you're in this state. If you were adamant that you weren't going to pursue this, you wouldn't be feeling so wrecked.'

'I've reached a point where I don't actually want to think anymore. My mind's exhausted. I'm drinking every night, I'm tired every morning. I've hardly exercised, and I ate all of Kasey's Christmas selection box. I'm going to have to replace that.'

Elliot laughed quietly. 'I think a good run in the morning will help you, in many ways.'

'Yeah, you're right. It always clears my head. I need to sort myself out. Get back on track. I'm complicating the issue.'

'No, you're not, Ned. It's perfectly normal for you to feel like you're cheating on Penny. As long as you know, you're not. Penny was a lovely woman. She would want you and Kasey to be happy. Deep down, you know that.'

Ned gestured towards the door. 'Go on. I'm all right now. I'm going to get some sleep.'

*Not sure I want to move. Maybe I should wait till he drifts off. He's got that look in his eyes. He wants me to go. Okay. I'll leave. He seems a lot better now he's got that load off his chest. I'll give him some space. He needs a good sleep.*

Elliot headed for the door. 'You know where I am.'

'Thanks, Elliot.'

'Goodnight, Ned.'

# 25

## *Ned*

Penny was floating on her back in the middle of the ocean. Long tendrils of strawberry-red hair splayed out around her. Her shimmering pink mermaid's tail flapped gently on the water. She was smiling as the sun started to set on the horizon behind her.

Ned was floating on his back by her side. Their fingertips brushing against each other's every time the motion of the waves gently moved their bodies.

'The water's so warm today, Ned.' Her soft voice soothed his weary soul, and every time her skin touched his, love rippled through his heart.

'Why are we here, Penny?'

'Why are we anywhere?'

'That's not an answer.'

'What do you want to hear me say, Ned?'

Water clogged his ears, making her voice sound muffled for a moment. She lowered her tail and bobbed close to his face. He felt her lips press lightly down onto his, and he closed his eyes and relaxed. Penny pulled him beneath the water level, and he opened his eyes to see her beautiful smile. He smiled back and kissed her again. Small bubbles left his mouth and a rush of air filled his lungs, allowing him to breathe beneath the ocean.

The sun had almost set by the time he resurfaced. Streaks of fire lit the sky, and the water felt colder.

Penny appeared in front of him and held on to his shoulders. 'I love you, Ned, but you have to go now.'

He shook his head. His heart was racing, and he started to feel anger bubbling. 'No. You can't leave me.'

'I'll never leave you. I live on in our daughter.'

'I want you to live with me.'

Penny wiped away some of the tears that were rolling down his pale cheeks. 'I wish I could, Ned, but it's time now for you to let someone else live with you.'

'No, Penny. I don't want anyone else.'

She tenderly kissed the tip of his nose. 'You're going to be fine, Ned. Everything is going to be fine. The flowers are blooming now. Look. See.'

He turned his head to see a beautiful field of hundreds of bluebells stretching far and wide.

A jolt shot through him, and he shot upright in his bed. His hands immediately touched his damp face. 'Christ!' He glanced over at the black alarm clock on his bedside cabinet. It was five in the morning. He swore under his breath and inhaled and exhaled slowly. 'Oh, Penny. What are you doing to me?' Flopping back onto his pillow, he stared blankly up at the ceiling and took another slow breath. 'Now I'm even crying in my sleep.' He wiped over his face, cleaning away the evidence. 'Sod it. I'm getting up. I need a run.'

The cold water that he washed in only reminded him of his weird mermaid dream, which he blamed on Kasey's obsession with The Little Mermaid. If he had to sit through that film one more time, he was sure that would be the next thing to make him cry.

He changed into his running clothes at record speed and headed down to the kitchen. He drank a mouthful of water to take away the dryness in his throat and went out to the foyer to warm up and set his fitness tracker. He felt as though he hadn't had a wink of sleep, and his stomach was rumbling, crying out for a full English.

He stepped outside into the cold and shivered, then powerwalked to the end of the driveway. It was dark and quiet as he went into a slow jog. The icy air hit his cheeks, and he wished he had put on his running mask. His gloved hands pulled down the dark woolly hat that he was wearing, covering his ears from the chill. He could see the air escaping his mouth and focused on his breathing as he picked up the pace.

*It's too cold to run. I shouldn't be out here. I don't care. Run. Just run. Let it burn. Let it hurt. Don't think. Just keep running.*

The snow had been pushed off the road along the bottom of Wishing Point, causing a mound to each side, which made Ned jog on the tarmac. He turned off and ran along bumpy grass until he met with the pathway that took him towards Sandly View. He was making good time and felt energised, even though the back of his throat was burning slightly. He focused again on his breathing technique and carried on along the roadside. A patch of ice caused him to wobble. His heart flipped as his legs sprawled in opposite directions. He managed to keep upright, which felt like a miracle, and stopped for a second to compose himself.

'Bloody hell!'

It was too cold to stand still, and he didn't want his body to start cooling down, so he side-stepped the icy patch and went to start running again, but something caught his eye. He squinted into the near distance at a small figure limping towards him.

*Is that...?*

As the woman came closer, he could clearly see that it was exactly who he thought it was.

'Belle?'

She stopped, doubled-over, and waved one hand in the air, as though she was attempting some awkward yoga manoeuvre. 'I'm fine.'

The fact that he had seen her limping, her hair was damp and stringy, she was clearly struggling with her breathing, and on closer inspection there was a large lump under her right eye proved she was lying about how she was actually feeling.

Ned grabbed her by the waist, giving her something to lean on. 'What the hell happened to you?'

She straightened from clutching her side and seemed relieved to flop on him for support. 'A speeding black sports car with a big fat exhaust that sonic-boomed me, that's what. It came that close to me, I swear it swiped the fibres on my sleeve. I jumped out the way, buckled on the side of a small ditch back there, and fell on my face. I think I've twisted my ankle. I can just about walk.' She looked into his eyes and smiled. 'So, how's your morning going?'

After his mermaid dream, he didn't really think his morning could get any weirder.

'Well, I just saved myself from a patch of evil ice that I believe laughed at me, and now I think we need to get you to hospital.'

She waved away his suggestion. 'I don't need to go to the hospital. I just need to get home, have a hot bath, and a nice cup of tea wouldn't go amiss.'

He sighed loudly, showing his annoyance at her stubbornness. 'Hold on.'

'To what?'

He quickly swiped her up into his arms as though carrying his bride. 'Me.'

Her blushing face appeared to at least warm her for a moment. Either that or it was ice burn. The bitterness in the air had certainly pinched his cheeks.

'You don't have to carry me, Ned. I can walk, you know.'

He rolled his eyes her way. 'Really?'

'Well, okay, it's painful to walk, but still. I feel like a right idiot. What if someone sees?'

He glanced around at their deserted surroundings, then stopped walking to grin at her. 'Just so you know, I really want to kiss you right now, but I can't feel my lips, so I won't, but if it weren't for all this snow, I'd place you down on the ground and do a whole lot more than kiss.'

Belle was clearly holding her breath for a moment, because her exhale rushed out in a desperate attempt to escape her lungs. 'Oh, Ned. I want you to do all that to me.'

He locked eyes with her and carried on walking. He had to get her home before they both froze to death. 'What are you even doing going for a run this early in this weather?'

She sniffed back the cold air as she arched her brow. 'I was channelling my inner Rocky. Rocky 4, to be precise. Although, Stallone can keep it. Running in snow isn't as easy as he made it look. Anyway, you can talk. You're out here too.'

'I needed to clear my head.'

Belle moved her face closer to his and pressed her damp nose into his cold cheek. He wasn't entirely sure if she kissed him. His face was that numb, she could have punched him and he wouldn't have felt a thing.

'What's going on in your head, Edward Renshaw?'

'You.'

Her arms tightened around his neck and he jolted her up to get a better grip. His shoulders were starting to burn from her weight and his leg was aching, so he was glad when Wishing Point came back into view.

'Why don't I try walking for a bit, Ned. You need a rest. I know I'm starting to get heavy.'

'I'm fine.'

'You're not. How about we shift the weight then. I'll get on your back.'

'Okay.'

Belle slid out of his arms as he gently lowered her feet to the ground. He turned, taking a silent breath, readying himself, and she clambered onto his back. Her face snuggled into his cheek again, making him attempt a smile, but it was held back by winter's answer to Botox.

'Thanks for this, Ned.' Her teeth chattered in his ear.

He glanced down at her hands below his chin and noticed for the first time that she wasn't wearing gloves. He huffed to himself. 'Take my gloves off me, will you. My hands are sweating.'

She did as she was asked and held them.

'You can put them on if you like, Belle.'

She quickly slipped her hands into his large gloves, and he smiled inwardly. 'Ooh, Ned, I can't wait to have a long hot soak in the bath.'

'Me too.'

Her ear nuzzled into the side of his hat. 'You can get in with me if you want.'

He laughed out loud, then winced as he felt the skin on his lips crack.

'I'm not joking, Ned. I'd love to have a bath with you.'

'Fine. I'll take you back to mine, and we can bath there. My bath's much bigger than any of yours, so it makes sense.'

She giggled in his ear, warming his blood. 'Are you really going to bath with me?'

'I think the term is, defrost with you.'

He was pretty sure she did kiss his cheek, or perhaps she was just warming her dripping nose. 'Then, after our bath, we're sorting out your injuries.'

'Deal,' she replied quickly. 'Although, I might want to take you to bed.'

'I think we'll see how that goes. You've sprained your ankle and will have a lovely shiner come up on your eye in a bit.'

'Oh, is it bad?'

'You survived round one.'

'Great! I hope it goes away by the time our show is on. I can't sing "Provincial Life" looking like I've just been beaten up by Gaston. What will the children think?'

'Well, at least you've stopped calling me Gaston.'

'Who told you that?'

He laughed along with her as they reached the top of their divided hotels.

*Come on, leg. Hold on. Just a few more steps. Almost there. Nearly home.*

'Do you really want to come back to mine, Belle?'

'Yes. I'm really looking forward to our bath now.'

'Okay, let's do this. We've got about an hour before everyone wakes up.'

'Ooh, a whole hour. What can I do to you in that time?'

He tried not to laugh. 'You're not doing anything to me, Mrs Renshaw. I'm going to look after you.'

*If I don't die first.*

Belle snuffled his ear. 'I look forward to it.'

# 26

*Belle*

After a quick detour to the kitchen to grab a tea towel and a bag of frozen peas, Ned carried Belle into his bedroom. He placed her on the bed, and she watched his eyes darken as he stilled for a moment. She grinned mischievously at him and only stopped smiling when he plopped the wrapped frozen peas over her eye. He then went off into his private bathroom to run the bath.

Belle tried to roll her ankle around but winced as soon as it moved. 'Ow! That's not good.' Her face was just starting to defrost and the peas weren't welcome. She removed them from her eye and bent over to untie her trainers.

Ned came out of the bathroom, wearing only a navy towel wrapped around his waist and another one draped over his arm.

*Oh, you look so good, Edward Renshaw. Do you even know what I'm thinking right now? Do you want to know?*

He awkwardly lowered himself to her feet, obviously feeling some pain himself.

'Ned, are you okay?'

'I'm fine.'

'You're not. Your leg is hurting.'

'Let's just get you sorted.' He helped remove her footwear and socks and placed the spare towel next to her on the bed and then lifted her hand holding the peas back to her eye.

She groaned, flinching away. 'It's cold.'

'It will help with the swelling.'

'I know, but it's cold.'

He paused for a moment, his hand hesitating over her thigh. 'Am I allowed to help you remove the rest of your clothes?'

A feeling of excitement outweighed any nervousness that dared to show. She was happy for him to remove everything. She was hoping he might forget about all the pain in the room and just rest her gently backwards on the bed and lean over her. He'd already seen her scars, and she was looking at some of his as he trailed his hand slowly over her knee. 'If you wouldn't mind.'

He grinned, leaned over her, forcing her body back a touch, and waited.

Belle made sure her warm and steady breathing was hitting him straight around his ear.

His lips slowly parted as he turned to meet her mouth. 'Lift your bum so I can roll your bottoms down your legs,' he whispered.

She swallowed hard and produced a small smile, which quickly disappeared when he reached her bad ankle. 'Ow!'

'It's okay,' he told her softly. 'Nice and slow.'

She watched him concentrate, then shake his head.

'We need to get this checked out, Belle. It's really swollen.'

'I will, I promise, just let me have my bath with you first.'

*I don't even care that I'm pleading with him. I know I sound like a soppy fool, but I just do not care. Not one bit. Look at him. Why would I? I'm having my bath, and he's coming with me. Sod this pain. I'm going to ignore it all. Ouch! It bloody hurts.*

His bright eyes rolled up to meet hers and a thump hit her straight in the heart.

*How does anyone get to be that gorgeous?*

'What are you grinning about, Mrs Renshaw?'

Belle couldn't resist. She pulled him close and went to kiss him, but the peas got in the way, and when she tried to remove them, he placed them back.

'I just wanted a quick kiss,' she mumbled, attempting a fake sulk, even though she felt like sulking for real, the amount of pain she was in.

He tilted his head and manoeuvred under the peas to find her lips.

It was only a slight peck, but Belle had well and truly melted.

Ned creaked his way to a stand and winced. 'Let me turn the bath off. You can wrap that towel around you. I'll be back in a minute to carry you in. Put the peas on your ankle for now.'

She tried to place the peas down her leg, but they slid off her toes and plopped to the floor. She ignored the bag and removed the rest of her clothes, struggling with her sports bra, which challenged her after any exercise. Her shoulders did not have the energy for the fight, but she persevered and finally whipped the thing off. Catching her breath, she wrapped herself inside Ned's soft towel and made a mental note to buy new ones for herself. She quickly checked the label to see where he bought his.

He limped back out of the bathroom and leant on the doorframe. 'You've lost the peas.'

She looked up, giving her best innocent expression. 'I had to use both hands to get out of the rest of my clothes, seeing how you gave up undressing me.'

'Hmm.'

'I'm ready now.' She hit him with a sweet smile and waited for his strong arms to hold her. 'Just help me. I don't want you carrying me. You're in pain too.'

'No chance.' He grinned as he swooped her up and held her close.

His bathroom was bigger than hers, way more modern, light and airy, and he wasn't kidding about having a large bath either.

'Goodness, where did you get that bath? It's huge.'

'I've always had a pet hate for the standard size bath. I think they should all be bigger, don't you? Now, do you want to keep the towel on?'

Belle looked down at the inviting water she was being held over. 'I want to take it off. Is that okay with you? I don't want to make you feel awkward. I know we haven't done naked yet, but if you're going to be my husband one day, then I say you need to get used to my body as soon as possible.'

'Is that right?'

She wriggled out of his hands to stand like a drunk flamingo and allowed her towel to drop to the floor. She pursed her lips together and lowered her eyes.

*Not sure if I'm feeling liberated right now or just dramatic. Anyone would think someone was about to draw me. Well, he hasn't looked away yet. And now he's stepping closer.*

'Hey,' he said, touching her chin. 'You make me feel blessed to be your husband.'

*Oh wow! Did he really just say that? He can be so sweet.*

She smiled into his palm, and he helped her climb into the bath. The hot water thawed her bones and relaxed her muscles immediately. She let out a low moan and draped her bad ankle over the side of the tub and turned to face him to see nothing but affection in his eyes, and it was that look that warmed her heart.

'Can I watch you drop your towel?' she asked quietly.

Ned didn't need to be asked twice. His fluffy towel fell to the floor and he stood there in all of his glory, waiting.

Her stomach flipped, as her butterflies had defrosted too. She swallowed hard, hoping he didn't notice, but she was pretty sure he did. 'Climb in behind me.'

Ned did as he was instructed, and Belle closed her eyes as she rested back onto his firm chest. Their fingers entwined as soon as his arms were around her, and his face was close to hers. She could feel how steady his breathing was. How relaxed he felt behind her naked body.

His fingertips slowly stroked over her stomach, sending waves of electricity to flow through her. He let out a relaxed groaning sound, causing Belle to open her eyes.

She raised his hand, turned it over to examine the difference in size to her own, and then lifted it to her mouth and lightly kissed his fingers. 'My lips can kiss properly again.'

His stomach rumbled into her back as he breathed out a laugh. 'That's good to know.'

'If I could just move my leg, I could show you properly.'

She felt his hand sweep her hair away to one side and his mouth rest on her cheek. She could also feel his need for her and it only made her wish even more that her ankle wasn't hurt.

*Flipping heck. Why do I have to be injured at a perfect time like this? This is so not fair. I really want to wrap myself around him.*

'Oh, Ned,' she whispered. 'I've got feelings for you that I've never had with anyone else before.'

His breath was mingling with the steam by her ear. 'That's because I'm your husband.'

She laughed, then winced. 'Ow! My face hurts.'

'Five more minutes, Belle, then we're getting your wounds sorted.'

'Yes, dear. But right now, this hot water is doing your leg the world of good.' She watched him raise her hand to kiss her palm.

'You're so beautiful, Bluebell Trent.'

'Renshaw,' she whispered.

'Renshaw,' he confirmed.

# 27

*Rosie*

'Blimming heck, Bluebell, you'll be the death of me.' Rosie draped Kasey's snowman blanket over her sister's lap. She looked at the crackling fire in the Renshaws' living room and sighed. 'What were you thinking going out in the ice?'

Belle glanced down at her bandaged ankle. 'My toes are cold.'

Rosie slipped her feet out of Elliot's slippers and removed her pink socks and placed them on Belle's feet. 'Did the hospital give you any painkillers?'

'No. They said the ones we had at home were fine, and Ned gave me some when he brought my lunch.'

'I wish you would have called me earlier. I could have come to the hospital with you.'

'I was fine. I didn't want to go, but Ned kept going on.'

Rosie gently tucked a piece of Belle's hair behind her ear. 'Look at your poor face. You look like you've been in a boxing match.'

Belle sighed. 'Feels like it too. It's not too bad, as long as I don't smile.'

'What about sing? We're supposed to be at rehearsals every night until the show.'

Belle shifted on the sofa. 'I can still go.'

Rosie watched Belle relax back when Ned's hand touched her shoulder.

'The doctor said you need to rest today,' he told her.

'It's just singing.'

'It's just for today. One night off won't make any difference.'

'He's right,' said Rosie. 'I'll call Sean and let him know, and I'll stay home with you.'

Ned smiled when Belle finally agreed. He sat down by her side and held her hand. 'You can both stay here again while you're healing.'

Rosie could tell that he really wanted that. His eyes were fixed on Belle, and there was a gentleness there that she hadn't seen before. She smiled on the inside at just how happy her little sister looked, even whilst in pain.

'We can't,' said Belle. 'You have guests arriving every day from tomorrow, and I know you're fully booked for Christmas. There's no room for us, and we'll just be in the way.'

'Of course you won't,' said Elliot, entering with a tray of hot chocolate drinks filled to the brim with cream and chocolate sprinkles. 'Rosie stays in my room, anyway.'

Rosie looked over at him and smiled with love. Oh, how she loved waking up in his arms. There was no way she was going to put a spanner in the works. If the Renshaws wanted them to stay again, she wasn't about to refuse.

Ned was gazing ever so slightly dreamily, in Rosie's opinion, at Belle. 'You can stay with me.'

'What about Kasey?' asked Belle. 'Won't she get a bit confused?'

'I'll explain things to her.'

Rosie picked up one of the chunky white mugs and handed it to Belle. 'So, what exactly is there to explain? I'd like some info myself.'

There was a slight flush in Belle's cheeks as she turned, and Rosie knew it wasn't because of the heat from the fire. She recognised that look, as she'd had it herself over Elliot.

Belle frowned at the cream on top of her drink. 'Ned and I are...' She paused, obviously searching for the right words.

'Destiny,' he added, and Belle's scoff blew some of the cream from her mug straight onto Rosie's top.

Elliot laughed and handed her a tissue from his pocket. 'Where's a camera when you need one? Sorry, babe, but your face.'

Rosie held off a grin as she wiped herself clean. 'Destiny?'

'It's in my tea leaves,' said Ned.

'Did Josephine tell you that?' asked Elliot knowingly.

'Ooh, is that the fortune teller?' asked Rosie. 'I want my tea leaves read. I'll have to make an appointment with her.'

'Belle's my Mrs Renshaw,' Ned told his brother, and Belle giggled until it obviously hurt to do so.

Rosie was looking at a grinning Elliot. 'Great, isn't it.'

Belle didn't look too bothered by the prediction. She was happily watching Ned use a long spoon to scoop out the remaining cream from her mug, transferring the melting dollop over to his own.

'I have a proposal for you all,' said Elliot, sitting up straight in the armchair and looking serious all of a sudden.

'Go on,' said Ned.

Elliot's eyes were on Rosie. 'It's about our hotels.'

'What about them?' she asked.

'How do you feel about going into business together? You and Belle with me and Ned. I'm talking about joining the buildings again and rebranding under the original name. We can buy half your business so that you have a lump sum up front but still own half the hotel.'

Belle was clearly as confused as Rosie. 'So, you want us to own half of our half?'

Even Ned looked perplexed at Elliot's idea.

Elliot shook his head. 'No. You'll own half of the whole business.'

Rosie looked at them all in turn. 'But we don't have a business, Elliot. You do. We should be buying into yours.'

'You will be, sort of. You're adding your inn to ours.'

'And you're going to pay us to do so,' said Rosie.

'Technically, you'd own three-quarters, and we'd be left with just the toilets.' Belle scoffed, and Ned held her free hand.

'No, not at all,' said Elliot.

'Elliot, you're not making any sense,' said Ned.

Elliot breathed out a long sigh. 'Look, I want the inns to be one and to have the original name. We can renovate the building, fix up the right side, and create a better business that we will all benefit from. We'll have equal shares, equal profit, equal say.'

Rosie frowned. 'If we do that, then we'll just join. There's no need for you to pay us. We can just come together.'

His eyes lowered slightly, as did his voice. 'I just wanted you to have some money.'

'We're not a bloody charity case, Elliot,' Rosie snapped. 'We have money, thank you. Just because we're not as wealthy as you, doesn't mean we're on the breadline.'

'I wasn't trying to offend you, Rosie.'

Rosie was silently seething. 'And where do you propose we all live, Elliot? Have you got that one figured out as well?'

Elliot swallowed hard. 'We have our home here, and we can keep your home over there. That doesn't have to change.'

Rosie's agitation was rapidly rising, and she wasn't quite sure what was bugging her more, his handout or the fact that he basically just said he doesn't want to live with her.

*So, is that your game after all? You really did get into bed with me just to get your hands on our hotel. I'm not sure how I feel about you right now. I don't know if I can trust you anymore.*

As if reading her mind, Belle spoke up. 'Jeez, Elliot, sounds like all you care about is getting your hands on our hotel.'

Elliot looked mortified. 'That's not where I'm coming from.'

'Really?' asked Belle, shrugging away Ned's hand. 'You told my sister that you love her, and now you've pretty much just told her that you wouldn't live with her though.'

'I would,' he snapped. His eyes were back on Rosie. 'You two are taking this the wrong way. I didn't want to insinuate anything. Rosie, you can move in with me right now if you wanted to. I just thought that you wouldn't want that yet. That you might both feel comfortable still having your own space.'

Rosie was only half hearing what he had to say, because her heart hadn't calmed down, and her head felt fuzzy and light.

'Rosie,' he added firmly. 'I would marry you right now if I could. That's how much I want you in my life. I'm doing this for you. To be with you. I'm giving you a share in my hotel, for Christ's sake.'

Rosie's head whipped up so fast, she felt a tight ping in her neck. 'Your hotel? I thought half of it belonged to me.'

Elliot breathed out a slow huff of a breath. 'You know what I mean.'

'No, Elliot, I'm not sure I do anymore.' Rosie turned to Belle. 'Come on. We're going home.'

'Erm...' Belle stared down at her comfortable foot propped up on a cushion on a footstool.

Ned shifted forward. 'Do you want me to carry you? I know the crutches are tricky, and I'm worried about any stairs and the ice outside.'

Rosie felt terrible. Poor Belle was in pain and was supposed to be resting, and there she was trying to move her. 'I'm sorry, Belle. You should stay. Ned will look after you. I'll pop by later when Elliot is busy.'

Elliot's mouth flapped open like a fish.

'No, Rosie,' said Belle. 'I'm not letting you sleep over there by yourself. What if something happens? What if you need me in the night?'

'I'll be fine, Belle.'

Elliot swallowed hard. 'I'm not letting you sleep over there on your own either.'

Rosie swung her head his way. 'You don't get a say in it.'

Belle turned to Ned. 'Can you two give me and my sister a minute, please.'

Ned glanced at Elliot, then nodded. He kissed her head and left with his brother.

Belle waited until they had gone. 'What the hell was that?'

Rosie nodded. 'I know, right. What a cheek he's got.'

'I'm talking about you.'

'What did I do?'

'Are you having a laugh? The man just proposed to you, and you ignored it as though it didn't happen.'

'I was too busy focusing on the part where it sounded like he was only interested in our hotel.'

'I don't think he explained himself properly, if you ask me. I think he was a bit flustered, but one thing's for sure, Rosie, that man loves you.'

Rosie picked up her hug in a mug and really wished it could hug her, because she sure as hell needed one. 'I feel confused, Belle.'

'Yeah, that makes two of us.'

'What are you confused about?'

Belle sighed deeply. 'Everything. We sold all of our things, upped sticks, and moved here to run a hotel when we have no idea what we're doing. We've both fallen in love with the enemy, broken the family feud, I've been told that Edward Renshaw is my future husband, and I've just been offered the job at the nursery. I'm singing Disney songs every day and cleaning dust out of my hair every night, and I've inherited a lazy cat, who clearly has never seen Tom and Jerry, as we still have a rat running around the kitchen.'

Rosie quietly sipped her drink, giving herself a cream moustache. She licked her top lip and smiled. 'It really has been the weirdest winter and it's not over yet.'

'What do you want to do about the hotel, Rosie?'

'Are you going to take the school job?' She could tell by Belle's face that she wanted to. Belle missed working with children, and Rosie knew that's where her sister's heart was. 'It's okay, Belle. You can if you want. We don't have to run a hotel, or partner with Elliot. We can just live there, or we could slice our hotel in half. Sell one half to them and make the other half a home. You can work at the school, and I'll start making pottery pieces again. That sounds like a nice plan. Sure, we'll be living next door to a hotel, but we can put up a higher fence or plant trees.'

'I do like that idea. Not the planting trees and prison fences. The house part. I want to stay living in Pepper Bay, Rosie. I love it here. It feels like home. It's just that inn we own. That doesn't feel like anything except stress.'

'At least we tried.'

Belle scoffed. 'We didn't get past the cleaning stage.'

'We threw broken things out. Plus, I learnt some hotel tips from Elliot. He's been teaching me a little every day.'

'And he wouldn't bother doing that if he wanted to just take your hotel away from you, would he?'

Rosie slowly shook her head in defeat. 'I guess not. I can't believe you're sticking up for him.'

'I'm not. I'm just saying what I see. The way he looks at you, Rosie. He doesn't hide it, you know. It's as plain as the nose on your face, which by the way has cream on.'

Rosie cuffed her nose.

'Did you learn much?' asked Belle.

'I'm not sure. I found it so boring, my brain kept falling asleep. He started talking about insurance at one point and I designed a whole new dinner set in my mind.'

Belle held her cheekbone as she laughed.

Rosie smiled. 'I love that he's passionate about his job, but it's not for me.'

'Then, I think we should consider his offer. At least tell him our idea about separating our hotel and selling him half. Goodness, what do we sound like? It's bad enough the inn was sliced in half in the first place, and now we want to cut up some more. At this rate, there'll be nothing left of the original building. Do you feel bad?'

'A bit. Not sure what Pops would make of this.'

'Not sure what I make of it.'

'Can we talk about you and Ned now?'

'I'd rather not, but where are we staying while my ankle heals?'

'You want to stay here with him, don't you? You don't have to answer. I know. I feel a bit off now. I don't know what to say to Elliot.'

'Have you told him that you love him yet?'

'No. I haven't said it out loud.'

'You could open with that. Make things clear.'

'I don't think he wants to talk to me at the moment. I just accused him of… I don't even know what word to use. Skulduggery.'

Belle breathed out a laugh. 'Skulduggery?'

Rosie shrugged. 'It's a word.'

'I think he was more worried he'd offended you.'

Rosie stared over at the fire. 'Is it wrong that I miss him already?'

Belle followed her gaze. 'Is it wrong that I miss that fireplace when we're over at ours?'

Rosie giggled. 'It's so cosy here, isn't it. I wish we did live here.'

'Well, we can, for a few days anyway.'

'Elliot invited us for Christmas dinner and Boxing Day as well.'

'Oh, Rosie, I'd like that. No fighting with our oven to get it to come on. No buying more food than we'll ever eat. No washing up.'

'We'd probably have to offer to do that.'

'No, we won't. Have you not seen the size of their dishwasher. Besides, they have staff working who won't want us interfering.'

'Well, I see you have your excuse ready.'

Belle flopped her head back and sighed. 'Oh, Rosie, what are we going to do?'

'Please don't worry, Belle. I'll sort it. You just concentrate on getting fit and healthy again.'

'What are you going to do?'

'Talk to Elliot.'

# 28

Elliot sat on the stairs listening to Rosie belting out 'Let it Go' so that her choirmaster could hear via their video call. He could also hear the other members of the choir coming out of the laptop in his living room. He had spent the rest of the day avoiding her, and she didn't come back to his hotel until after dinner. He hoped she had eaten. The thought of her sitting alone in that dingy place next door filled him with sadness. He had saved her a pasta dish in the fridge, just in case, but he still didn't know if she'd eaten it or not.

Kasey flopped down at his side. 'Are you okay, Uncle Elliot?'

He put on his best fake smile and held her hand. 'Of course. Now, why are you dressed as a mermaid? Shouldn't you be in your pyjamas by now?'

'I want to join in with the singing. Can I go inside?'

'Don't see why not. Come on.'

He warily opened the door to see Rosie sitting on the floor in front of the laptop, and Belle still glued to the sofa. He smiled to himself at how normal it felt to see them in his home.

'Go and sit quietly with Belle for a moment,' he whispered. He watched Belle place an arm around his niece as soon as she sat down, then he left.

'Is Kasey in there?' asked Ned, appearing behind him.

'Yeah, she's sitting with Belle.'

Elliot walked off up the stairs.

'Where are you going?' asked Ned.

'Bed.'

'I'm waiting to take Belle up, and now Kasey. Is Rosie going to stay?'

Elliot shrugged. 'I have no idea.'

He entered his room, got into his pyjamas, and sat in bed with his book. He knew he wouldn't be able to concentrate, but he had to try something.

*Why did I have to open my mouth? Everything was perfect between me and Rosie, but now she doesn't trust me. How did it all come out so wrong? I had rehearsed it in my mind as well. Argh! I'm such an idiot. What am I going to do now? I told her I'd marry her today and she didn't even bat an eyelid. She doesn't feel as strongly as I do, that much is clear.*

He stared at the page in his book, but no words were entering his brain. There were many attempts to read the first paragraph, but the story wasn't taking hold, so he picked up his phone from the side and called his aunt.

'Hello, Mandy, sorry it's late.'

'Hello, my lovely. It's not that late. Anyway, I was just putting some of my arts and crafts away. I've just made a lovely candle holder out of a small log. It's not a yule log, but still, it'll do, and I managed to get some real mistletoe today, so I'm well chuffed. I'm on table decorations this year. William is making the chocolate log, which I'm pleased about. I'm no baker. I think they've finally realised that.'

Elliot smiled at his aunt's chuckle of a laugh. It really was infectious.

'I can't wait to see the photos, Mandy.'

'I can't wait to see you. Now, tell me the reason behind this call.'

There was no hiding anything from her. She could read him like a book. She could read everyone like a book.

Elliot attempted a hushed sigh, but it was still noticeable. 'I messed up with Rosie, and now I think she actually hates me.'

'What happened?'

'I was trying to join our inns, and it all came out wrong, and now she thinks I'm only pretending to love her so I can get my hands on her hotel.'

'Did you explain it properly afterwards?'

'I haven't had a chance. She's been avoiding me. I even proposed, of sorts, and there was nothing from her. No acknowledgement or anything. See. She hates me.'

'I'm sure she doesn't.'

'You didn't see her face.' Elliot realised he had the top part of the quilt scrunched in his hand as though trying to strangle it, so he loosened his grip. 'I'm just a Renshaw to her, at the end of the day. That will always be the bottom line, won't it?'

'That's up to you, Elliot. You choose what you want the world to see. You have to remember, you're not a reputation. You're you. What do you want her to see?'

'Me. Just me. Not the stupid family feud. Not that divide between our properties. Just me.' He lowered his head to one hand and closed his eyes for a moment.

'Breathe, Elliot.' Mandy's voice was gentle and calm. 'It's going to be okay. What do I always say about miscommunication?'

'Talk things through.'

'And you haven't done that yet, have you?'

He shook his head, knowing full well his aunt couldn't see, but knowing her, she probably knew.

'What are you doing about the situation at the moment, Elliot?'

He glanced up at his room through his fingers. 'Sitting in bed, trying to read.'

Mandy chuckled. 'Oh dear. Well, that won't do. What would be more productive?'

'Talking to Rosie.'

'Then, why are you still on the phone to me?'

He smiled and said goodbye.

It seemed quiet outside his bedroom, but he still peeped around his door. No one was about. Not even Ned. He pulled himself together and made his way downstairs to find the living room was empty.

*Where is everyone?*

He figured Ned had taken Kasey to bed, and probably Belle too, but had Rosie gone back to her own hotel? He hoped she hadn't.

*But if she thinks she's staying in that gloomy hole alone, she can think again. Right, that's it. I'm going over there and sleeping on the floor outside her room if I have to.*

Full of defiance, he marched over to the Inn on the Right, knowing there were only two ways it would go. She'd either kick him out or he was in for a rough night on old wooden floorboards. The thought alone gave him backache, but he was determined to make a statement. She had to know he loved her. That he cared about her so much.

*Sometimes, I really hate these bloody hotels.*

He stood on her driveway, glaring at the divide.

*So stupid!*

The door was unlocked, which made him shake his head at the lack of security. He had night staff that worked in his hotel when they had guests, so he could leave the front door unlocked. Plus, his family had private quarters that were closed off from the guests. There was no way that Rosie was going to go to sleep allowing entrance to all and sundry. Not on his watch.

Standing in the foyer, he wasn't sure whether to call out or just go to her room. The dark empty space around him was uninviting, and he wasn't quite sure if she would be the same. He didn't want to creep around though. What if he scared her?

'Rosie,' he belted out, jolting himself.

As there was silence, he called out again, this time louder. He wasn't entirely sure, but something resembling a rat scurried around the skirting close to the reception desk.

Rosie made him jump as she looked over the not-so-sturdy banisters. 'Elliot?'

He glanced up and then approached the bottom of the stairs. 'Were you planning on sleeping here alone tonight?' He didn't give her a chance to answer. 'If so, I'm staying right here all night.'

She appeared to huff, although he couldn't be sure. Her shadow disappeared as she moved away from the landing. She sat on the top step and glared down at him.

Elliot glared back.

*I'm not giving in to your stubborn streak, Rosie. I'm sleeping by this front door if I have to. No one will get by me.*

He sat on the bottom step and lowered his eyes submissively. 'About earlier, Rosie. It all came out wrong. I haven't got any tactics. All I want is for us to grow together. I know you're not happy with this place, and I don't blame you. This wasn't your dream. To be honest, my hotel wasn't mine, but I enjoy it now. I've seen the way you almost fall asleep when I'm talking hotels, and I've just been trying to figure out a way that would help you and

Belle. Yes, I know, it helps me too but... Oh, nothing I say sounds right.'

'Did you mean it when you said you would marry me?'

Her soft words caused his heart to miss a beat. He quickly looked her way. 'I did.'

'But you haven't known me five minutes.'

'I don't care. I love you, and I'd do anything for you, Rosie. I want to help. Let me help.'

She was twiddling her fingers in her lap, not looking at him. All Elliot wanted to do was sprint up the stairs and hold her.

Their silence lingered for a while.

Rosie finally spoke. 'Belle and I have an idea about what we would like to do. Not sure how doable it is but...'

'Tell me. I'll make it work.'

It was dark, but he was pretty sure she smiled.

'Well, we were thinking about dividing our place into two. One section you could have for your hotel, and the other we would make into a house for us to live in. Belle has accepted a job at a local nursey, and I want to go back to my pottery. I already have customers wanting new pieces, and I can use the outbuilding at the bottom of the garden as my workshop. With the money from the sale to you, I can set up my business again. What do you think?'

'Can I throw in another idea?'

There was a low grumbling noise that either came from her or his stomach.

'What idea?' she asked quietly.

'How about instead of the house for you and Belle, you build two houses, side by side. Then, you'll have one each. I'm sure you won't want to live with each other forever.'

'I guess. What with Belle and Ned destined for marriage, and me marrying you, it makes sense for us to have our own homes. There's enough land for that, and your hotel will have more room available once you Renshaws move out. Plus, you'll have half our hotel joined back in place with yours. I think it might work.'

Elliot's smile couldn't stretch any wider. His heart was absorbing her warmth and future plans. 'Did you just agree to marry me?'

'I'll see if we still like each other by the time my new home is built.'

He lowered his head as he laughed to himself.

'Do we have a deal, Mr Renshaw?'

'We do, Miss Trent.'

A silence that was filled with a wonderful fizz of excitement sat between them.

Elliot went to say something, but she beat him to the chase.

'I love you, Merman.'

Unable to hold it together any longer, he sprinted up the stairs to wrap her up into his arms.

*I'm definitely always going to love you.*

# 29

*Ned*

'Try to keep still, Belle. Hold on to the chair. I'm trying to do this thing up?' Ned stared at the back of Belle's Disney costume. 'Nora could have just put in a zip. That would have been easier. Also what would be easier is if my hands weren't seizing up. It's freezing in here.'

Belle peered over her shoulder as he balanced on one foot. 'It's a pinafore, Ned. Just pull the ribbons into a bow.' She glanced over at Daphne. 'I'm just glad I'm not playing Jasmine. Poor Daph looks like she might turn into a snowman any minute.'

Ned looked around the large grey tent at everyone in the choir, who were all faffing around, quickly getting changed. There were curtained-off sections, clothes strewn far and wide, loads of chattering teeth in amongst the hustle and bustle of the show's dress rehearsal, and every so often, someone would burst into song, then some others would join in, each time making him jump.

Belle started peppering kisses along Ned's neck as he leaned over her to help straighten her dress.

He grinned widely and quickly kissed her back. 'Without those kisses, I wouldn't have agreed to help out here.'

'Oh, you love it really. I can tell. And I've heard you sing a few notes. You could join if you want. It's not too late to get you up to scratch, Gaston.'

He laughed as he stepped behind her, stroking down her arms. 'You would love to see me dressed up as him, wouldn't you?'

The eruption of laughter that came from her confirmed what he'd already guessed. She awkwardly leant over to one side to pick up a flyer from a nearby wooden chair.

'Look, Ned, did you see the flyers we had made advertising the show? See. Your hotel is on the back. Top sponsor slot.'

He took the piece of paper from her and turned it over. 'Only sponsor, more like.'

She tenderly kissed his cheek. 'Thanks, Ned.'

'Hmm.' He arched an eyebrow as his mouth curled. 'Good thing I like you, Flower Girl.'

'I'm not Flower Girl today. Today, I am Belle from Beauty and the Beast.'

'I'm glad you told me. I thought you were Dorothy from the Wizard of Oz.'

She started to sing 'Somewhere Over the Rainbow', immediately gaining backing singers from at least three other people.

Ned shook his head and glanced over to see his brother twirling Elsa around next to a makeshift dressing room. 'So, what happened to the town hall?'

'We can't rehearse there because they have a burst water pipe. We might not even get to do the show there. It'll be okay though. Sean has secured us use of the dome here at Hope Park. Apparently, it only gets used by the local theatre company, so there's no reason we shouldn't be allowed to use the place. We're part of the art community too.'

He smiled at the way her face was scrunched in annoyance about the fight to be noticed as equals to the am-dram lot, as she called them. 'You're the best part of the community, in my opinion.' He kissed her neck and gave her a cheeky wink.

Belle lost her smile as she glanced down at his leg. 'Are you okay in this cold, Ned? I know it hurts your leg.'

He was pretty sure he had hidden his wince, but obviously she had noticed. 'I'm okay. Let's worry about your ankle. How is it feeling today?'

The nonchalant shrug didn't fool him. He lowered her onto the chair.

'Take the weight off till it's your turn.'

'It's all my turn, Ned. We stand on the stage together. I have to just step forward for my parts, and I only leave to get changed.'

'How many costume changes have you got?'

'Four. So, as a stagehand, expect a lot of carrying back and forth.'

He saluted her. 'Yes, miss.'

She laughed and slapped his hand away as he tickled behind her ear. She gestured towards her sister. 'Rosie looks great dressed as Elsa.'

'Yes, I think Elliot is impressed.'

'Can you believe those two. They've pretty much wrapped up our future between the two of them.'

He grinned as he squatted down to her side. 'I'm looking forward to the new homes being built. Just so you know, Kasey got wind of it and has already started planning her new room, so if she approaches you with mermaid bedroom ideas, I do apologise. I haven't said we're moving in with you, but she thinks we are.'

The reality was, neither of them had discussed their future, let alone bring Kasey into the mix.

'Aww, she can have a room at mine. I don't mind. It's a good way for us to come together slowly. You can both have sleepovers, if you want.'

His hand was already on her cheek. 'Oh, I definitely want.'

Belle leaned over and rested her mouth on his, and every part of him melted into her.

A shriek of a scream jolted their embrace. Another loud cry came from the opening of the tent, followed by a few swear words, and then darkness fell as the tent caved in, covering everyone inside.

Ned felt Belle slip from the chair. He blindly reached out to fumble around for her hand.

'Ned?' Her voice was strained and seemed distant.

'Belle?' His hand slapped around him, but the only thing it connected with was one leg of the chair.

Muffled noises, hefty weight, and chaos weren't on his mind. Finding Belle took priority. She had to be close. He could hardly move, so she couldn't have got far, especially with her bad ankle. His adrenaline was pumping, causing panic to toy with him.

He called out her name again, but his voice was faint in amongst all of the other noises going on. He swore he could hear his brother calling him, but maybe he was imagining things. Something had hit his head, and he was starting to feel queasy and a bit dizzy.

*What the hell is on my back? I need to get out of here. I can't see a bloody thing. Where is Belle?*

He called for her again whilst stretching out one arm.

'Ned?' her voice croaked.

*Thank God.*

'Belle, where are you? I can't see anything.'

'I'm right here.'

His hand stroked over the ground, finding a clump of material. He tugged at the cloth but it didn't shift. Fingers lightly brushed over his knuckles.

'Ned. Is that you?'

He quickly huddled her hand into his. 'Yes, it's me. Try not to move. The tent has collapsed. It's all right. Everything will be okay. Someone will get us out in a minute.'

'I can't see you, Ned.'

The broken tone in her voice battered him completely. He used every ounce of strength he had to move his pressed-down body over towards her. Pain ripped through his leg and acid built in his stomach. He stretched and crawled, slithered, twisted, and wriggled. His head was thumping almost as loudly as his chest. He couldn't throw up, and he couldn't pass out. If he could just lose the weight on his back, he figured he would make it. Somehow, he managed to slide to her side. His vision was cloudy, but her face was in sight.

Belle almost cried as his arm draped over her shoulder. 'Oh, Ned.'

'Shh! It's okay, Belle. We're going to be okay. It's just a tent. We're fine. Are you okay? Does anything hurt?'

She coughed and moved her head a touch so that her face was closer to his. 'I can't breathe properly.'

His hand managed to move to her hair, brushing it away from her eyes. 'Does your chest hurt?'

'No. There's just no air.'

He knew that. He also felt suffocated by all the dust and the lack of room. 'Okay. Just try to relax so you don't struggle for more air. We'll be out of here soon.'

Sorrowful, anxious eyes were looking back at him. The last time he'd seen a look like that was the day he woke in the hospital. Elliot was sitting by his bed. His eyes distressed and sad. That was the moment he found out Penny was dead.

*This isn't happening to me again. I'm not losing someone else I love to a stupid accident that could have been avoided if only other people weren't so bloody thoughtless. Okay. Stay calm. It's just a tent. A hefty tent, but a tent all the same. There'll be a few bruises, probably, but no one should be badly hurt from this. It's just a tent. Just a tent. She's fine. Elliot's fine. Everyone's fine. Okay, just breathe, Ned. Breathe. Slow and steady.*

Belle's eyes looked blurry, and she hadn't stopped looking at him since he found her. He needed to see her face relax. To see her smile.

'Hey,' he whispered.

'Hey,' she whispered back.

'How you doing over there, Mrs Renshaw?'

'A lot better now you're here.'

He smiled as strongly as he could, trying anything to comfort her. His back was killing him, and sharp bolts of pain kept firing through his leg. His stomach had settled a touch, and his racing heart was slowing, but his head ached, and his shoulders were bruised.

'Ned, I'm worried about my sister.'

'I know, but I bet she's fine. Elliot is fine. Everyone in here is fine.'

'This tent is really heavy.'

'Yeah, I know. It's that heavy-duty canvas type. That's why it feels heavy. But it's still just material. Someone will cut through it soon.'

The sound of a siren in the distance brought air to his lungs and peace to his heart.

Inside the tent became silent for a moment.

'Ned?' came Elliot's voice, startling him.

*Oh, thank God he's all right. I knew he was. I just knew.*

'We're both fine,' he called back.

A few other voices started calling out names until Sean told everyone to shush. He wanted to do a roll call. Once it had been confirmed that everyone trapped under the tent was alive and seemingly well, Kris started to quietly sing 'Defying Gravity', and one by one, the choir joined in.

Belle's shaky voice was singing softly by Ned's ear. He was pleased to see her tears had dried on hearing Rosie answer to Sean. He lightly squeezed her hand and used his other to stroke the side of her face.

'I love you, Bluebell.'

She stopped singing and kissed his fingertip that was close to her mouth. 'If I get out of here before you, you know that means I beat you at something, right?'

He grinned. 'We'll see.'

# 30

*Belle*

Belle and Ned climbed into his bed together and held each other tightly.

'Are you okay, Ned?'

His chest lifted beneath her and slowly sank back down. 'It's been a crazy day. I'm glad it's over.'

'I'm glad everyone was all right from that stupid tent falling in on us. Sean's thinking of suing the council. They put it up, but they said it was the local theatre's fault. Apparently, it belonged to them. They were supposed to take it down after their panto last week. There's a lot of blame flying around.'

His hand brushed over her hair, causing the tension still trapped deep within her to disperse.

'How's your back, Ned? Is it still hurting?'

'No. It's doing okay. Just a bit bruised. That canvas material was pretty heavy. I'm not sure if it was just that or something else whacked me. Probably one of the posts. I didn't get to see when I was being carried out.'

Belle leant up on one elbow to look down at him. As soon as his bright eyes met hers, her heart fluttered and she felt on the verge of tears. His hand reached up and cupped the side of her face, and she closed her eyes for a moment and rested in his palm.

'How are you doing, Belle?' His voice was soft and warm, embracing her as much as his touch.

She opened her eyes, unafraid to reveal the dreamy look she held. 'We've had a hell of a time, haven't we?'

The corners of his mouth twitched into a gentle smile. 'Turned out all right in the end.'

Smiling down at his chest, she had to agree. Never in a million years did she see any of it coming. The move. The Hotel. Falling for a Renshaw. Being in his arms. So much had happened in such a short time, and so much more was to come, thanks to her sister breaking the family feud, and all from driving a lawnmower into next door's pool. Just the thought made her giggle on the inside. She still couldn't get over it.

Ned flopped her back on him and pulled her closer. 'I feel a bit blown away by it all, if I'm honest.'

She stroked her fingertips over his skin. 'I know what you mean.'

After a moment, he said, 'So, you took the nursery job.'

'Yep. It's where my heart is, Ned. I love working with kids.'

'You're great with Kasey. She loves you.'

Belle smiled and rolled her head up to face him. 'I love her too. You've got a good kid there.'

'I know. Let's hope she stays that way. I'm dreading the teenage years.'

'What were you like as a teen?'

'Hmm, well. I was the good one, which means I wasn't my dad's favourite.'

'Do you think he treated you two differently?'

'He definitely did. Elliot was so destructive, and Dad lapped it up. I just wasn't attracted to trouble. I didn't like what it brought. So, I was pretty quiet as a kid. I was a good boy.'

'You look like trouble to me.'

He frowned playfully. 'I thought that the first time I saw you.'

She laughed and reached up to kiss him. He pulled her back to him as she went to slip away. The slight brush of lips took less than a second to heat and less than that to cause a wave of electricity to rush over her. Climbing on top of him, with her hands clasped in his hair, did little to lessen the tingling sensation.

*Oh, Ned. I can't believe this is happening. You, of all people. How did we get here? I'm so glad we did. You feel so good. I don't want to ever leave this bed.*

His kiss swept her away to somewhere so remote, nothing else in the world existed during that moment. His large hands were at the sides of her face, holding her hair away from them both, pulling her deeper and deeper into the connection.

They gasped for air, then kissed some more and parted again for more air, and he gave a low moan that vibrated against her bottom lip. She looked up and could see the affection he had for her sitting right there in his eyes, and the look warmed her heart. They kissed again, and he rolled her onto her back where he took a moment to gaze down at her.

'You're in pain, Ned.'

He gave the slightest of nods. 'It's not so bad now.'

'I'm worried about your back.'

'The doc said I was fine. How's your ankle?'

'Safely tucked up in bed.'

'Good. You ready for another kiss?'

She smiled softly at him, feeling little strength to do much more. Every look and touch that came her way was rendering her even more useless by the second. He was beautiful, and he loved her, and he was right there with her, in bed, holding her in his arms.

*I'm definitely marrying him. I don't need tea leaves or magic to tell me that. I just know. I can feel it. Look at the way he's looking at me. He can feel it too.*

Remembering how he had looked at her when they were side by side under the heavy weight of the tent brought a tingle down her spine. The goosebumps were visible on her bare arms. She glanced at her skin, deciding to remove her tee-shirt.

*I want to feel you. Every part of you. Your skin on mine. Goosebumps and all.*

Ned sat up slightly so she had room and helped her out of the garment with ease.

The feeling of his skin on hers caused her to still for a beat as he lowered himself over her. She closed her eyes and drifted back to his mouth. The warmth. The tenderness. The affection.

'I love you, Ned,' she whispered on his lips.

The kiss deepened and moved to her cheek, then to her neck where he trailed his mouth all the way down to her collarbone.

She could hear herself breathing out his name and feel herself wanting more from him. Wanting everything.

They fumbled with their pyjama bottoms, discarding them quickly and tossing them to the floor. Now she could feel all of him. Nothing was between them.

He lifted himself up to look at her face, and she smiled and pulled him back to her.

*I don't even want air between us. I don't want to feel any space. Just you and me, joined forever. Untouchable. Unmovable. God, I love you, Ned. Stay this close to me always.*

Their kissed slowed. He was taking his time, and she was lost in him, coming undone at every movement.

Wishing the moment would never end. Hoping he would never stop.

'I love you, Flower Girl.' His gentle words tingled her lips, and she was sure there was no part of her left to melt.

His breathing changed, and she gripped him tighter, holding him as close as she could, wishing it could be even closer. But they could not be joined any more than they were. Wrapped around each other, clinging on as though their lives depended on it, their quivering bodies sank breathlessly into the mattress.

Belle could feel his damp face pressed into her neck. His warm breath was heating her skin. He was keeping his weight from crushing her as his heart pounded on her chest. She clutched his biceps to her face and held her mouth there for a while. His other arm tightened around her, and he slowly raised his head.

'Don't move, Ned.'

He blinked slowly whilst attempting a slight nod.

'Stay with me,' she whispered.

He swallowed hard and took a steady breath. 'I'm not going anywhere.'

Their eyes remained locked for the longest amount of time. Belle had no idea just how long. It seemed like forever. Time was standing still for them. Life had stopped moving forward. The moment was silent, with a tranquil peace filled with sheer bliss, longing, and the purest of love.

He lowered his head and kissed her mouth, mumbling on her lips, repeating his words, 'I'm not going anywhere.'

# 31

*Rosie*

The folded red check blanket beneath Rosie was stopping her bottom from going numb in the coldness of midday. She had another one wrapped around her, even though she was wearing jeans and a jumper. She had been sitting by the side of the swimming pool for ten minutes, just staring down into the water.

*Why is this so hard? All I want to do is place my legs in there. It's not as though I'm going to attempt to swim. I just want to dangle and perhaps one day be able to paddle in the sea again. Oh, flipping heck. Stupid phobia. Go away. I hate you. Come on, Primrose, you can do this. It's no different to being in the bath.*

Her shoulders drooped along with her heart. Her fear of the water was something she really wanted to get rid of. She loved the beach and missed splashing in the sea. Going for a paddle would be a dream come true.

The smell of the swimming pool water was making her stomach churn, but she refused to move. Her jeans were rolled up to the top of her shins, and her cold, pale legs were waiting further instructions.

*I hope no one sees me and comes out. I want to do this by myself. The last thing I need is pressure from anyone else. Goodness, Elliot will think I'm so lame if he sees me. He probably won't. I will just feel daft in front of him. Maybe I should have asked for his help. He would sit with me. Comfort me. So would Belle. Nope. This is best left to me and only me.*

'What you doing, Princess Primrose?' asked Kasey, stepping onto the blanket.

Rosie jumped, slapping one hand to her chest. 'I… erm.'

*What should I say to her? I can hardly tell her I'm petrified of the water. I don't want to make her feel scared of the pool.*

Before she had a chance to reply, Kasey plonked herself down by her side. Rosie opened her blanket and tugged the child closer to her to snuggle inside.

'It's cold, Kasey. Why are you out here?'

'I wanted to look at the pool. I come and look sometimes.'

Rosie glanced down at her with an amused frown. 'Why?'

Kasey's aquamarine eyes were staring up at her. 'After I nearly drowned in the river, I've been scared of the water. That's why I come to look. It's not really scary, you know.'

*And she just blurts out her fear without any attached shame. Puts me to shame. I know how she feels about being afraid after nearly drowning though. Poor kid.*

Rosie gave her a gentle squeeze. 'I nearly drowned once too. That's why I've come to look at the water. I don't want to be afraid anymore.'

Kasey smiled weakly. 'There are no mermaids in the pool to help you.'

'No, there aren't.'

'I'm a good swimmer.'

'That's good. I haven't been swimming in years, so I have no idea if I can still do it.'

Kasey giggled, and it helped Rosie to relax.

'My daddy is the best swimmer. He taught me when I was little.'

'My dad taught me too.'

A smile hit her heart as she thought about her parents. Her old life seemed a million miles away sometimes. Growing up with Belle, family time, and then going to live with her ex. The whole lot was a distant memory. Throughout her time in Pepper Bay, all she had done was focus on the here and now. The closest she came to thinking outside the safe box she had created for herself was the time she spent discussing a possible future with Elliot.

*Elliot Renshaw, where did you come from? Right here. All this time, you've been right here. I certainly was not looking for you when I arrived. I didn't even know I was going to come here for a while. It was Belle's idea. A change of scenery will be good for us. Yeah, I remember that conversation. She was right though, wasn't she? Look at us. Our lives. Our future all mapped out. Flipping heck, I feel like I'm in a weird dream.*

She gently sighed, trying not to disturb Kasey.

*Oh, Elliot, your arms holding me all night. Your whispered words. The worry in your eyes from the stupid tent.*

A smile crept onto her face as the memory of being trapped with him under a heap of thick canvas came back to her. The way he had shielded her from the impact. His body cradling over hers. That moment when he said his wedding vowels and they both said *I do.*

*Magical. Scary, but he made it magical. Funny how I didn't have the same feeling I have now looking at this swimming pool. Maybe if he was here with me, whispering his sweetness in my ear, I wouldn't be afraid. Maybe. That's not something I should rely on. I need to do this by myself, for myself. I can't let Elliot be a crutch.*

Kasey leant forward and started to roll up her own jeans.

'You'll be cold if you do that.'

The little girl beamed her way. 'I want to be like you.'

Rosie couldn't help but smile.

*I could do it for her. Be a role model.*

She tried not to reveal any fear through her voice. 'I was thinking about putting my legs in the water, but I'm a bit scared.'

Kasey nodded. 'Do you want me to help you?'

Rosie's heart flipped for two reasons. The kindness of a child, and the fear of the water.

Kasey shifted closer to the edge and peered down. 'I can get Uncle Elliot to help you. He said he would do anything for you.'

'He told you that?'

'I heard him telling Daddy.' She rolled her bright eyes up to meet Rosie's. 'He would do anything for me too. He told me.'

Rosie nodded. 'Yes, he would.'

'And I don't even have a fairy name.'

'I like your name, Kasey.'

She shrugged and scrunched her button nose. 'It's okay, but I still want a fairy name.'

'Well, in that case. How about I give you one. You can add it to your other names.'

Kasey turned so fast, she wobbled and almost fell sideways into the pool. Rosie's quick reflexes put a stop to that.

'What name can I have?' The excitement was top level and making Rosie laugh, which was a relief after her near heart attack seconds before.

'Hmm. I'm thinking... how about Poppy. Poppies are red like your hair.'

Kasey grinned from ear to ear and then turned back to the pool and plopped her feet into the cold water without a second thought. 'I'm Fairy Poppy.'

Rosie's eyes were wide as she watched the child happily swing her legs back and forth, creating gentle ripples.

*Wow, she just went for it. It's that old saying... Don't think, just do. Sod it.*

She quickly lowered her legs into the pool before her brain had time to overthink the subject anymore. The icy liquid soon took charge of her mind. 'Whoa! That's cold.'

Kasey giggled. 'It's a heated pool.'

'Doesn't feel like it.' She took a breath, steadying the pounding that hit her heart.

It didn't take long for her body to adjust to the temperature. Her legs were as numb as her mind almost was. She could hardly believe she was doing it. Dangling her legs in a swimming pool. What next, diving from a cliff? She laughed to herself. Adrenaline was lifting her higher, making her feel so good. Proudness owned every inch of her and relief of not panicking overwhelmed her completely. A lone tear rolled down her cheek. Luckily, Kasey was too busy watching her own feet moving in circles in the water to notice.

'Can anyone join in?' asked Belle.

Rosie didn't need to speak. Her sister knew of the major moment. Belle simply plonked herself down by her side, rolled up her bottoms and slowly lowered her legs, showing obvious signs of being careful not to splash.

'Whoa!' she cried. 'It's cold.'

'You'll get used to it,' said Kasey, not bothering to turn her head.

'Are we having a pool party that I wasn't invited to?' asked Ned, appearing over Belle's shoulders.

'Daddy, I have a fairy name now. Poppy, because my hair is red.'

Ned breathed out a quiet laugh as he sat by Belle's side. 'Oh, is that right?'

Kasey was still swirling her legs gently in the water. 'Yep.'

Rosie could see Belle leaning into Ned and smiled inwardly when his arm came up and wrapped around her sister's shoulders.

*Oh, I love them. I'm so happy that she's happy. So funny that it's Gaston, of all people. I don't think I'll ever get over that.*

'What's going on out here?' asked Elliot.

She turned her head to see him walking towards them, carrying some towels. 'I saw you lot from the window. You'll all freeze.'

'The water feels warm, Uncle Elliot.'

He plopped the towels down by her side. 'Yes, that's because your legs are now numb, Kasey.'

Rosie caught his eye as he sat down next to his niece and dangled his legs, showing no signs of feeling cold. He flashed her that sexy smile of his that she loved so much.

*My merman, back in the water with me.*

He winked, and she felt her cheeks warm.

*Does he know what I'm thinking? I bet he does.*

'One more minute,' he told them all. 'And then we're out of here.'

'Two minutes,' said Kasey.

Rosie held up two fingers, looking as though she were giving him the peace sign. He gave the slightest of nods and reached behind his niece to place his hand over hers.

'This is fun,' said Kasey.

'Yes, it's really nice,' said Ned, kissing the top of Belle's head.

'I like having fun with my new family,' said Kasey.

Rosie's heart warmed. If someone had told her a few years back that she would be so happy, so at peace, and so in love with an incredible man, she wouldn't have believed them. Her past with her ex was beyond soul-destroying. There was a time when she thought she would never smile again.

*And now look. Look at my beautiful life, and all because I took a chance, made a change, and took that shaky step forward. Oh, Rosie, I am so proud of you.*

# 32

*Elliot*

'Aunt Mandy's here,' called out Elliot from the front doorway.

Kasey went running out to the drive, quickly followed by Ned.

Rosie and Belle were hanging back, but Elliot grabbed Rosie's hand and brought her to his side. He could tell she was nervous, but she had no need to be. His aunt, who favoured long shirts draping over long skirts, naturally dried hair, and no makeup was the friendliest person he knew. There was no way Mandy would make anyone feel unwelcome.

Elliot stopped smiling when he saw his aunt clutching at her chest. Her eyes were partially closed, her forehead crinkled, and her lips pursed. He let go of Rosie's hand and sprinted towards her little blue car.

'Mandy, what's wrong?'

She raised one hand and clutched his jumper. 'Elliot. I don't feel well. My chest hurts and I can't breathe properly.'

He straightened from leaning over her and turned to Ned. 'I'm taking Mandy straight to the hospital.' He took her car key from her and helped her back inside the vehicle.

Ned pointed back at the main door. 'I'll make sure everything is sorted here, then I'll meet you down there.'

Rosie rushed to the car. 'I'll come with you.'

The drive to the hospital didn't take that long, but Elliot felt he had been driving for ages. Every traffic light went red as he approached, there seemed to be more traffic on the roads than usual, and his aunt's old car refused to go over the speed limit.

He slumped into a hard chair in the waiting area as his aunt was taken away for tests. A slight disagreement was quickly defused by Rosie when Elliot was told by a nurse that he wasn't allowed to go with his aunt.

His fists were clenched tightly on his lap, only relaxing once Rosie placed her fingers over them.

'She's in good hands now, Elliot. Stay positive.'

What Rosie was whispering to him made perfect sense, but it was so hard to think straight let alone any other way.

*Please don't take my aunt away from me. Please. Not her. She's such a good person. She doesn't deserve to be in pain. She brings goodness to this world. Helps everyone she meets. Don't take her. Help her.*

He rolled back his tears as he sat back and took a breath. Rosie lifted his hand to her mouth for a tender kiss, and his eyes followed her every movement.

'Thanks for being here with me, Rosie.'

'You don't have to thank me.'

'She means so much to me, you know. I sometimes wonder what my life would be like now if it weren't for her.' He glanced sideways. 'I sometimes wonder what we would be like if you had grown up next door to me.'

Her smile warmed his heart.

He looked down at their entwined hands and hoped the shaky feeling inside wasn't rattling through. 'I would have hated you, Rosie. I would have been cruel to you.'

'You don't know that.'

'What are the odds? I can remember my grandfather well. He wasn't a pleasant man. Bitter and never smiling.'

'Maybe he was just sad.'

'What, because he was in love with your grandfather? Who knows. Maybe. I don't remember too much about my grandmother, as I was young when she died, but my dad held all of their hate towards your family. That much I do know. I was raised to be the same way. My dad hated your uncle, with a passion. There was definitely no love there.'

'It still doesn't mean you would have hated me, Elliot. We might have felt the same way about each other as we do now. Maybe we were meant to be and that's why we fell so quickly for each other. I remember the first time I saw you. I wasn't afraid. I didn't know who you were or where I was, but I wasn't worried. Okay, so I was a bit drugged up, but still. Something inside of me was relaxed in your presence all by itself. If I were drawn to you then, I reckon I would have been drawn to you at any time. Surely that's how it works.'

He turned to gaze at her gentle face.

*God, you're so beautiful, Primrose Trent.*

'If my dad was still alive now, there is no way he would allow this relationship.'

Rosie breathed out a quiet laugh. 'He wouldn't get a say in it, Elliot. We're grown-ups.'

'Oh, you'd be surprised at what that man could achieve. He'd find a way to destroy us.'

'I'm glad he's not here then.' She drew breath and widened her eyes. 'Sorry, Elliot. I didn't mean that how it sounded. Of course I'm not glad you lost your dad, I just…'

'Hey, I knew what you meant. It's okay.'

A fresh waft of disinfectant surrounded them as a cleaner opened a nearby toilet door.

Rosie was staring blankly over at the metal trolley filled with cleaning products. 'I've also wondered what we would

240

be like if I grew up next door to you, Elliot. I bet Belle and Ned have thought about it as well. It's hard not to.'

'I find it hard thinking about how I might have hurt you.' He quickly met her eyes. 'Not physically. I would never...'

She leaned closer and kissed his cheek.

Elliot sighed deeply and took a moment. He closed his eyes and breathed her in. Her faint rose scent, the mild coconut shampoo coming through her hair, the fresh laundry smell on her top. The combination of Primrose Trent's aroma had quickly become his favourite fragrance. Everything about her was loved by him.

*I have to believe I would have fallen for her even back then. How she would have changed me. Helped me. Perhaps I wouldn't have been as bad. She could have been my way out. My saviour. We would have joined our hotels years ago. Everything would have been wonderful years ago.*

'What a different life we could have had, Rosie.'

'It would be great to see some sort of parallel life, wouldn't it? It would definitely be interesting to see you when you were young.'

He shook his head and a laugh huffed out. 'It wasn't pretty.'

'Maybe I would have been nasty to you, had I grown up here. Can't be sure. It could have been me doing the hating if my dad had got involved. Who knows.'

*You step over ants. I couldn't see you being hateful to anyone. God, I would have had to protect her even then. My dad would have slaughtered her. Would I have stood by and watched that? No. I have to believe I wouldn't have. I wouldn't let anything bad happen to her. I just know I would have felt the same back then. I can't even imagine it.*

*Just thinking about it makes me hate myself. I'm glad I didn't know her then. Just in case. It's worked out for the best this way. We're ready for each other now. I'm so ready for her.*

He grinned as another thought sprung to mind. 'Do you ever think they're all up there somewhere, silently fuming at us?'

'Well, we haven't been struck by lightning yet, so there's hope.'

They laughed and shared a peck on the lips.

'I think we were meant to meet, Rosie.'

She smiled warmly. 'I think that too. I just wish I'd met you earlier, Elliot, then I wouldn't have gone through what I went through.'

He gave her hand a gentle squeeze and tugged her closer to his side. 'I hate what you went through. If I could go back in time, that's the thing I'd focus on changing.'

They held each other for what seemed like hours but was merely moments. Elliot felt trapped in a past he didn't have. He was holding on to memories that weren't his. Rosie's past did not belong to him. There was a tightness in his chest and a breath caught at the back of his throat. He was on the verge of tears. Tears for his life, her life, the past they could have shared.

*Who knows, perhaps we were supposed to go through a whole heap of crap for some reason. I know it sure as hell makes me appreciate her even more.*

'Hey, Rosie, I'm so glad I met you.'

The light touch of her fingertips brushing over his stubble soothed his weary mind. His dreamy gaze fixed on her face. He really couldn't believe his luck.

*Is this fate? Were we always meant to be? I have to let go of the what ifs. All that matters is now. Look at what I have now. I can't believe that I found love. And she's a Trent. It's actually funny. I'm just so glad she's here.*

'Elliot, do you believe in serendipity?'

'Is that when something good happens to you by some sort of chance encounter?'

'Something like that. Some say it's the universe getting involved in your life.'

'Well, if that's what brought us together, then, yeah, I'm a believer. And I'll thank anything that made this happen.'

Rosie muffled her giggle by placing her mouth over his biceps. 'The lawnmower.'

He had to laugh. 'Not too sure I was laughing that day.'

She snuggled further into his arm. 'You'll always be my favourite merman.'

'Hey, I'm your only merman.'

She kissed his cheek and rested her head on his shoulder. 'How you doing, Merman?'

He looked over at the doorway where his aunt was rushed through. Two nurses were chatting whilst looking over the paperwork one of them was holding. 'I'd be doing a lot better if I knew what was going on, but thank you for trying to help keep my mind distracted.'

Rosie patted his hand. 'Wait here. I'll go and ask that nurse over there. See if we can get an update.'

As soon as she was gone. He felt the coldness of loneliness hit him. He could see her standing at the desk, but she seemed so far away. Everyone he loved seemed so far away. A small stabbing pain pierced his heart. The thought of losing his aunt hit him again. Then, he took a moment to think how he would feel if he lost Rosie. He clutched his chest and forced himself to breathe, to think positive, and to get a grip.

*Stop it, Elliot. You hear me. Stop this now. No more negative thoughts. No more going over crap that didn't even take place. No more thinking about loss. Mandy's going to be all right. Rosie isn't going anywhere. The stupid family feud is finally over. Pepper River Inn is making a comeback. Life is good. Everything is fine. There's Ned.*

He stretched up his arm to get his brother's attention.

Ned quickly sat at his side, catching his breath. 'What's happening?'

'Don't know yet. We were told to wait here. It's been a while. Rosie's just gone to ask for an update.'

Ned leant forward and cradled him into his arms, as though knowing that was what he needed.

Elliot buried his head deep and allowed a few tears to finally fall. He immediately felt the relief. Warmth was coming from Ned's head being so close to the side of his own. He couldn't remember the last time he had cried on his little brother.

Ned gently tapped his back and gestured towards Rosie.

Elliot sniffed as he raised his head. Wiping his eyes, he watched Rosie talking to a doctor who had appeared from somewhere. It was the first doctor he had seen since their arrival. Rosie glanced his way, then through the doorway. She nodded at the doctor, then waved towards them.

Ned nudged his arm. 'Come on.'

Elliot approached her, reaching for her hand automatically. 'Any news?'

'She's just through there. You can go and sit with her now. The doctor will come and see you in a minute. He said she's doing okay. It was an angina attack, not a heart attack. She's going to be prescribed medication.'

Elliot felt parts of him floating on water, but other parts were still tense and on full alert.

Rosie tugged his hand. 'Go on. Go and see her. I'll wait out here.'

'I want you to come too.'

'Family only.'

'You are my family.'

She smiled and let go of his hand. 'Only two allowed around the bed. Just go and see your aunt. I'll get a coffee and call Belle.'

Elliot stilled as Ned walked through the doorway. For some reason his feet refused to follow his brother.

Rosie nudged him out of his trance. 'Hey, I'll be right here, Elliot. I'm not going anywhere.'

There was something deep about her words. The ones she chose. The way she spoke. It was as though she was gently stroking his hair and singing him a lullaby. Her sweet smile encouraged him to move away. He glanced once more over his shoulder at her as he turned a corner.

*I'm definitely going to marry her.*

# 33

*Ned*

After everything that had happened with the tent fiasco, the council decided to bring some cheer to the area by giving the choir use of the dome in Hope Park for their concert. With the temporary ice-rink close by and a few of the Sandly Christmas Market alpine huts put back out, everything suddenly looked Christmassy and joyful. Hot chocolate and mulled wine, iced cookies and candy canes, spiced fruit cakes and cheese with crackers were being served to the excited visitors.

Kasey was one of the most excited people there. She clung on to Ned's hair for dear life as he carried her through the crowd on his shoulders. Her fishtail flapped down his back, and her long hair draped over his eyes every so often.

'Daddy, I want to sing with the others.'

'You can join in from the seats.' Not that he was sure there would be any seats. He glanced to his side at his brother and aunt. 'Will there be any seats? I'm thinking we should have brought a blanket now.'

Elliot glanced at the ground. 'It's a bit cold to sit on the floor, Ned.'

'And I'm all right. I don't need a chair, if that's what you're worried about,' said Mandy, handing a chocolate coin to Kasey.

Ned rolled his eyes up. 'Do you need the loo before we get settled at the dome?'

Kasey wriggled her head from side to side. 'No. I just went.'

Elliot grinned. They both knew that meant nothing.

Kasey leaned down towards Mandy, causing Ned to fight for some balance. 'Aunt Mandy, I know all the Disney songs that Bluebell and Primrose are going to sing. I've been rebursing with them.'

'Rehearsing,' said Elliot.

Kasey tried to say the word again but it still came out wrong, so she moved on to her next statement. 'When I'm older, I'm going to be in the choir as well.'

Mandy smiled warmly up at her. 'Oh, I can't wait to watch you sing.'

Ned glanced over at the stage under the dome. Someone had been busy with tinsel and baubles. He figured the council wanted to make up for the recent disaster by going that extra mile. Plus, the local news reporters were mooching around taking notes, so it was a good look for the place to be filled with festive cheer.

Much to his relief, there were many chairs facing the stage. He had little desire to hold his daughter on his shoulders all through the show. He wasn't entirely sure just how long it was going to go on for.

They plonked themselves down on some foldaway chairs to the side, and Kasey immediately announced she needed the toilet.

Elliot breathed out a laugh and said he would take her.

Mandy reached over and patted Ned's hand. 'This is nice, isn't it?'

He glanced up at the cool sky. 'Yes, it's quite mild today. Not bad for Christmas Eve.'

'Not the weather, Ned. I mean this life you have now.'

He turned and smiled at her twinkling eyes. They always looked to be filled with mischief. 'What do you think of the Trents?'

She gave a slight nod of approval. 'I like them. They give off good vibes. I can see the energy between Elliot and Rosie. It's so strong. They definitely knew each other in a previous life.'

'And what about me and Belle? What's going on there?'

She snuggled closer to his arm and gently tapped his chest. 'There's something so magical when you're given a second chance at love. That doesn't happen for many. Oh, folk think they're in love every time they meet someone, but it's not true love each time. They say that true love comes around only once in a lifetime, but does it really? I think there are a special few who get to experience it a second time.'

*I loved Penny with all my heart. We gave each other everything we could. Never in a million years did I expect to ever feel that kind of love inside my heart again. I'm not sure why I have been given another chance when so many don't even find one love. I'm so grateful though.*

Mandy gave his hand a slight squeeze. 'You feel thankful for her, don't you, Ned?'

He pursed his lips and smiled whilst nodding. 'It blows my mind a bit when I think about it, if I'm honest. I never thought I'd fall in love with someone, let alone this fast, and certainly not with a Trent. It really is bizarre.'

Mandy laughed. 'I think life in general is bizarre. We just join in and give it our best shot.'

'Yeah, I guess we do.'

'So, what's next for you two and the Trents?'

Elliot had discussed so much with Rosie, Ned felt as though he was just going along for the ride.

'Well, Elliot wants to join the hotels, take back the original name, and move in with Rosie. Actually, that's marry Rosie. They've planned two houses, a workshop for Rosie's pottery, and the hotel extension. So, it's all systems go in the new year. Honestly, Mand, I've never seen him so excited.'

Mandy smiled warmly, staring him straight in the eyes. 'And now tell me what you want.'

There was no point trying to hide anything from his aunt. He learnt that years ago. She was the one person who he truly believed could read minds. He couldn't lie to her. She just knew. She always knew.

'I'm trying to slow things down with me and Belle. Unlike my brother, I'm not planning on moving into her new home before it's even been built. However, Kasey has already designed her bedroom over there. I don't know where she got the idea from that we're moving in with Belle, but she's all for it.'

'Have you and Belle discussed your future?'

'Not really. Although, Josephine Walker reckons Belle's my destiny. Apparently, we're going to be married.'

Mandy laughed. 'Oh, I do love old Josephine.'

'Hmm.'

'What about you, Ned. What do you see? How much do you love Bluebell Trent? Enough to marry her?'

*That moment she glared at me over the fence when we first met. Her eyes holding so much contempt. And when she came up to Elliot's room to check on her sister. She stood so close to me on the stairs, I could smell the sweetness in her hair. She can outrun me if she wanted to. I can tell. She holds back, worried about my leg. I went from trying to make her nervous when I reached for the tea to her making me nervous when she played solitaire with me. I*

249

*don't think I'll ever get over every moment we've spent together. That's not something I want to end. She's sticking around. She has a new job and home and, well, me… I guess. I love her, and she loves me.*

'Yeah, I'd marry her.'

'I'm so pleased, Ned.'

'So am I.' He glanced up as Elliot plopped Kasey down onto a chair.

Mandy pointed at the stage. 'Sit down, Elliot. The show's about to start in a sec. Look, some of the choir have come out.'

Kasey squealed with excitement. 'There's Bluebell and Primrose.'

Ned caught the look of pure love in his brother's eyes, then he turned to the dome to look for Belle.

She was standing in the front row, looking keen to sing her first song. He smiled at her blue dress, remembering helping her with the ties on the pinafore before the tent collapsed on them. Belle noticed him in the crowd and smiled a smile he knew to be just for him.

With the warmth of her filling him, he settled back into his hard chair and watched the show.

Kasey joined in with the other children there, singing all the songs, knowing all the words.

Elliot and Mandy joined in too with some songs whilst Ned couldn't bring his mouth out of the wide smile it was fixed in.

*How brave is she standing up there singing to a crowd. That's not something I can do. She's got me beat there. I wonder… Does that count? Has she finally beat me at something? Hmm.*

He leaned his arm over the back of the chairs and tapped Elliot. 'Watch Kasey. I won't be a sec.'

Elliot nodded and moved his legs so that Ned could squeeze by.

Ned walked along the side, making his way over to one of the alpine huts. He knew what he was looking for. Stopping at the cheese stall, he called over to the big muscular man behind the counter. 'Hey, Nate, can I borrow that board you have back there?'

Nate turned to the large white card that had *Pepper Pot Farm* written on it in thick black letters. 'Erm, what for, Ned?'

'I just need to borrow it for one minute. I'll bring it back with a full explanation, I promise.'

Nate took a deep breath as he combed one hand through his dark hair. 'Okay.'

'Great.' Ned beamed happily and leant over to take the board.

Nate's grandmother, Josephine Walker, was sitting in a foldaway chair at the back of the hut. She gave Ned a mischievous wink before lowering her head.

Ned smiled at Nate. 'Cheers for this, mate. Have you got the pen you wrote this with?'

Nate handed over the black marker. 'I definitely want a full explanation, Ned.'

Josephine grumbled something under her breath. She rolled her shrewd eyes up to her grandson. 'Oh, leave him be, Nate. He's got important business to take care of.' She looked at Ned. 'Well, go on. Get on with it, kid.'

Nate's face was bursting with curiosity.

Ned flipped the board on the counter and wrote on the back. He slowly rolled his eyes up at Nate, who was peering over.

Nate grinned from ear to ear and boomed out a laugh. 'That's made my day.'

Waving the board at him, Ned walked away. 'Merry Christmas, Walkers.'

Nate's reply was lost in amongst the people mooching around the huts.

The show had finished just as Ned awkwardly scrambled back to his chair, knocking everyone in his row with the large board.

'Ned, what have you got there?' asked Elliot, frowning at the dairy farm's name.

Kasey jumped up and started waving towards the stage before he had a chance to answer.

Belle and Rosie had finished bowing and was waving over at everyone they knew.

Ned glanced around. He saw Joey with her husband, Josh, standing to cheer alongside the owners of The Book Gallery, Anna and Jake. They were clapping loudly whilst Nate appeared to stand beside Tessie, who was waving at the stage, along with their two daughters, Robyn and Daisy, and Dolly's son, Dexter. Scott and Dolly were in an embrace close to the front, chatting and laughing with Tilly and Rory and the rest of the Sheridan family from Dreamcatcher Farm. Ned smiled as he looked back at his own family.

*I love all my friends from Pepper Bay. I'm so glad Belle is happy here, because there's nowhere in the world I'd rather be. Okay, Bluebell Trent, let's do this.*

'Hey, Elliot, hold my chair.'

Elliot frowned with amusement. 'What are you doing, Ned?'

'Watch.'

He climbed up on the chair so that he was towering over the crowd. The choir was still taking in the appreciation from the audience as he balanced with his brother's help.

He raised his arms up into the air. Holding the board as high as he could. Then he waited.

Belle was smiling and waving over at Elaine Sparrow, sending love heart symbols with her fingers in front of her chest.

Rosie's eyes went wide and her mouth gaped. She nudged her sister, and there it was. Belle's eyes connected with the sign.

Ned flashed her his best smile as she slapped one hand over her mouth.

'What's going on?' asked Elliot, who couldn't see the sign, due to holding the chair.

Mandy peered up to see what Ned had written. She smiled down at Elliot. 'It's a proposal. Says, you beat me at singing, Bluebell Trent. Will you marry me?'

'Oh my God,' said Elliot, and Kasey cheered.

All eyes turned to the stage.

Belle lowered her hand, broke into the biggest smile, and nodded over at Ned. She quickly bent over and retrieved one of the microphones. 'Yes,' she shouted into the mike, pointing one hand over towards him.

At which point, pretty much everyone in the audience turned to look at Ned.

Belle spoke into the microphone again. 'Yes, Edward Renshaw, I will marry you.'

A round of applause filled the whole area as Ned lowered the sign to his knees.

# Epilogue

Summer had arrived in Pepper Bay, and the warm, dry weather helped move along the new development over at Pepper River Inn. Elliot couldn't stop grinning as the new sign went up, but his smile still wasn't as wide as it was when his wife's workshop opened.

Rosie was back at the potter's wheel, as happy as a pig in mud, or in her case, up to her armpits in clay. There was some mess to clear up one night after Elliot thought he could re-enact the scene from the film Ghost. Rosie was less than impressed, as her equipment wasn't to be played with, but she had still succumbed to his touch.

Ned and Belle stood at the gateway to the hotel, watching the gardeners at work. They both had the same idea at the same time and laughed.

'I still can't get over the fact your sister tried to do the gardening in November on that monster of a mower.'

Belle smiled. 'I know. She has these mad moments from time to time.'

He leaned over and kissed her head. 'Don't we all.'

She nudged his ribs. 'Oi, you. You'd better not be referring to marrying me.'

'Would I?'

'Hmm.'

Ned stopped smiling for a moment as Elliot and Rosie came over. He gestured towards the hotel. 'Can you believe it, Elliot?'

Elliot shook his head. His face filled with amazement. 'Nope. If someone had told me this time last year that I would be in this situation now, I'd never have believed them.'

'Nor me,' said Rosie. 'Mind you, I never thought I'd end up as the owner of a derelict hotel on the Isle of Wight. But that happened.'

Belle laughed. 'Oh, I'm so glad that is behind us. What a nightmare.'

Elliot glanced up at the clear blue sky. 'Do you reckon anyone up there hates us now we've finally put the hotel back together again?'

Rosie placed her arm around his waist. 'All that matters is the happiness we bring to this place. The past is in the past. There is no more hate here. Pepper River Inn is back on the map, and life is good.'

He smiled as he nuzzled his nose into her hair.

'I love you, Merman,' she whispered, so only he could hear.

He placed his hand over her small baby bump and told her that he loved them both.

Belle snuggled further into Ned's hold as his arm came around her, pulling her close.

He could see her looking lovingly at Rosie's stomach. 'Hey,' he whispered, watching his brother lead Rosie away to look at some new plants that had just gone in the ground. 'You want to start looking into adoption procedures yet?'

She lifted her head and pulled his face closer to hers so she could lightly brush over his lips with her own. 'Not yet.'

He kissed her back and smiled on her lips. 'Whenever you're ready, Flower Girl.'

'I'm thinking maybe in a couple of years. I just want to settle in with all this first.'

'Sounds like a good plan.'

Belle had a sudden thought. She drew back and frowned at him. 'Hey, I've just realised something. Ever since we got married, you haven't called me Mrs Renshaw. You used to call me that all the time.'

Ned laughed. 'I don't need to now. You know what your name is. I was just trying it out for size back then. Plus, I was letting you get used to it.'

She gently poked his chest. 'You're such a liar. You wanted me. You know you did. You liked how it sounded.'

'You liked how it sounded.'

She pulled him to her mouth for a kiss. 'I did,' she mumbled on his lips.

'I know,' he mumbled back, gaining another poke from her.

'Come on. I'm taking you to bed.'

Ned laughed and nudged her nose with his own. 'It's the middle of the day and we're surrounded by gardeners and builders.'

'We'll lock the door and close the windows. No one will know.' She gave him a cheeky wink.

He grinned widely, wanting to take her up on her offer. 'We can't, I'm afraid. We have to go and pick Kasey up now from Dolly's.' He kissed her again, trying not to heat things up further. 'But, later on, Mrs Renshaw, you are all mine.'

Belle melted into his arms where he held her tightly.

Elliot called over. 'Shall we grab some lunch when we pick Kasey up? I was thinking we could eat at the pub, then go for a paddle.'

Ned and Belle were locked at the lips.

Elliot cleared his throat. 'When you two are ready, that is.'

Rosie giggled and pulled him around to face the new sign above the hotel's doorway.

'I'm having one of those surreal moments again, Elliot.'

He nodded. 'I have them all the time.'

She looked at the side of his face and smiled to herself. 'I'm glad I met you.'

He turned and smiled back. His eyes twinkling with love. 'You, Rosie Renshaw, are the best thing on this planet.' He rolled his eyes over at Ned and Belle. 'Just don't tell those two I said that.'

She laughed into his tee-shirt. 'Oh, Elliot. Look what we've created here. What a dream come true.'

His arms curled around her. 'And neither one of us saw it coming.'

'I'm not sure if I took a wrong turn or a right one to end up here. I just seemed to get here.'

He kissed the top of her head and then glanced back over at the new sign. 'Yeah, I know what you mean. Life can be funny, can't it? Maybe we just end up exactly where we're supposed to.'

Rosie smiled. 'Yeah. I guess Pepper Bay was always a part of my destiny.'

* * *

If you enjoyed this story, why not come back for another visit to Pepper Bay with Lexi and Bryce.

Silver Blooms Flower Shop

Lexi and Bryce have never been friends. She views him as her childhood bully. So, she finds a way to stick it to the fancy-schmancy businessman by using his name as her pen name for the erotic romance books that she writes. That way, when potential clients try to check him out online, all they will see is fishnet stockings, sexy CEOs, and steamy sneak previews. But, when Not-Nice-Bryce comes back home to confront her, their past comes flooding back, and maybe it wasn't as bad as she remembers.

Printed in Great Britain
by Amazon

38627403R00148